# *My Favorite Cloud*

# *My Favourite Cloud*

"It all sounds a bit like you're living in the plot of a scary movie, yet in one sense I kind of understand," Bill replied. "Is it like you're in some sort of waking dream, analysing yourself? Have you ever thought about asking a psychologist or someone who studies the brain?"

Polly frowned. "Are you implying I'm mad?" she asked with mock indignation.

"No, not..."

"Something happens," she continued, "and it stirs you from this strange mental treacle you're trapped in. Something or someone might touch your body and you realise you *do* exist. Your nerve endings jolt you back to reality. I often think the only sure way we know we exist is though pain. When you feel pain, you truly *know* you are alive. It fires the senses; it wakes the brain like a scream in your ear."

To Bill, the expression on her face was one seeking approval or empathy. For his part, he was struggling to fathom how someone so physically perfect could be so complicated. The only thing certain to him was that his fascination with this beautiful, complex life-form was multiplying by the second. It was an intense feeling he had not experienced before. "I don't think I can agree with you about pain, Polly. Pain is subjective, but it can destroy, change, bring hatred. Surely there are other things that can make you feel alive...food, friendship, love?"

Gently she rolled over onto her stomach. With her back

arched, she propped herself up on her elbows and cupped her chin in her hands. Her face had assumed a childlike expression. Her eyes danced from Bill's eyes to the brook and back to Bill. "I'm sorry, I'm rambling on," she apologised. 'I can hardly believe I'm baring my soul to a—"

"Stranger?" he volunteered.

# *What They Are Saying About My Favourite Cloud*

If I didn't have any idea what went on in the world of journalism, I do now. I have learned, through Polly Jordan, that it's tough, and to be a valued part of it, a woman needs to become one of the boys. After the first few lines, my interest was captured. Polly's rapport with the man we later know as Doc, is gritty and feisty, and her confidence in standing up for herself is displayed in no uncertain terms.

Her job as a reporter leads her from one questionable situation to another and she is seemingly a law unto herself when being faced with sexual advances. Her behaviour is sometimes shocking and yet I found it impossible not to admire her. This story follows Polly's adventures across the world and shows how easy it is to become involved in unsavoury and criminal activity when your heart rules your head.

I totally recommend this book. It is an interesting, intriguing and compelling read.

—Emma Martin
Retired SRN UK


The author seems to have an insight to newspaper life of yesteryear and casts Polly Jordan as an attractive, free-wheeling reporter in the sixties who enjoys her job, sex and drink. Thanks to a predacious and vindictive female boss, Polly's career crashes when by chance she lands a scoop involving a world-famous musician—a Beatle.

What follows is a dramatic series of events...tragedy, a near nervous breakdown, heartache, crime, treachery and finally love.

The story is compelling and makes good use of contemporary social and moral themes. Some parts may surprise, perhaps shock, but there is hardly a page that doesn't hold something to keep the reader engaged. I hope Mr Campbell offers us a sequel.

—Joshua 'Jock' Lennox
Retired Civil Servant
Edinburgh, Scotland

# My Favourite Cloud

## Gordon Campbell

A Wings ePress, Inc.
Historical Novel

# Wings ePress, Inc.

Edited by: Jeanne Smith
Copy Edited by: Brian Hatfield
Executive Editor: Jeanne Smith
Cover Artist: Trisha FitzGerald-Jung
Camera from Pexels, Woman: Pixabay

*All rights reserved*



Wings ePress Books
www.wingsepress.com



Published In the United States Of America

Wings ePress, Inc.
3000 N. Rock Road
Newton, KS 67114

# Dedication

To my darling wife, Vera, for her support and encouragement, and to my parents, Florrie and Stephen, whose dream for me was always to succeed.

# One

Polly Jordan shivered with cold as she put her foot on the doorstep. Thirty-three Pitt Street was a modest little house in Cardwell, a cotton-spinning town in England's north-west. It had been home to several generations since Queen Victoria's reign. Not much distinguished it from the other terraced two-up-two-downers, except its front door: it was painted purple. Neighbouring doors had brass or cast-iron knockers, or new-fangled door bells powered by batteries. Polly's target had nothing—it was plain...and purple. To many people in the north, purple was unlucky—the colour of shrouds.

Polly cupped her small hands and blew vigorously between her thumbs. A smile lit her pale lips as warm breath rushed with a faint whistle through her hollowed palms. She rapped four times on the purple door and grimaced as her cold knuckles stung and she silently determined, *Polly, memo to self. Buy a pair of gloves next time you're in town.* Gently she massaged her hand. Another rap, a little harder. Another grimace. No reply.

The tired, weak sun was on the point of sinking behind the moors surrounding Cardwell. With its healing light all but gone, dozens of tall factory chimneys reverted to grimy reminders of the town's industrial might. That, too, was all but gone. She glanced at the afternoon sky. An unusual formation of streaky-barred clouds was gradually turning a pale marmalade colour. With numb fingers, Polly clutched a notebook and pencil she clumsily fished from her shoulder bag. In squiggly writing she jotted down, *Fantastic mackerel sky. High. Amazing colours. Bloody freezing!*

A car door closed with a clunk. Polly spun to see who had arrived. For an instant, her pale face vanished behind a carousel of long, blonde hair. A tall figure locked the driver's door of the Mini Cooper S and drew closer. Polly took exaggerated sniffs at the air.

"Doing your Bugs Bunny act again?" The voice had the rasp of a rake through gravel. "Come on, babe...not even a what's up, Doc?" the tall one said, laughing and letting out a cloud of foggy breath and smoke. "What's up, Doc! Get it? It's a Bugs Bunny joke! Looney Tunes cartoons."

"Shut up!" Polly snapped. "There's only one loony around here and I'm looking at him."

She stuffed her notebook back into the bag and slung its chain over her shoulder. "You're late. Have you been moonlighting again?"

"Didn't you think my joke was funny?" the newcomer probed, gently stroking aside wisps of Polly's hair that had snagged on her lip gloss.

Polly rolled her eyes and bobbed her head sideways to avoid the unsolicited grooming. "Stop it, Doc! You're always bloody touching," she complained, pushing away his big, gloved hand.

"You know you love the attention," he said, pressing his body to Polly's and snaking a long arm around her shoulders. "You love me too, don't you? When you roll your baby blue eyes like that, I melt."

The banter failed to amuse. The gnawing cold, unusual for early August, and the nature of her assignment were testing

Polly's patience. "Christ Almighty, you big Irish lump, you're smoking dope again," she barked. "Can't you go just one hour without that garbage?"

Gerry 'Doc' Docherty, always smartly dressed, handsome in a rugged way and a little over six feet three inches tall, towered over the petite young newspaper reporter. He was a man who took an unashamed pride in his appearance and whose wardrobe, as those who knew him well would vouch, was an Aladdin's cave of expensive, high-end clothes.

A bulky German Rolleiflex press camera swung from a strap over the right shoulder of his leather jacket.

"New jacket?" Polly enquired. "How much?"

"Seventy quid, give or take a few shillings. Like it? Saw it in George Brothers in Manchester. Couldn't resist."

"You're kidding. That's more than a month's wages for most people in Cardwell. I don't know how you photographers make so much money. It's not from working at *The Cardwell Express*, that's for sure. And put that joint out, Doc. It's foul, it's illegal and we're on company time."

With a disapproving grunt, Doc flicked away the offending marijuana joint. As it hit the flagstone pavement, he crushed it under the sole of his left foot. It was a gesture of unambiguous indignation. "Cool it, babe, don't sweat it. It's 1963, you know. Get with the times! Pot power and all that." His grumble betrayed an unmistakable lilt that gave away his Northern Ireland roots.

"Sweat it? In this weather? It's like flaming winter," Polly croaked, rapping the door again.

"No one's home, Doc. You'd better go to your next job."

"Give it one last go," Doc insisted. "I've had to dash away from a very lucrative private little commission for this job, so one more knock, eh?"

"Jeez, no wonder you're loaded. Do all you press photographers do sneaky private jobs on the side, or is it just you?"

Doc's smug grin accentuated the crows' feet wrinkles that formed tiny deltas at the corner of each sparkling green eye. "I ask you now, how could a poor toiler such as myself know that? I'm not *all* photographers, am I?"

"Poor? That'll be the day," Polly sniggered, tapping out another tattoo on the door. "Perhaps the old girl's died on us. At least that would save me wasting time here."

"Tut tut! You're all class, Polly," Doc scolded as he swung his camera from his shoulder and flipped open its leather case. "And by the way, it's high time you stopped having a go at me over my smoking habits. You're no bloody saint, sure you're not!"

Polly was unsure whether Doc was serious or joking. However, his poker face surrendered to a crooked, roguish smile. "You should try a bit of grass sometime."

"No way! That junk can't be good for anybody. In any case, smoking anything is for idiots."

"Don't knock it till you try it, babe. It'll unwind you, especially when you have your monthlies and you're all irritable."

"Wow! Just listen to God's-gift-to-women, Professor Pothead," Polly retaliated acerbically. "What makes you such a bloody expert on young girls' body clocks...especially mine?"

"People in the know say a few drams of whiskey and a few drags of Mary Jane are the best sensation you can get with your clothes on," Doc preached. A flash of annoyance in her eyes caused him to back off. "Oops! Truce! You're a feisty wee thing when you get your buttons pushed."

"It'll be a cold day in hell before I let you get close enough to touch *my* buttons."

There was an awkward pause. Each searched the other's eyes for a cue before they laughed out loud amid a fleeting cloud of misty breath. In a typically Irish way, Doc enjoyed the verbal cut and thrust with Polly but had learned, many times to his cost, that his young colleague could give as good as she got.

"Let's go!" Polly said, then added, "Hey, Doc, did you see those crazy clouds a few minutes ago?"

"Clouds? No, who looks at clouds? Only drunks and poets."

"Aren't photographers supposed to be artists? Don't you ever look up...at the sky?"

"I saw it once, but I reckon everything I need is right here on the ground. Anyway, what's the fascination with clouds? They're just big lumps of water wafting about waiting to burst and ruin some poor souls' day while they're trying to make love on the grass." He nudged her arm playfully. "It's just pie in the sky, Polly."

"You're hopeless," she said wearily. "No sense of romance. Oh, blimey, what have I just said?" she groaned playfully. She knew at once she had inadvertently fed him a line. His response was as predictable as it was schmaltz.

"Ah, zat iz where you are wrong, Mademoiselle Jordan," he growled in a comically futile attempt at imitating a French accent.

"Don't give up your day job. A Belfast boyo trying to sound like Maurice Chevalier? I don't think so, mate."

Doc returned serve. "Technically inaccurate. I'm a Carrickfergus boy...but it's close to Belfast."

"Whatever," Polly continued, aiming to keep the upper hand.

"What's the big attraction with clouds?"

"I'm sure I've told you this before," Polly grumbled. "My dad was a meteorologist and he used to point out all the different cloud formations and teach me about the weather. Some kids collect stamps. I collected clouds."

"I always knew there was something queer about you."

"Get stuffed...in the nicest possible way," Polly fired back.

Theirs was a strange relationship. It had begun two years earlier when Polly, aged almost twenty-three, moved jobs from her native Isle of Man. Doc, sixteen years her senior, soon saw promise in the smart, young reporter. In no small way, her pretty face and shapely figure helped him make his judgement. They were obvious attributes readily appreciated by just about every male member of staff at the *Express*, Cardwell's influential evening newspaper.

They were a formidable team with a well-deserved reputation for breaking big news. Hardly an edition was published that didn't have a story and picture from them, more often than not on the front page. Doc wound his long, red scarf around his neck. Peering down into the twin-lens camera and cranking the handle to load the next frame, he took aim at Polly. The shutter's click brought a mock frown to her face. "Just testing!" he teased. "You were in perfect focus too."

Polly was well aware of her good looks and had quickly learned they could be a valuable asset in charming information from reticent interview subjects. Had she not ventured into journalism, she might easily have found work as a model, and the rascally Doc was forever telling her so. With a tut, the frown became a grin. The grin turned to a pout then two delicate fingers stabbed a V-sign at the camera. "Did you get *that* in focus?"

"Not posing for me today, babe? Listen, I've got one more job to do, then we could sneak in for a couple of quick drams at the Nag's Head, or we could go back to the office and have a different kind of quickie...in the darkroom. Waddya say?" he proposed with a wink. Before Polly could reply, Doc switched from clowning to serious. "How come *you* got picked to cover this crappy looking-back story? You're supposed to be the paper's golden girl."

Polly's reply was rapier fast. "Okay, okay, genius...by the same token, how come you got picked to take the pictures?"

*Hmm, I'm playing with fire again,* Doc thought before adding, "*Touché!* What's the brief anyway? What's the big deal about this old lady?"

Polly did a little skip on the spot and stamped her feet to warm them. "You may or may not know the *Express* is preparing a big special supplement to aptly mark the twenty-fifth anniversary next September of the start of World War Two."

"Yeah, of course I know all about that. I'm in the loop," he huffed. "I didn't realise they were starting so early."

"Apparently, it's going to be massive—a glossy supplement separate from the *Express,* not just a pull-out section. I've been put in charge of collating people's memories of those days," Polly said proudly. "Apparently Lizzie Flint has some cracking wartime stories to tell. Were you ever in the armed forces, Doc, or wouldn't they trust you with live ammunition?"

"If I was, it was all a blur," he said with a cheeky wink.

"I'm not sure what that means, but I reckon if you'd been taken prisoner, you wouldn't have folded under questioning," Polly quipped. "Now, Mr Docherty, to get back to your evil little plan...watch my lips. News flash: I'm not your babe, so stop calling me that. You're engaged, in case that dope-addled walnut you call a brain has forgotten. God knows how you conned that poor girl into saying yes, you philandering rake."

Doc goaded her. "I'm *always* watching your lips. Mmm, and all your other parts."

"Shut it, Doc! News flash two: I'm newly single and loving it. News flash three: you said *we*. There is no *we*. *We* are just work buddies, get it?"

Melodramatically, the cameraman slapped his right palm on his chest. "Stabbed through the heart! Yesterday's man!"

"Another news flash," Polly continued. "Since I dumped my useless boyfriend Joe, who thought more about fishing than anything remotely connected with other activities starting with *eff*, our pain-in-the-arse news editor Jocelyn Duckworth has been stalking me…big-time. I made a big mistake and confided in her about my break-up. She hasn't left me alone since. So I'm feeling mighty pissed off, and for your information, my mood has nothing to do with the time of month."

"Well, that's *me* shot down in flames," Doc conceded. He fingered the perfectly executed Windsor knot he always used to fasten his tie. "Oh, that queer auld cow," he offered knowingly. "Never liked her, she's an eejit."

"Tell me more," Polly interjected. "I might be interested in your opinion of that woman." There was a hint of venom in her tone as she spat the last two words.

"I was always very unsure about her," Doc continued, "but she tried to drop me in the mire last year when that circus elephant escaped and ran riot through Cardwell Market stalls. She told the editor I had missed the event because I was doing private work."

"She didn't! Polly gasped.

Doc nodded slowly. "I had the drop on her, mind you. I was the only photographer who snapped the jumbo stopping in its tracks to take a banana from a seven-year-old school kid, which, by some miraculous intervention, just allowed the trainers to recaptured it. It made the front page. Most of the big national papers bought my photo from the *Express*. Jocelyn Duckworth was left red-faced." He paused and inhaled deeply. "Mind you, it was all a pure stunt. I got the tip-off from the circus publicity officer, an old pal from Londonderry. Harry from Derry," he said, amused with his own attempt at rhyme. "The kid was actually the animal trainer's nephew, but nobody found out. And I got a note of thanks from the managing director. Old Duckworth was livid and had to back down with an apology."

"She's not that old, about forty I reckon, but your use of *queer* is the right word. She's definitely not into men. I made it crystal clear I wasn't being *her* babe when she came on to me at the Christmas party last year. And if you recognise that as fighting talk, you are dead right!"

"Aye, there was some scuttlebutt in the office. You know how rumours fly like the wind in any newspaper office," Doc replied matter-of-factly.

"Duckworth insisted on dancing with me. I refused. Later she cornered me in the ladies' loo and told me in no uncertain terms she wanted to get me into the sack. She started to run her hands up my, er, chest. Can you imagine anything so repulsive, even if you *do* butter your toast on the other side?"

Doc theatrically pretended to stick two fingers down his throat. "Yuk! She's got a face like the back end of a cow and probably weighs as much as one."

Polly shook her head and tossed back her hair in a gesture of pique. "She's bloody dangerous, a serious predator. I warned her—one wrong move and I'd strangle her with that bloody pendant she wears around her neck. That was a seriously bad move. Now she's vindictive. She's totally turned against me. The only sack in her mind now is getting me fired."

"What about going to the journalists' union? Surely they can step in."

"The sly witch is cunning. She knows I couldn't ever prove anything. It's all very subtle, very circumstantial," Polly complained. "She's taken to rostering me on extra late-night jobs and giving me menial feature stories like this one. It's a big project, but it's far from being a page one scoop."

"Don't put up with it. Talk to the editor. Old Ronnie Day will sort it out. I've always found him amenable."

"Easier said than done. Duckworth's well in with the board of directors. She has family connections high up the food chain.

Anyway, I've heard Ronnie's ready to retire, so he won't want to rock the boat." Polly rubbed her hands together. "My fingers feel like they're about to drop off. Go and do some work, Doc, and if I get finished in good time I might, that's *might* with a capital *M*, see you in the Nag's Head."

"Okay, see youse later." Doc slid his big frame into his Mini Cooper, carelessly tossed his camera and flash unit onto the back seat and roared off in the direction of Cardwell's town centre.

"One more knock, and if there's no answer, I'll be off too," Polly muttered as she gingerly delivered a last rap. *That smarts. Hmm...nobody home. Goodbye, Pitt Street. Hello, new gloves.*

Just at that moment the purple door slowly opened, but only halfway. A pale, bespectacled face appeared from the gloom. It was etched with life's toil and crowned with snow-white hair. Faded blue-green eyes blinked at the world outside. "Who's there? What do you want?"

Polly Jordan switched at once to reporter mode. "Mrs Flint? Mrs Elizabeth Flint?"

# *Two*

Doc glanced at his watch. It was eight-thirty and he was alone as he sipped his third Irish whiskey. He was sitting in the corner seat he always made a beeline for when he drank in the snug of the Nag's Head. The tall Scottish barmaid with a ruddy, happy face, knew him well and loved to tease. As she dried glasses behind the bar, Annie Campbell called out, "I see you're drinking with all your mates tonight, Doc."

The photographer reached over to a heavy glass ashtray on the table and stubbed out a cigarette, trying to stifle a smile. "I think I've just worked out who they named this pub after. What in the name of all that's holy would a haggis-bashing beanpole like yourself know about mates?" Doc growled playfully. "If you were back north of the border, they'd toss you at the highland games, sure they would."

Annie let out a hearty laugh as she held a clean glass to the whiskey optic. "Same again, hen?"

"Aye, go on." Doc ran a hand through his hair and checked his watch again.

Always ready for a bit of banter, especially with journalists who called the Nag's Head their *real* office, Annie unleashed another wisecrack. "You'd know all about tossing, Doc. All your *Express* pals reckon you're the biggest tosser to come out of Belfast!"

"*Touché*, Annie," Doc conceded, "but I'm too tired for a decent joust with youse tonight."

"Worn out counting your money?" she joked. "Hey, by the way, are you still doing jobs on the side?"

"I do a few, now and then. Why?" he replied cautiously.

"A friend of mine has just had twin girls and wants a good photographer to take some shots that won't cost the earth. Are you interested?"

Doc stroked his sculpted chin. "Working with babies is a pain in the arse, to be honest. And twins? I'd have to charge double."

Hands on hips, Annie gave him a stare that would make the boldest of men go weak at the knees.

"Just kidding," he told her. "I'll see what I can do. Give me the details later. If she's a friend of yours, I'll look after her.'

"Thanks, Doc. I knew I could count on you."

As he reached into his jacket pocket and pulled out a silver cigarette case, Polly walked in. "About time! I'd just about given up on you, babe. Oops, sorry, un-babe, or whatever you wanna be called! Poll? Polly? Jordy?"

"Anything but blasted *Babe*. How about Polly...my name? I banked on you still being here," she said, grinning "How's my favourite bohemian shutterbug?"

"Don't tell me I'm back in favour," Doc said, striking a match and lighting a cigarette. "Have you been drinking already?"

"One or two, in the spirit of press-public relations." Polly grinned with slightly glassy eyes.

"Did you get to interview the old girl?"

"Yes, she was lovely. We had a great chat, but it went on far too long, that's why I'm late. Boy, she loves her whisky."

Polly took a seat opposite him at the small round table and waved her hand towards Annie. She slipped off her coat, draped it over the seat of an adjacent chair and carefully placed her cassette tape recorder on top of it. "*You?* Back in favour? Let's not get carried away. I might just tolerate you if you buy me a beer...no, make it an Irish whiskey."

"Two doubles, please, Annie," Doc called out. "On my tab, darlin', if you will."

He turned back to Polly. "Are you all right? You look a bit frazzled."

Polly fished in her handbag and pulled out a compact. She flipped the lid and checked her make-up. "God, look at my eyes!"

"Blue and beautiful as ever," Doc chimed in.

"Don't you *ever* give up? It was a good interview. Old Lizzie Flint had some great war memories. It'll make such great reading in the supplement."

"Well, golden girl, here's your chance to show Duckworth you're the best. Still the best."

"I am the best, Doc, aren't I?" Polly exclaimed, downing her drink. "Bloody hell, I can't believe I've just gulped that in one go. I'm gonna be so drunk. I had more than one decent scotch with Lizzie Flint during the interview. For an old biddy that lady sure can drink."

"Come on, you can take it," said Doc. "One for the road, then we'll go back to the office. You can knock out your yarn and I'll process today's batch of brilliant, award-winning pictures for tomorrow's paper."

Polly swung her right foot onto the chair and rested it next to the tape recorder. As she did so, her short, black skirt rode up her shapely thighs. "Like 'em?"

Doc licked his lips. "Delicious! I've always said you have the best legs in Cardwell."

"Not those, you pervert...the boots, the boots!"

"Oh, yes, kinky boots turn me on. Are *you* secretly kinky, Polly?"

She rolled her eyes and groaned with exasperation before leaning forward to stroke the shiny cream leather of the fashionable, calf-length footwear. "The boots, kinky? To a grubby mind like yours, yes okay. Me, kinky? That's something you'll just have to wonder about. They were *really* expensive. Twelve quid at Roland and Baxter's, but worth every penny. Everybody's wearing them. I was wearing them this afternoon, but you were too stoned to notice."

"I wasn't stoned," Doc protested, "just relaxed. You into fashion, babe?"

"If you *babe* me again, I won't be responsible for my actions."

"Sorry! I apologise, ever so humbly."

"You're not the only one who likes good clothes. Problem is my salary and yours are at different ends of the pay scale."

"Trendy, eh?" Doc teased.

"I'm a bit trendy, I suppose. Heard of Mary Quant, fashion goddess? She's fab...absolutely *it* at the moment in London."

"You're asking Mr Fashion about Mary Quant? The question is...has *she* heard of *me*?"

"Stop taking the piss. As I was saying...short skirts, boots, short hair. Can't say I'm big on short hair, but I'm definitely a Quant girl. Hey, there's something I need to ask..."

Annie quickly came over with two more doubles. Polly paused while the barmaid put down their drinks and took away the empty glasses.

"Doc, I've drunk too much—will you drive me to the office?"

"No problem, ba...oops, sorry, I nearly said it again."

"S'all right," Polly said with a vacant grin. "To be honest, I'm past caring at the moment. In fact, I'm a bit titsy. Hell, did I just say what I thought I said? I meant tipsy, Doc, *tipsy!*"

As they rose to leave, Doc handed Polly her coat and tape recorder from the chair.

"Thank you, kind sir," she said demurely. "Chivalry lives on!"

While she awkwardly fought her way into the coat, Doc unashamedly ogled her bosom, bulging from inside a thin yellow cardigan. Their eyes met and he flashed a roguish wink at his colleague. "Are you cold?"

"What makes you think I'm cold? It's warm in here, especially with all the booze swilling around inside me."

"Either they're your nipples poking out, or you've sewn thimbles into your bra."

She held his gaze and fluttered her eyelashes. "I'll never wear a bra, it's all me. And trust *you* to notice, you pervert!"

Doc's expression hid his thoughts. *I'm not sure if she's feigning indignation or flirting.* He breathed in deeply. *Stop this, Pol. You're feeding my imagination in ways even I can blush at!*

"You can look, buster, but you can't touch."

"I'm a photographer, I have an eye for detail. And I'm definitely looking! When are you gonna do some cheesecake shots for me? You know damn well you have a sensational body."

"Ssshhh!" Polly whispered, putting her right forefinger to her lips. "Don't tell anybody."

Doc persisted. "I've done loads of spreads for men's mags," he boasted. "I know quality when I see it. You're the perfect package." His ruggedly weathered face suddenly wore a look of hope.

Polly was a little the worse for wear, but neither her reasoning nor her wit seemed impaired.

"Listen, pal, there's no way you'll get me *spreading* for some grotty men's mag you'd find in a barber's shop. I'm not desperate. Even if I wanted to be a model, at five-foot-three, I'm too short."

"No way! You're the perfect size. Anyway, you've got it all wrong, Polly. I just want to do some private artistic...tasteful...shots." He paused and eyed Polly up carefully. There was no response. Her face had paled and she seemed to be staring right through him. They turned towards the door and walked silently into the night.

Polly stopped dead. She used her nose like a dainty little vacuum cleaner to suck the cold air into her nostrils. She wobbled and quickly made a grab for Doc's left arm. "Phew! I'm gonna have to leave my car here. Can you drive me to the office, please, Doc? I've drunk tar foo much!"

"You've already asked me that. Yes, I'll drive you. My pleasure. As the Bard said, you've drunk well but not wisely."

"Bard? What's a bard? Have we been barred from the Nag's Head?"

"It's a saying. Oh, just forget it, babe. I can see it's a waste of time talking to you about anything at the moment."

They walked to his car. He unlocked the passenger door and held it open while she tumbled clumsily onto the leather seat.

"Phew, it stinks of marijuana in here! What if the police pull you over?"

"Not a problem," Doc replied with cavalier confidence. "I always carry a couple of containers of darkroom developing chemicals in the boot. If I'm stopped, I tell them it's the chemicals they can smell and get 'em to sniff the contents. By the time they get a nose full of that, it kills any other smell. Anyway, I know most of the cops in town and heaps of them owe me favours for one thing or another."

"You cunning devil. I always knew you photographers lived on your wits...and your big fat expense accounts."

# *Three*

It was Tuesday evening and there were few people in Cardwell town centre, so Doc had no problem finding a parking space on the usually busy Malthouse Lane. This was where most of the district's upmarket fashion and furniture shops were to be found.

Towering above them was the imposing office of the *Express*. It boasted a grand, rust-red brick facade with sculpted bone-coloured sandstone sills and window arches. A nineteenth century edifice, the former brewery was acclaimed by many savvy locals as an architectural icon and was topped off with a huge circular clock that hung majestically three floors above the pavement from an ornate, wrought-iron arm.

Doc locked his car and put his hand under Polly's left arm to support her as they walked towards a large plate-glass door.

"I'm all right, you don't have to carry me," Polly said petulantly.

Doc just smiled. He pressed a buzzer set into a brass plaque on the adjacent brickwork. Within seconds, a uniformed security guard appeared. He recognised the pair and let them in with a cheery, "Blimey, you two are working late."

"Thanks, Clifford," Doc and Polly said in unison.

"Only the ground floor's lit," the security man said, "but give me a minute and I'll switch on the lights in photographic and the reporters' room." With a scurry, the guard flicked a few switches on the wall. "There you are, folks, all the lights should be on up there now. Have a good evening. How long do you reckon you'll be?"

"Dunno," said Polly, trying to gather her senses. "Doc's got pictures to do and I've got a big interview to bash out...could be a couple of hours."

"Okay," Clifford said and returned to the paperback novel he'd left open on the security desk.

The newsroom was deserted when the pair entered. Polly went to her desk. Like many a reporter's work station, it was all but hidden beneath a jumble of newspapers, phone directories and old notebooks. All around were desks with typewriters, telephones, books, and other clutter that typified reporters' rooms the world over.

Polly's desk had an uncovered typewriter, wire trays and a jam jar stuffed with pens and pencils. She threw a few papers and an empty chocolate box into a nearby waste basket and set up her tape recorder in the newly cleared space.

"How are you feeling?" Doc asked with genuine concern.

"I have to be honest, Doc. I feel wasted. I shouldn't have raced those whiskies down. I think I'll write all this stuff tomorrow. If Duckworth complains, I'll..."

"Knock her out?" Doc offered with a sly grin.

"Something like that. Hey, I'd better let you get your pictures processed. Can I come and watch? In all the time I've been at the *Express*, I haven't seen inside the darkroom."

"Be my guest. It smells a bit chemically, but I'll be glad of the company." He fumbled in a trouser pocket and pulled out a key.

"How come it's kept locked?" Polly inquired.

"Because."

"Because what?"

"There's thousands of pounds of equipment in here: cameras, printers, lenses, plus all the photographers' personal gear. Thousands! Old Wally Parsons, the chief photographer, would have a heart attack if anything went missing." Doc waited for Polly to enter the photographers' dimly lit office. "After you...make a sharp left turn!"

In the half-light, Polly turned as instructed and walked straight into a heavy black curtain. She let out a shriek. "Bloody hell, you could have warned me about that."

Polly's scare made him laugh. "Part of the light trap. Now, even though we're totally alone, I'll lock the door and switch the glow on."

"The what? What's the glow?"

"The dim red light we work by. It won't ruin exposed film and it's connected to a warning light outside so people know the darkroom is in use."

It took a moment or two for Polly's eyes to get accustomed to the eerie red gloom. She found a table in one corner. Not seeing a chair, she hitched up her skirt and managed to jump up and sit on the table top. She wriggled to get comfortable.

Doc, meanwhile, donned a rubber apron and gloves and busied himself preparing film to put in a developing tank.

"You were right, Doc, it does smell chemically in here...it's like...stale vinegar. How do you work in this? Does this get on your clothes and overpower the stink of weed?"

"Polly, I'm going to have to disappear for a minute. There's another little room over to our right that's totally blacked out. The hole, we call it. It's where I have to load the exposed film onto spools. We do everything by touch. I won't be long. Don't get scared, there's no bogeyman."

"I bet you're a good toucher," Polly muttered to herself. "Got anything to drink in here? I want a drink!" she squawked.

"You've had enough, lassie."

"I've got the taste tonight. I'm feeling very, very something...very..."

A disembodied voice cut her off. "Very pissed. Just sit there and behave. There's nothing in here except stuff that will make you very sick. So do NOT touch anything!"

"Yes, Daddy. I'll be a good little girl, Daddy!" Polly slurred sarcastically. "Jeez, I'm sick of being good!"

A voice boomed out again from the darkness. "I really shouldn't be telling you this, but if you find your way to the photographers' lockers and look on the shelf above them, there's a bottle labelled *fixer*. It's the one with the skull and crossbones on it."

Polly slid down from the table and made her way through the gloom. "Is it a short, stubby bottle...clear liquid?" She reached up on tiptoes and tapped the bottle to the shelf's edge with her fingertips. "Got it," she said, double checking the label and running her fingers over the crude Jolly Roger drawing. "Do you want it?"

"No, it's for you," Doc answered.

"Waddya mean?"

"Open it and have a taste."

"Are you mad? You trying to kill me?"

"Try it, it's vodka. If you can find the pile of plastic cups out there near the shelf, pour me one, too. And if you tell *anybody* about this, the photographers will lynch you. And if you throw up in here, I'll—"

"You'll what, Doc?"

"Never mind."

Polly unscrewed the lid and tipped a little of the liquid onto her left hand. She sniffed it, then cautiously dipped the tip of her tongue into the tiny pool that had collected in her palm. "Bloody hell, it *IS* vodka!" She licked her hand and put the bottle to her lips, tipping her head back eagerly. She coughed and spluttered, then took another, longer swig. "I definitely should not be doing this, Doctor...Doc. I shushpect I am utterly pished and this red light isn't helping. It's making everything really weird. I feel weird, I think *I am* weird...everything's friggin' weird tonight."

There was no reply.

"Doc's ignoring you, Polly,' she grumbled to herself. "I'll show you how to get his attention!"

After a while, Doc emerged from the hole. He gasped with shock and almost dropped the film spools he was carrying. "Christ! Polly!"

In the soft red light, he found himself peering at Polly sprawled across the table and propped up on her right elbow. Apart from her flimsy cotton blouse, dangling earrings and boots, she was naked. The rest of her clothes lay on the darkroom floor.

Doc was dumfounded. "What the hell...?"

"You wanted to take me...well, here I am," Polly whispered provocatively.

Doc put down the spools and hurriedly tore off his apron and gloves. He put his hands on his hips then quickly threw them up to his head in a quandary.

"Do you like what you see?" Polly teased. She swung her feet down to the floor, wobbled on three-inch heels, then slowly began to unfasten her blouse.

Doc's eyes widened in disbelief.

With fumbling fingers, she undid the buttons. As the blouse swung open, Doc eagerly drank in her shape—her narrow waist, shapely legs, her oval navel and most of all, her magnificent breasts which jiggled and swayed from side to side tantalisingly with every move she made. The darkroom's red light accentuated the rosy hue of her nipples.

"You wanted to take me...take me!" she said huskily.

Doc was both mesmerised and tongue-tied. Flustered, his thoughts ran riot. *Polly, what are you doing? Are you asking me to take a photo, or are you offering yourself on a plate to me? Don't do this to me...please.* As he tried to untangle his thoughts, he sighed deeply. *There must be a reason for this shock metamorphosis.* He cleared his throat and composed himself before he said, "I thought..."

"Better not think, Doc. Do it!" Polly urged. "This is a once-in-a-lifetime opportunity. Take notice, Doc, I'm a Gillette girl, that's me!" she said, referring to the trade name of the famous razor blade manufacturer. "Polly Gilly. Gilly Polly, Ha ha! If Mary Quant can shave her pubes, then so can Polly Jordan! Did it yeshterday. Only problem is I couldn't do a heart shape like Mary's. I made a total mess, so I hacked everything off. First time I've been bald since...since I was in junior school." She breathed heavily and displayed an air of self-satisfaction.

Doc, on the other hand, sat and watched what was unfolding before him. *What the hell do I do now? You have reduced me to an incompetent teenager, Polly Jordan. I can't think straight. Should I, or shouldn't I? Oh, bloody hell, woman!*

"If you're going to take pictures, do it now, Doc. You asked, you begged. It's your first and last chance. But if you do, you have to print them right here and give me the negatives. That's the deal, Doc. I know what a Rolleiflex holds. You've got twelve exposures." It seemed for an instant her lucidity had returned.

"Polly, why are you doing this? You're driving me insane but..." His mind raced. *You have never confronted me like this. Why now? What's going in that pretty little head of yours? How am I supposed to know what you really want? You've turned this normally confident Irishman into a blithering idiot.*

Polly cupped a dainty hand under each breast and proudly pushed them up and towards him. "How about these? What do you reckon? Magazine material?"

At that point something seemed to resuscitate Doc's stunned nervous system like a jab in the ribs. "Thirty-four Cs!" was all he could splutter.

Polly frowned. "Ha, ha, ha! Wrong, wrong, wrong! Thirty-two double-Ds actually. Tut-tut! I thought you had an eye for detail," she mocked as she jiggled them from side to side. "That's according to my one and only bra. Told you, I can't stand bras. They're so restricting. I love my boobs swinging free. There's something incredibly sensual about feeling their weight pulling at you. I'll tell you another little secret...ssshh! The pill has made them grow. When I'm home alone—"

"Stop! Stop right there!" Doc pushed back his long brown hair and slowly drew closer to her. "Why are you doing this to me? What if somebody comes in?"

"We're the only people up here. In any case, the little light's on over the door, you said."

"Oh, Polly! What the hell am I going to do with you? I know journos are a bold lot and very daring, if I'm being honest. They have to be, I guess, in order to get their scoops, especially when, at the risk of being sexist, you women want to get there first, but you're really going over the top tonight." With his hands on her bare shoulders, he tenderly pulled his inebriated colleague to him. She lurched forward on unsteady legs. Her heaving bosom flattened against his chest. Through his shirt, he felt her heat and her heart thumping. He smoothed back her hair and gently took her face in his hands. It was so angelic, shining back at him, radiating unsullied innocence. "Polly...babe...this truly has been the most incredible, bizarre and wonderful night of my entire life, and God knows, I've had more than a few of those. My testosterone is running riot."

He stooped and kissed her lightly, gently on her lips. For a moment their eyes questioned each other's, then he kissed her once more, this time on her forehead, lingering and tenderly, in the way a father kisses his daughter. "Sorry, babe, you've drunk way too much," a resigned Doc said quietly. "Get dressed and I'll take you home. My news pictures can wait until tomorrow."

With one last defiant flourish, Polly cupped her right breast in her right hand. "Say goodnight to the nice, lovely Mister Doc."

Doc swallowed hard.

She repeated the process on her left side. "Say goodnight to Doc. Say night-night, I think we're all going home!" She looked sleepily into Doc's face and smiled. No more words were exchanged. The nothingness, the numbness said it all.

After fumbling to pull on her clothes, she let him put his arm around her shoulders. Wriggling his jacket free of a coat-hanger, he draped it around her shoulders and over her own coat. He opened the darkroom door, flicked off the lights and locked up. They walked out silently into the night. Doc smiled to himself, his thoughts clear. *I know I've made the right choice. Maybe I'll remember it fondly, or maybe I'll regret it for the rest of my life, but somehow I feel good. Yes, I feel good and it feels so right.*

# *Four*

Polly Jordan's spectacular plunge into the bottle, ending with her impromptu darkroom striptease, had begun earlier that afternoon.

"Mrs Flint? Mrs Elizabeth Flint?" the blonde stranger asked, almost apologetically.

"Yes, I'm Lizzie Flint, and who might you be? Do I know you?"

Hardly stopping for a breath, the young reporter blurted, "Hello, Mrs Flint, I'm Polly Jordan from *The Cardwell Express*. We're preparing a huge feature for next year to mark the twenty-fifth anniversary of the start of the Second World War and we've been told you have lots of stories about life in that era. Can I come in and do an interview, please? I won't stay too long, I promise."

"What I've got to say after all these years will hardly be news, dear, but come in. We can sit in the parlour."

Polly followed dutifully.

With shaky hands, Lizzie buttoned her cardigan up to the neck. "It seems very cold outside. I'll put the kettle on. Would you like a cup of tea?"

"No thanks, Mrs Flint. I'm not a tea drinker. You have a lovely little home here. It's so cosy. May I call you Lizzie?"

"Lizzie's fine, dear, everyone calls me that, but not Liz. I don't like Liz. I don't like them calling our Queen Liz. It's disrespectful."

Putting her subjects at ease was a reporter's skill Polly had down to a fine art. Her eyes darted about the room—to the fireplace, the polished walnut sideboard, the neatly-arranged ornaments and photographs, searching for anything to small-talk about. "Wow, I love your big clock. I've never seen one so beautiful."

Lizzie looked up at her timepiece with obvious pride. It was about three feet tall. Its face was edged with bold Roman numerals and its wooden body was crafted from a tightly grained wood which clearly had enjoyed a lifetime of care and polish. Behind a protective glass window, a pear-shaped brass pendulum elicited a loud tick with every swing.

Polly got up to take a closer look. Little figures of stags and boars had been carved into the wood and in Gothic lettering under twin holes in the face for the winding key was *Munich, 1903*.

"It's the same age as me," Lizzie said with obvious delight. "My son Billy brought it back from the war. He didn't come home until 1949. He was evacuated from Dunkirk. Have you heard of that? Thousands of our troops were cornered, and Winston Churchill, he was the prime minister then, arranged to bring them back home on hundreds of boats, or the Nazis would have killed them."

Polly quickly said, "Oh, yes, Dunkirk, I know about that." It was a little lie. Most of her knowledge of World War II had come from her father who was in the team that advised the Allies on weather prospects for the D-Day invasion of France. That occurred three years after the evacuation took place.

"Billy was on a small boat with some other soldiers when the Germans machine-gunned it from an aeroplane. The bullets missed our Billy but one man was killed and two others fell overboard wounded. Billy rescued them."

"Wow! What a hero," Polly said obligingly.

"But something happened. The boat sank or capsized or...well, I don't remember...but Billy must have hit his head or something. He lost his memory and doesn't remember anything after that. He woke up one morning in a hospital on the Isle of Man. He doesn't know to this day how he got there."

"Oh, that's a coincidence. I'm from the Isle of Man," Polly volunteered eagerly.

"It must be horrible on that island. They whip people with a birch, don't they?" Lizzie asked with concern. "Did they birch you at school when you were naughty, Polly?"

"No, Lizzie. I was always a good girl," Polly said reassuringly. "Actually, it's only criminals who get the birch. The courts order it, but only for violent crimes."

"Oh, that's all right then. Criminals deserve to suffer pain. I can't light a fire because I forgot to order coal. If you don't drink tea, I'll get us something else."

She left the room and came back holding a bottle of Johnnie Walker scotch whisky and two glasses. "This'll warm us up."

She lowered herself into the settee, smoothed her apron over her knees, then poured two generous whiskies.

"Cheers!" Lizzie toasted and drank it in one.

Polly gulped hers down too and clutched at her throat as the scotch burned its way south. "Whoops, I shouldn't have done that," she spluttered.

~ * ~

Later in the Nag's Head, Doc had taken a slow drink and lit a cigarette while Polly enthusiastically recounted her interview with Lizzie Flint.

"That woman has so many stories to tell. She'll need a whole supplement to herself. She told me about being a Land Army girl and seeing her best friend, Rose Thorne, killed. What a great name!" She smiled, more to show sympathy than happiness. "They were out helping a farmer plough a field up at a place called

Edgemoor Farm. Rose spotted a skylark's nest among the grass. It had chicks inside. Lizzie said Rose shouted to the ploughman to stop so she could save the little birds from being trodden on." Polly looked at her companion, eyes shining with enthusiasm.

"Sounds good," Doc interjected, "Did you manage to tape it all?"

"Shush," Polly scolded. "The farmer stopped the plough and Rose crawled behind the horses. As she went to rescue the chicks from being killed by ploughshare, there was a sudden freak clap of thunder. She said one of the two carthorses snorted with fear and kicked out with its back legs. A hoof hit Rose full in the face. The horses were shod with steel shoes. Lizzie reckoned Rose was dead before her body hit the ground."

Doc lit another cigarette and sank back in his chair with a half-smile as Polly recounted more.

"Then she told tales about flirting with young American GIs who were stationed near Cardwell. I'll bet she was a handful back then. She used to lead them on a bit and accept gifts of nylon stockings, cigarettes and coffee. They could get all sorts of things that were either rationed or unavailable to everyday English people. Some of the GIs were little more than boys, and came from places in the United States most people would never have heard of. Only a few had ever been out of their county, let alone overseas."

"I know many of our boys were conscripted as soon as they were eighteen," Doc added. "That's no age to be fighting for king and country, is it?"

"Lizzie said she felt sorry for them because they were so innocent, and were probably on a one-way trip without ever enjoying pleasure with a woman. But she insisted she never gave them *everything*. She let them fondle and kiss her, but if they pressed her for sex, she'd ask them to wait a couple more days until her rash went away." Polly nudged Doc's arm and then continued. "Lizzie has a wicked sort of chuckle and recalling those times seemed to bring back a sparkle to her eyes. Mind you, half of that could be put down to the whisky."

"I'm sorry I wasn't there to get pictures," Doc said.

"Don't worry. I saved your bacon. I managed to borrow a lovely black and white snap of Lizzie and Rose in their Land Army uniforms. Lizzie was quite a looker back then. No wonder the guys homed in on her."

Doc looked at the photo and smiled, raising his eyebrows knowingly.

"She said we can use it in the supplement, but you must promise to look after it and be careful with the frame. It's decorated pewter and it's her pride and joy."

"No, worries," Doc said confidently. "When have you ever known me to stuff up? Actually, don't answer that! Another scotch?" he urged.

"Oh, all right, but I've already had plenty, so don't let me drink too much more."

"Don't worry, I'll keep my eye on you."

"You've been eyeing me for ages, Doc. Don't think I'm not onto you," Polly said with a laugh. "Cheers, you Irish perve!"

"I think I prefer rake to perve. Rake sounds a bit more roguish," Doc parried, "and cheers to you."

~ * ~

The phone in the bedroom of Polly's first-floor apartment rang and rang until she woke with a groan. Rolling to the edge of her bed, she carelessly flung out an arm, sending the handset flying from her bedside table and crashing to the floor. With her face partially buried in the pillow, she managed to fish around on the floor for the receiver. Slowly she put it to her ear. "Whoever it is, leave me alone. I'm dying."

"How are you, babe?" The caller's accent was unmistakable. "Do you know what time it is?"

"Christ, Doc, I feel so ill," she moaned. "I've puked I don't know how many times in the night."

"Do you remember *anything* of last night?" Doc asked with genuine concern.

"I can remember some things. I know I made a complete arse of myself. I'm so embarrassed. Promise you will never...ever...*EVER* tell anyone, Doc? I mean it. Do I have your word?"

"Of course," he replied. "Like you said in the pub, chivalry lives on. I've just got one question...why? What got into you, apart from too much booze?"

"I've been asking myself that. Something came over me that made me want to do something totally wild. Don't know whether it was the alcohol or some hidden me trying to get out like a mad bloody genie. I'm talking trash, Doc, ignore me."

Doc stayed silent.

"I think I'll stay in bed and maybe go to work this afternoon."

"Well, that's going to be difficult."

"Why?"

"It's already afternoon. It's two-thirty."

"Oh, shit! That creep Duckworth is going to have my guts for garters. I'll ring in sick. Well, it's the truth. I'm sick as a dog. Truly, I'm sorry about last night, especially now my head's throbbing like a bloody jackhammer."

"It's all right, babe, don't sweat it."

Suddenly Polly's anxiety turned to panic. "Hey, you didn't take any pictures, did you? Tell me you didn't, Doc. I'm sorry I was a complete bozo."

"Nothing to forgive and, no, I didn't take any pictures."

"I'm so ashamed."

"Couldn't take pictures in that light. Can't use flash in a dark room. Anyway, my hands were trembling so badly I couldn't have held a camera still. But, hey, you put on a show that I'll remember when I'm old and grey."

"I hope you don't tell your fiancée about it."

"That's never going to happen. Lesley and I have broken up. She just decided she wanted to go to Canada to teach."

"Oh, my word, I had no idea. I'm so sorry, Doc. I didn't even know she was a teacher."

"She has friends over there and they've been telling her for years about the lifestyle and better standard of living."

"I'm sad for you, Doc."

"Obviously, she prefers the Mounties to the old Doc," he quipped light-heartedly.

Polly dragged herself off the bed and, with her eiderdown wrapped around her, shuffled over to her bedroom window and peeped out. As she parted the curtains, she accidentally tripped on the phone cable and sent the cradle crashing to the floor a second time.

"What was that?" Doc asked.

"Oh, just the phone falling. So...that means you're single. How come you didn't try to screw me when you had the chance? I was totally vulnerable. It was the chance of a lifetime and you passed."

"It would have been too easy, babe, but where I come from, we leave the raping and pillaging to the heathens. You were so far gone, it would have been only one step away from...well, you know."

"You sound like you really mean that, Doc. I'm impressed. I owe you." She threw the eiderdown on the bed and tugged at the hem of her silk shorty-nighty. "Not every man would have had such control."

"I'm not every man."

"You're not, Doc, you're definitely not. You're a wonderful human being and in another life, I could love you. Shit, I'm getting all sentimental," Polly conceded. "You're not queer are, you? Don't answer that! You *are* a saint, though. A total freak, but a saint. Saint Gerald. Crickey, I don't think I've ever called you by your first name," she giggled. "Hey, thanks for calling and thanks for being a good friend. I'm going back to bed."

"Okay. I'd better do some work. See you."

"Hey, wait a minute," Polly called anxiously. "How did I get home?"

"I drove you."

"So...how did I get into bed? More to the point, how did I get into this nightie?"

"It's not the first time I've undressed a woman and put her to bed, babe."

"Well, I don't suppose it matters after my burlesque show," Polly replied with an air of resignation.

Doc silently chastised himself, shaking his head to clear his thoughts. *Imaginative pictures of last night's antics are not needed here.* "Hair of the dog tonight?"

"Haven't you seen enough of me?" Polly croaked. "Christ, what am I saying? You've seen bloody *all* of me—twice. I've got no secrets now."

There was no answer, just a click on the other end of the line.

Polly flopped back onto her bed. As she pulled the eiderdown up to her neck, the phone rang again.

"It's me, again. Just letting you know your car's in the company executives' car park."

"How did you swing that?" Polly asked. "I'm impressed."

"I was driving past the Nag's Head this morning and a cop was just about to give you a parking ticket. He owes me a favour or two. He went to the cop shop to get one of their special bunches of keys...they open just about every make of car. Then he drove it round to the office and I fixed the parking with a mate of Clifford's in security. So no problem, just immaculate timing."

"Wow, thanks. It's good to have contacts, eh? The second Docherty miracle. One more and I'll be writing a story about your canonization. Hey, for your third miracle, why not give up smoking dope?"

"No way! Never! That's a negative, Polly."

She laughed, then put her hand to her forehead. "Negative, very funny, ha, ha, I get it...a photographer's joke. See you." Click! *Please, Lord, let there be some headache tablets in the bathroom cabinet.*

## *Five*

It was almost two weeks before Polly returned to work at the *Express*. The miserable feeling of being hung over was just the start of a run of illness that ended with a heavy bout of the flu. As she scanned the reporters' diary to see what her assignments were for the first day back, she could almost feel Duckworth's glare boring into the back of her neck.

"Jordan, you're on courts for the rest of this week. Didn't know when you were coming back," Duckworth bellowed across the newsroom.

"Suits me," Polly replied. "There's always a decent story or two from court cases."

"Yeah, well don't expect any by-lines. Your name won't be on any court stories. Any junior reporter could just sit on their arse and write notes."

Polly seethed as she was belittled by the news editor in front of her colleagues, but refused to take the bait. She knew Duckworth was spoiling for a fight and looking for any excuse to get her sacked.

It was almost six-thirty in the evening by the time Polly finished typing up her last court story. Suddenly she remembered she still had to compose the Lizzie Flint feature and submit it for the commemorative war supplement. She slid open the top drawer of her desk to find the small cassette containing the taped interview with Lizzie. Slightly panicked, she thought, *Where the hell is it?* As her fingers busily searched the jumbled contents of the drawer, Polly recalled a young reporter at the *Express* talking a few weeks earlier about how he took his tape recorder to cover the retirement dinner of a renowned public school headmaster. For readers in Cardwell, the retirement was big news. When he returned to the office, all he could hear on tape was the rattling of cutlery, the chinking of wine glasses and the drone of scores of voices. The headmaster's farewell speech was inaudible. He recounted how Duckworth went purple in the face as she screamed and hurled abuse at him. Somehow the *Express* managed to cobble together a story, but the reporter confessed he had been a whisker away from being dismissed on the spot.

She fished around and finally found the cassette. "Phew! Still there. Losing that would be the last straw with Duckworth," she muttered. She also came across a brown envelope from the photographic department. It contained a note from Doc and the framed photo she had borrowed from Lizzie: *Found this pic on your desk. Know you got side-tracked on night of interview. Handed it in to features editor. He's had it processed and wants me to return it. Reckon it's something you'd like to do yourself. Best, Gerry D.*

"I'll do that first thing tomorrow before work," Polly reasoned.

Next morning, she was up early. The weather was mild so she threw her coat onto the passenger seat of her Triumph Spitfire and set off in the direction of Pitt Street, about a ten-minute drive from her apartment. She steered her car at a crawl looking for Lizzie's distinctive purple door. She parked, picked up the pewter photo frame and went to knock. The curtains were closed, both upstairs and down. Older generations of Lancashire folk would know the significance of curtains drawn in the day, but Polly was not from those parts. Before she got chance to knock, the purple door swung wide open.

"Hello, there!" A tall man whom Polly guessed to be in his early forties opened the door. "I saw you through the curtains. Are you selling something?"

Polly smiled politely and asked for Lizzie. She explained about the interview almost three weeks earlier and that she had come to return the photo.

"You'd better come in." His voice was gentle and reassuring. It immediately put Polly at ease, so she followed him into the parlour.

"Please sit down," he said, holding out a hand in the direction of Lizzie's settee. "I'm Mrs Flint's son, William, Bill. I'm sorry, but I have some bad news. My mother passed away five days ago."

Polly gasped and threw her hands to her chest. "Oh, that's such a shock. What happened? Was it an accident? She seemed so healthy and happy when I interviewed her."

"The doctor said her heart just gave out. She had a bit of a rough time in the war, many people did, and I know she drank a little too much scotch. She died in her sleep, so that was a blessing. One of the neighbours raised the alarm when he came to give her his newspaper and couldn't get an answer."

"I'm truly, truly sorry. Please accept my condolences and those of *The Caldwell Express*. Do you want me to scrap the interview? Would it upset you to see it in print?"

"No, please don't do that. I'm sure Mam would want her little bit of fame. When will it be published?"

Polly told him about the time-frame for the supplement.

"I don't think I'll see it. I'll be well and truly back home in Australia by then."

With the supplement in mind, Polly wanted to ask about his wartime heroism and the missing years since the evacuation of Dunkirk, but thought it a private family matter and a completely inappropriate time. Even so, her reporter's curiosity was working overtime. She casually asked him instead about his life down under and showed keen interest when he told her he was an artist. "I'm glad you're in the media too," she chirped, trying to lift the gloomy atmosphere. "I suspect your skills are far greater than mine and in a different branch. Do you draw, or paint...or sculpt?"

"I've studied sculpture, but don't, or should I say *can't* claim any prowess at it. The other two fields are what I specialise in. I own an art gallery in Melbourne and travel quite a bit. I don't come to the northern hemisphere that often, so I always make a point of visiting Mam when I'm within striking distance of here. My mother might have mentioned me. Maybe not. Her memory let her down sometimes. It seems odd talking about her in the past tense. You always assume your parents will last for ever."

He reflected silently for a moment and wrung his hands. "I haven't come to terms yet with her death. She was only sixty, which isn't considered old these days." He pulled a handkerchief from his pocket and dabbed at his eyes. "I'm sorry. Men shouldn't cry." He looked around wistfully. "I can't believe she's not here. I spent a lot of my younger years in this house."

"Don't apologise," Polly reassured him. "It's perfectly natural when you lose someone close."

He was quite handsome in a way that Polly silently summed up as being just short of pretty. His light brown hair was streaked with wisps of grey at the temples. Bright blue eyes lit up his suntanned face. She found the way he showed emotion oddly disarming and warmed to him immediately.

"After all the red tape and procedural stuff, it's finally her funeral tomorrow. It's at Overdale, the local crematorium. I don't believe in burials. Neither did Mam. They just leave graves behind for others to tend."

"Yes, I know Overdale," Polly replied. "I've covered quite a few goodbyes there…you know, famous celebrities and people in the news. Were you close when…?"

He was quick to anticipate the question. "No, I was at home in Australia. I closed the gallery and flew out straight away. I still haven't recovered from the flight. That journey always seems interminably long. President Kennedy in America is talking about putting a man on the moon by 1970, yet we can't get across the globe in much less than two days." He managed a nervous smile and Polly empathised with a subdued laugh.

"How are you going to get to Overdale? You obviously won't have a car."

"It's just going to be a quiet send-off. Mam wouldn't have wanted a fuss. There'll be a few neighbours and me. Nobody else that I know of. I'll get a lift if somebody has a car, or get a taxi."

Unhesitatingly, Polly found herself saying, "I'll drive you, if you like. Tomorrow's my day off."

"No, I couldn't expect that of you," he replied, "especially on a day off. You don't want to be going to a stranger's funeral."

"Funny, but I don't regard your mum as a stranger, Mr Flint. We spent a lovely afternoon together and I feel I got to know her. I thought she was a wonderful, kind and knowledgeable person. It would be a pleasure."

"Call me Bill, please, and thank you so much for your kind words. I don't think I can refuse after such a compliment."

The two made arrangements to meet the next day and Polly attended the service in the crematorium chapel. The service for Lizzie was short, but suitably respectful and dignified. As Polly and Bill walked from the chapel into the mild afternoon air, there was an awkward silence. Polly searched for something to say as she unlocked the doors of her car. "I always find it sad but spooky when the coffin disappears behind that purple velvet curtain, don't you?"

Bill opened the passenger door but offered no reply. He seemed lost in reflective thoughts.

Polly sensed her observation had fallen short of the mark. After leaving Overdale's grounds, she threw her Spitfire into top gear and pushed it well over the thirty miles per hour speed limit along Charnock Avenue, the main road out of Cardwell. Bill dangled his arm out of the passenger window.

"Nice car."

"It's not bad," Polly replied. "I've just managed to make the final payment. It's second -hand. I couldn't afford a new car on my wage. Most people my age can't wait to own a Leyland Mini. I wanted to be different. That's me all over...Miss Different. And that might cost me. My mechanic tells me the gearbox needs some work and it sounds expensive. I might trade her in next year. Our motoring editor reckons there'll be a revamped version with overdrive."

"Yes, thought I detected a bit of a clunk going through the gears. You like driving fast, then?"

"I have to admit to liking a bit of a thrill, yes. I was visiting an ex-colleague over on the Wirral a few weeks ago and I got done for speeding in Wallasey. I have to go to court soon, which will be an absolute drag, driving all that way back and taking time off work." As she endeavoured to keep the conversation light, Polly sensed Bill's grief. "Maybe we could do something to brighten this sombre day a little," she suggested. "Do you fancy going for a spin over the moors, Bill?"

He turned his head and seemed to take a little time to weigh up this interesting girl at the wheel. There was a flicker of a smile. "Why not? I haven't been over the moors for years. To be honest, today's been more stressful than I imagined it would be. I'll miss Mam, even though I didn't see much of her since I went to live in Melbourne. Hey, Polly, I'm really glad you came to the service. Thanks for your support."

She smiled and nodded, but stopped herself from adding the customary, *my pleasure.*

As the little sports car flashed past the farms' gates and hedgerows along the back roads of Cardwell's rural fringe, Bill recognised a landmark. "Isn't that Edgemoor Farm over there beyond that thicket? Yes, I've spotted the old stone farmhouse."

"Oh wow!" Polly exclaimed. "I remember your mother talking about that place in her interview. The farmer hanged himself in the barn two years after your mum's friend was killed by a horse."

"Yes," said Bill. "I heard about it years later, just before I emigrated."

*Hmm, that's strange,* Polly thought. *Surely he couldn't have missed such a big news item if he lived in Cardwell. On the other hand, maybe I'm being too curious. The reporters' curse.* "I don't believe this," she exclaimed. "Look up! Is that the sun trying to push through the clouds?"

Out of the blue, Bill said, "Why don't we pull over and go for a walk. I used to go for walks up here in my younger days. If my memory serves me well, there's a path somewhere near here that leads down to a little brook."

With the Spitfire safely locked, Bill and Polly began their afternoon stroll. Before long they located the path. It was partly overgrown but easy to follow. Within two hundred yards, they found the brook still trickling its way down from the hilly moors skirting the town and they walked along its bank until they came to a flat grassy embankment. The path took them past a sturdy clump of hawthorn bushes. Most of the flowers' white petals had withered, and in their place, plump red berries hung waiting to sustain a host of birds through the coming winter months. The sound of the shallow brook babbling over beds of smooth, time-worn pebbles was all that could be heard, except for a skylark singing cheerfully. It was so high in the sky it was almost lost from view.

"This is so peaceful," Bill said. "You sometimes forget that grubby old Cardwell has such beauty spots. I didn't know skylarks sang like that so late in the year."

The mention of skylarks sent a shiver down Polly's spine as the story of Rose Thorne's awful death flashed into her mind. She took a moment to compose herself. "Did you come here often...before you went overseas?" she asked as she flicked a small pebble from the brook's edge into the water. "Brrr! The water's so cold."

"Now and then," replied Bill and felt the ground with his right hand. "The grass is actually dry. Shall we sit for a while? What about you, Polly, are you a country girl at heart?"

"I don't get time, Bill. I'm always too busy chasing stories. I wish sometimes I had another job, but I haven't a clue what I would do."

"You sound as if you're a bit lost," Bill observed.

"In a way I am. I can't explain it, but my life is at some sort of crossroad," Polly confided cryptically. She stared at the sky and hesitated before saying, "I've never asked anyone this before, but do you ever get a strange feeling when you, sort of, ask yourself who you are?"

Bill's face conjured a quizzical expression.

"It's hard to explain but in quiet, contemplative moments, sometimes you don't know yourself. It's as if you're a sort of ghost or spirit or something looking at yourself from outside your own body. You wonder if you are really you, as if you're in a weird, timeless dream. You catch yourself staring into space, trying to work out if you actually exist and whether you are imagining life. Am I some imaginary ethereal entity in a body someone's picked out for me?" She paused before she stated, "I don't even know if I can put the feeling into words. It's crazy...as a journalist, I have all these words in my head, yet I can't find the right ones to describe the feeling." Pausing again, she carefully chose her words before she continued. "Is it a problem of philosophy or even existentialism? Not that I know much about either," she said. "It's all too hard. I'm a simple newshound, not an intellectual."

"It all sounds a bit like you're living in the plot of a scary movie, yet in one sense I kind of understand," Bill replied. "Is it like you're in some sort of waking dream, analysing yourself? Have you ever thought about asking a psychologist or someone who studies the brain?"

Polly frowned. "Are you implying I'm mad?" she asked with mock indignation.

"No, not..."

"Something happens," she continued, "and it stirs you from this strange mental treacle you're trapped in. Something or someone might touch your body and you realise you *do* exist. Your nerve endings jolt you back to reality. I often think the only sure way we know we exist is though pain. When you feel pain, you truly *know* you are alive. It fires the senses; it wakes the brain like a scream in your ear."

To Bill, the expression on her face was one seeking approval or empathy. For his part, he was struggling to fathom how someone so physically perfect could be so complicated. The only thing certain to him was that his fascination with this beautiful, complex life-form was multiplying by the second. It was an intense feeling he had not experienced before. "I don't think I can agree with you about pain, Polly. Pain is subjective, but it can destroy, change, bring hatred. Surely there are other things that can make you feel alive...food, friendship, love?"

Gently she rolled over onto her stomach. With her back arched, she propped herself up on her elbows and cupped her chin in her hands. Her face had assumed a childlike expression. Her eyes danced from Bill's eyes to the brook and back to Bill. "I'm sorry, I'm rambling on," she apologised. 'I can hardly believe I'm baring my soul to a—"

"Stranger?" he volunteered.

"No! Well, yes. But you don't strike me as a stranger even though we've just met." She watched Bill intently as he juggled small pebbles then tossed them high in the air and skilfully caught them. In his dark suit, he looked handsome, but not in a rugged way. Not like Doc. She knew already that she was curiously attracted to this artistic being from the other side of the world. At that moment, she felt contented, happy. This new man was a thinker, intriguing and with the right kind of emotions. He was a far cry from the man she had cast off a few months ago, whose first thought just about every weekend was to go fishing with his mates.

They maintained a silence for a while as they stared across the brook and idly watched a family of rabbits dart in and out of a gorse thicket.

Breaking the silence, Bill said, "Lie back on the grass and look up."

Polly slowly complied and asked. "Why? What am I supposed to be looking at?"

"What do you see?"

"I see a tiny speck up there, a skylark. And some fluffy cumulus clouds."

"Cumulus? Yes, I think you're correct. You surprise me. Do you know much about clouds?"

"Oh, yes, they're definitely cumulus humilis," Polly affirmed. "I love clouds...so many shapes and forms and hues, and they're free to wander. No cares, no responsibilities. Just wandering about, shopping for rain then leaking every once in a while. My dad worked in the met. office during World War II. In fact, he was on the team that provided weather forecasts for the Allies so they could launch the D-Day landings in France. He taught me about clouds. I must have driven him mad with my questions. Even a bedtime story had to have clouds in it." Her expression was pensive, yet her eyes sparkled with happiness. "The really amazing thing about clouds is that they can hold millions, possibly billions of gallons of water up there, defying gravity. They must be the only things in the world that can do that. Of course, ultimately, the magic show ends and...*poof!*...it rains and..." She stopped mid-sentence. "Sorry. I'm rambling again like a babbling idiot."

"No, no, you're not. I'm loving hearing your life story, at least the childhood bits. That's a very poetic way of putting it, you know, about clouds."

"Yeah, right! It's a load of rubbish. It sounds like something from a child's story book."

"I too have often wondered how all that water can stay up there, floating around then suddenly come crashing down."

"I'll tell you one day," Polly said with a smile. "The thing that puzzles me is not clouds and rain, but why we call our planet Earth, you know...soil, solid ground, when about seventy per cent is water. Our home should be called Aquarius, not Earth. How old is water? It must have been recycled for millions of years. Maybe billions. It all starts and ends with clouds—they're like delivery drivers."

"Good point," Bill replied enthusiastically.

They gazed quietly at the pale blue sky as its cotton-wool clouds scudded by.

"Wow! Up there! Look! I've found my favourite cloud," Bill said softly. "Can you see yours?"

"My favourite? How can you have a favourite cloud? One minute they're there, next they're gone. No one cloud stays the same. They form, then transform."

"Ah, that's where you're wrong," Bill explained with gentle authority. He put his hands behind his head for support and gazed up into the infinity. "Clouds change shape, that's true, but they are entities, just like you and me. Once they drift out of view, they regroup, re-form and journey on. They go right around the world in an endless orbit and come back round time and time again. It never stops. It's just that we don't notice. Pick one out and commit it to memory and next time you look up, try to find it. We can all have a favourite cloud."

Polly laughed. "Bollocks!" It was the first time she had been able to fully let go with Bill and she enjoyed the moment. "You're a crackpot," she giggled. "You said you were an artist. You're definitely a bullshit artist!"

"Don't you believe me? The Australian Aborigines know all about clouds. They have stories about them in their Dreaming. Their clouds have names and lives and powers."

Polly couldn't argue with something she knew nothing about. "Mmm...maybe, but a favourite cloud here, in grubby old Cardwell? I don't think so, Mister Flint." She was startled when she felt Bill roll on his side and rest his strong frame against her body. "Hello you!" was all she could say and suddenly felt uncharacteristically shy.

Bill looked into her eyes, searching, questioning, almost pleading. She gazed back, knowing that an attraction to him was slowly beginning. There was a mystique about him that appealed to her. Somewhere below that tanned skin there were layers to peel back and she suspected that if she were given the opportunity, she would find an artist's sensitivity, but she guessed there was also vulnerability. Her senses tingled. She was confused. He wasn't like any other man she had known. "Time to go," she announced, the lack of enthusiasm obvious in her tone.

"Okay," Bill said. Having risen first, he stretched out a hand to help her to her feet. They brushed themselves clear of grass and a few early autumn leaves and started to walk back to the car. Bill's thoughts were of the longing he felt to hold Polly's hand. *I fear if I touch her, she might reject me. It has been a memorable interlude in an otherwise morbid day, but I don't want to ruin it by making a wrong move.*

Polly was deep in thought too. *What do I really know about this new man? Virtually nothing. Is he married, engaged, divorced? Should I even think of becoming remotely involved with a man who lives literally on Earth's far side? The one thing I can allow myself to think is, he seems trustworthy.*

Back at his mother's home, Bill invited Polly in. "Let's have a drink to mark Lizzie's farewell," he said. "There's only scotch, I'm afraid, unless you want a cup of tea."

"Scotch's fine, but make it a small one. I have to drive home."

It wasn't the driving so much as the fractured memories of the last time she drank whisky. Over-indulgence had led to her raunchy performance in the *Express* photographers' darkroom. In her mind, alarm bells were sounding loud and clear. She glanced at Lizzie's wall clock to check the time.

"You like that clock, don't you?" Bill observed. "My mother wrote to me after your interview and told me how you had admired it. It turned out to be the last thing she ever wrote."

"It's fantastic," Polly reaffirmed.

"I'm glad you like it, because I want you to have it. Mam would have liked you to enjoy it."

"I couldn't possibly take it."

"If you don't, it'll just end up on the tip...I can't cart something that size back to Australia."

"I suppose if you put it that way, I'd be happy to oblige. I accept gratefully, thank you, Bill." With that, Polly rose from the settee impulsively and planted a kiss on Bill's lips. "Thanks!"

In a flash, Bill put down his drink, threw off his suit jacket and hugged Polly. She felt totally trapped in his powerful arms, but did nothing to resist. He kissed her passionately time and again, and she responded in kind. They fell backwards onto the settee locked in an embrace. Polly raced to undo his shirt buttons. She was all fingers and thumbs. She pressed her body against his as she fumbled and panted, "Married?"

"No...never!"

The anticipation was electric. Bill suddenly grasped her lightly by the wrists. "Not here, not in Mam's place. It doesn't seem right."

"That's cool—my place then," Polly gasped with urgency.

The ten-minute drive to her apartment seemed an eternity. Bill placed the clock carefully on her apartment's kitchen table.

"In here!" Polly ordered, heading for the bedroom. "Now!"

They launched themselves onto her still unmade bed.

"I can't believe this is happening," Polly spluttered.

"Neither can I, but what the hell!"

Within seconds they had shed their clothes and paused only momentarily to take in each other's nakedness. Polly closed her eyes with unabashed pleasure as Bill's eager hands found her breasts. She welcomed the feel of his palms; they were large and clearly had strength, yet soft, with not a trace of a callus, the hands of an artist. She writhed and rolled her head from side to side as his sensitive fingers descended slowly over her downy belly. His fingers continued to roam delicately across the expanse of sprouting stubble.

Polly anticipated Flint's curiosity. "I shaved. Failed attempt at a Mary Quant," she said, breathing heavily.

"Mary Quant?" Bill echoed.

"Oh, I forgot you're from Oz. I don't suppose you've heard of her."

"We're not *that* far behind the times," Bill said. "It's the sixties there too, you know."

"Shhhh, no more talking," Polly whispered huskily.

Instantly they were exploring each other's mouth with their tongues.

As they locked together, Flint rolled so that Polly was suddenly on top. She felt his fingernails dig into her buttocks with each powerful push.

Flint was blind to self-control.

Polly let out a scream that transitioned to a long, low moan followed by a contented sigh. Panting after the short, spontaneous and energy-sapping collision, they pulled themselves apart and rolled onto their backs. In silence they stared at the ceiling. Slowly their gasping for breath subsided.

"I can't believe we just did that," Polly exclaimed.

"Neither can I," Bill said remorsefully, "but what kind of man am I, enjoying sex with a young woman on the day of his mother's funeral?"

Polly was quick to reply. "Would you rather I'd been a young man?"

"What?" Bill snapped, taking the bait. "Not today," he joked.

"Mr Flint, if anyone's to blame, it's me. It was me who suggested going up to the moors."

"That's true," Bill conceded, "although I don't think you had *that* in mind when you suggested it. Anyway, I hope you don't regret it, because I certainly don't."

"No way! It was the best sex I've had in months, years. In fact, it's the only sex I've had for ages, although I..." She didn't get to finish her sentence.

Bill's lips pressed against hers and his soft, smooth hands wandered all over her body.

Silence reigned until Polly sat up with a jolt. "Bill, what happens now? One minute we were at your mother's funeral, then bingo, we end up here, making love. This has been a beautiful experience, but I want you to know I'm not the kind of girl to jump into bed with every wild colonial boy. For all I know, I might never see you again. If I had to write a story about you, I couldn't fill more than one page in my notebook."

Bill sat up. His expression was serious in a blank sort of way, like a poker player about to play a hand that would either ruin him or break the bank. "Up on the moors, you said you were at a crossroad. Well, in the last half-hour, I think I have reached a crossroad too. I don't know what to do, Polly, or what to think. I believe my life has just taken a right-angle turn, maybe a U-turn. I'm supposed to fly back to Melbourne in five days."

"Hell's bells, five days. Will you go? You *have* to go back, don't you? I mean your life is over there, on the other side of the world. This is it, isn't it? All there is, all there ever will be." She wanted to ask if it was *'just a funeral fling'*, but it might sound like a cheap newspaper headline, tacky and hurtful. She silently scolded herself. "Today's Friday, so you'll be taking off on...Tuesday?"

Bill looked deep into the blueness of her eyes, now slightly damp, and read what he took to be sorrow. She was about to speak again when he quickly put his right index finger to her lips. "Shhhh! Don't analyse this. Let's sleep on it and see how we feel in the morning."

Polly simply stared, expressionless.

"By sleep on it, I meant, well, you know, think it over, not sleep here, not literally." As he became more tongue-tied and confused, his embarrassment grew.

They laughed together. It all felt so right.

Suddenly his mind became sharply focused. "Hell, we didn't take any precautions...we were in such a frenzy."

His bout of panic was met with a giggle. "Don't worry, Bill, I'm a modern girl," Polly announced. "I've been on the pill for the last six months, not that I needed it with my stupid ex-boyfriend. By the way, don't ask me any questions. I don't know what happens in Australia, but here in England, doctors are only allowed to prescribe it for married women, but I have...let's say...contacts."

Polly wrapped the eiderdown around her bare shoulders and picked up her watch from the bedside table. "Maybe we should call it a day, Bill. No, that came out all wrong...not call it a day and go our separate ways but, you go home and...'

"I thought I was the one getting confused and befuddled," Bill said with a warm smile. He breathed in deeply. "Oh, speaking of time, I checked out Mam's old clock and it doesn't chime. If you like, I'll have a look at it tomorrow and see if I can fix it. She loved it chiming, although apparently the neighbours weren't too upset when it took its vow of silence."

"You have a way with words, Bill Flint. I like that in a man."

"Are you working tomorrow?" he asked.

"No, for once, Duckworth, my news editor, a right bitch by the way, has given me a Saturday off. Why? Do you want to meet up?"

"I thought you might like to come round to my mother's house, which I suppose is mine now, and help me tinker with the clock, unless you've something planned."

"Nothing planned," Polly enthused. "And sure thing! I'll come and watch the artist handle time."

"Love it. You say I have a way with words, which is understandable in your line of work. I love a girl whose brains are not in her blouse. Oh dear, I've put my foot in my mouth again. That wasn't a crude reference to your, er, bosom. I was just trying to say..."

"Bill, shut up and kiss me," Polly commanded. They locked in a lingering embrace.

"Now go!" she said pointing to her bedroom door, "and don't forget to take the clock. I'll be round tomorrow morning between nine-thirty and ten. I have to nip into town first."

As the bedroom door closed with a click, Polly threw herself backwards onto the bed. She wriggled and rolled over, burying her face in the pillow where Bill had lain after they made love. Then, curiously, she sniffed the bedclothes like a bloodhound trying to catch the faintest scent, the merest trace of this new man's presence. *Mmm, Bill Flint, what the hell have you done to me?* Her mind raced with thoughts of a man from ten thousand miles away whom she barely knew. A long, deep sigh overwhelmed her and exhaustion lulled her into a deep sleep.

# *Six*

It was just before nine the next morning and Polly found herself rapping on the purple door of the Flint home once again. Her mind wandered back to her first visit and her interview with Lizzie. However, this time she was not chasing a story for the *Express*.

Bill was prompt in answering the door. "Hey, g'day, Polly. Jeez, you're early. I didn't expect to see you here so soon."

Polly's face was pale and bore a look of worry. "I'm in a quandary. I've just checked my diary and I'm due in court on that speeding summons on Monday...in Wallasey, which is the other side of the River Mersey from Liverpool, bloody miles away."

"Yes, I know Wallasey," Bill countered in a low, calm voice. "I went there on a Wolf Cubs' camping holiday when I was about ten. I remember crossing the Mersey on a ferry. Fantastic memory!"

"Yes, but that means I'll be away for most of Monday, which is the last day before you fly out. I was convinced the court case wasn't for another two weeks. Damn! Damn! Damn it!"

Bill stroked the stubble on his chin and stared at the kitchen table on which he had just started to take apart his mother's clock. "Okay," he began, "I was sort of planning to take you out for lunch somewhere, or even dinner, but this puts a new complexion on things."

"I haven't been to town yet," Polly told him. "As soon as I realised Monday was court day, I rushed over to tell you. I was going to ring, but I didn't remember seeing a phone in the house."

"No, Mam wouldn't have one, which was a pain in the you-know-what when I was on the other side of the world."

"I'm so sorry, Bill. This is something I can't duck out of."

"No, of course not, but I could always come over to Wallasey with you, if you wanted me to accompany you. In fact, I have something to do, too."

"What, in Wallasey?" she asked with a puzzled look.

"No, here in Cardwell. I have to pick up my mother's ashes from the crematorium. If you were to pick me up about eight-thirty, we could collect them. I realise it's a bit macabre, but then we could drive on to Wallasey for the court case."

Polly paused for a moment and thought about Bill's impromptu plan. "You mean drive to Wallasey and back with your mother...with the ashes...in the car?"

"Does that spook you? If it does, tell me and I can arrange to go there by myself."

"No, no," Polly reassured him. "It's not a problem. I was just taken aback at first. Are you planning to take them back to Australia?"

"That's the only thing I can do. I hate the thought of leaving them behind, or scattering them somewhere. That's what some people are doing now, but it gives me the creeps."

"Okay," Polly said. "Anyway, it's brilliant of you to come with me to court, and on your last day, too." She threw her arms round his neck. "You're the best," she said. "Well, for an Aussie."

"I'm not a real Aussie yet. I haven't been naturalised."

"Sounds like some weird surgical procedure," Polly quipped and then continued, "Yes, okay. It will be good to have company and if they decide to throw me in jail, you can drive my car back and let everyone know," she joked.

"I was hoping I could be more than just good company."

"Mr Flint, whatever are you suggesting? Unless you're a contortionist, there's very little you can accomplish in a Triumph Spitfire."

"Let's get your court case over with, then we'll think of something. What sort of punishments do they hand out for speeding in England these days? In Australia, things are pretty lax, especially out in the bush, although the courts are starting to crack down in the cities, especially on drink-drivers."

"Sounds like a plan. Okay, I'll see you later, William Flint." She fired up her car and roared off down the street, narrowly missing a black cat that was crossing the street with a mouse dangling from its mouth.

Bill finished a cup of tea he had made earlier and rinsed the cup under the kitchen tap before he went back to tinkering with the clock. He unhooked the pendulum and probed with his deft fingers up into the mechanism. As he poked and prodded around, there was a click and a whirring from the chimer spring, as if the old clock was about to find its voice after a year of silence. He stood it upright on the table and a small brown envelope slid down the inside of the casing, landed with a clunk and fell out onto on the table top.

"Well, well, well, are you the cause?" He mused. He carefully laid the clock on its back and tore open the envelope. Inside was a tarnished key. It was nothing like the one he had found on his mother's sideboard that wound up the old timepiece. After gently hanging the clock on the hook on Lizzie's parlour wall, he inserted the winding key into both slots and gave them each five measured turns. Then he set the ornate brass pendulum swinging. Finally he set the hands to one minute to one o'clock and closed the glass cover that kept dust off the face. Sixty seconds later, the clock whirred into life and produced a resounding solitary *dong*. The chime was restored.

Almost simultaneously, Polly knocked at the door.

Bill flung it open. He grabbed her wrists and pulled her to him. His voice displayed a boyish excitement. "It's working again! I've got the clock working!"

"I know, I heard it *boing* just as I reached the door. It's really loud," Polly said.

He tried to kiss her but she shied away.

"Wait! I have to tell you something before we go any further. I've been into town and my mind has been going haywire." She looked at him wide-eyed. "Bill, we don't know each other, not really, not properly, but there's something happening. Right?"

"Yes, most definitely," he replied readily.

She searched his eyes for some sort of sincerity. They were glossy, damp and she felt all her resolve beginning to melt. She smiled, pressed against him and he silently held her head to his chest. He held up the key from inside the clock and put it next to his heart with a symbolic turn. "Could this be the key to your heart, Polly Jordan?"

With a chuckle she hugged him even tighter and said, "Ever thought of changing jobs and becoming a farmer? And for your information, that last question was pure corn."

# Seven

**M**onday morning was particularly cold. It was eight o'clock when Polly tooted the Spitfire's horn. Bill quickly appeared and lowered his long frame into the passenger seat. Polly noticed he was clean-shaven and she breathed in the fragrance of Old Spice.

"Mmmm, you smell good."

"I was about to say the same of you," Bill replied. He eyed the driver. "What's the perfume?"

"Houbigant Chantilly."

"Jeez, that scent does things to me."

"Don't get any ideas, wild colonial boy. There is serious business to be done today," she said, releasing the handbrake and engaging first gear with a clunk. Ten minutes later, the wheels of the sports car were crunching over gravel as Polly turned into the winding, poplar tree-lined drive of Overdale crematorium. She drove at a slow, respectful pace to the foot of the sandstone steps that led to the funeral chapel's entry and parked amid the fallen leaves. "I'll wait here."

Bill clambered out and climbed the short flight of steps. As he approached the large glass outer door, a short, stocky man in a dark grey suit came out to shake his hand. He handed over a navy-blue cube-shaped box and went back inside. Bill clutched the box and returned to the car. "Where shall I put them?"

"Give them to me. I'll secure them in the boot so they don't slide about or tip over."

Polly took the box, then stopped by the driver's door for a moment. "They're quite heavy. I thought ashes would be light."

"I said the same thing to the undertaker," Bill said in a low, calm voice. "He told me the weight of a person's ashes is virtually the same as that person's birth weight. Isn't that weird?" The comment was met with a pensive silence. It seemed Lizzie Flint was in their thoughts.

As they continued on their way to Wallasey, the Spitfire slowed at a bend in the road and a large stone building came into view. Mature elm trees beginning to shed their leaves and a matching stone wall around it added to its impressiveness.

"Blimey, that building reminds me of my old school back on the Isle of Man," Polly chirped excitedly.

"Looks nice," Bill said.

"Nice? Not the word I'd use for my school. It was girls only and the headmistress was a real iron-fisted battle-axe. Step out of line and you'd cop it."

"And did you cop it, Miss Jordan?"

"Er...only once. Got the strap. On the hand. Not on the bum, although a few girls did get benders."

"Oh."

"Oh? Is that all you have to say?" Polly asked, not hiding that she needed more from his response as she thought, *At least show some sympathy, won't you?*

Bill was still finding Polly an enigma, a puzzling mixture he could not fathom.

"When I was interviewing your mum and I told her I was from the Isle of Man, she assumed school kids got the birch if they misbehaved. I told her it was only vicious criminals punished that way."

"Right," Bill replied cautiously. "I think I'd heard that about the Isle of Man..."

Suddenly Polly hit the brakes and veered to the left. "Damn, I almost missed the turn-off for the tunnel. I blame you, Mr Flint, you have had my mind running in all directions." The conversation about Manx justice came abruptly to a halt. "Here it is. The Mersey Tunnel. Onwards and...downwards!" They both laughed at her play on words.

After leaving the tunnel and weaving their way to Wallasey, the pair finally arrived at the court building. It was a grim-looking place. Its weathered stone was a grubby grey, with scattered patches suggesting it was once a cream colour. The nearest parking spot Polly managed to find was about a hundred yards down the street. Still, she walked purposefully towards the main entrance, her eyes taking in every detail. *This looks more like a prison, and those windows look like black eye sockets in an old skull.*

"I'll come with you," Bill said, "but if you don't mind, I won't come into the courtroom. I don't fancy listening to all that court procedure stuff."

"Not a problem. I'm just glad you've kept me company."

"If I'm not here when you come out, I'll be sitting in the car if you'll leave me the keys."

Polly fished in her handbag and handed him the keys. "For Pete's sake, don't lose them or we're in for a long walk back."

He laughed, drew her to him and kissed her lightly on the cheek. "Good luck."

"Thanks, I might need it."

~ * ~

The court building hummed with the murmur of defendants,

witnesses and lawyers and a few members of the public who had turned up, some out of curiosity, to watch proceedings, as almost all English courts allowed them to do. Weaving through them all in the main corridor were court officials flitting to and fro in black gowns, keeping the wheels of justice visibly turning. Being well versed in court procedure, Polly made her arrival known to an usher who pointed her in the direction of court three. "That's where they're holding the motoring hearings this morning," he advised. Polly nodded as she thought, *his cheery smile strikes me as being more suited to the face of a jolly local butcher rather than the quintessential po-faced legal proctor.*

She pushed through the large wooden door of court three and quietly made her way to a section she assumed to be the press gallery. It was a short wooden seat resembling a church pew, with what could only be described as a narrow wooden shelf running its length about a foot above knee height. Polly bowed her head courteously to the presiding magistrate and took her place next to the only other person sitting there.

"Press?" she whispered.

The thin-featured, middle-aged man who had been writing carefully in a notebook looked up and nodded silently.

In less than five minutes, Polly's name was called.

"Call Mary Frances Jordan."

A subdued ripple of amusement permeated the traditionally hushed court atmosphere as she rose from the press section and took her place in the dock. The court was just like every other she had ever attended. It was lined with wooden panelling and furnished with wooden seating, and a wooden bench, dock and witness stand; in fact, everything was wood and all with that familiar musty odour of age. Within one minute, the case was over. The summons was read out, Polly pleaded guilty to speeding and the magistrate, a local councillor, Alderman Hanaford, fined her eight pounds and admonished her. "Young lady, you must learn to slow down on the roads. Be more responsible!"

The fine was quite a slap on the wrist and would make a hole in Polly's twelve-pounds weekly wage, but she thanked the bench, smiled, bowed her head and returned to the press gallery to collect her handbag. Just as she did, the court usher summoned the next defendant.

"Call James Paul McCartney."

Polly pricked up her ears. *Did he mention a Paul McCartney? But a James Paul McCartney? Surely it couldn't be. It had to be coincidence.*

She looked at the other reporter whose face was giving the impression of total boredom. The fellow scribe stared back momentarily, then carried on writing.

The courtroom door opened and in strode Paul McCartney, *the* Paul McCartney. It was him—the boyish good looks, the helmet of black hair. *It's the Beatle!* Polly silently whooped with joy. *A scoop!*

To a reporter such as Polly, this was a godsend, a scoop of huge proportions. The Beatles were the biggest name in pop music and McCartney was already the idol of millions of teenage girls in Britain. Beatlemania was the buzz-word. But today, fame did nothing to save singer and guitarist Paul McCartney from the wrath of the law.

The court was told it was the mop-haired musician's third speeding offence in the year, and Alderman Hanaford was in no mood for mercy. He fined McCartney twenty-five pounds, but worse was to come. The officious magistrate imposed a one-year driving ban on the Liverpool lad and told him, "It is time you were taught a lesson."

Polly had rummaged in her handbag and found her notebook. She would need to verify the name of the magistrate, glean more information from the prosecuting police officer and, if she could swing it, dash outside and grab a quick interview with McCartney himself. She glanced at the other reporter out of the corner of her eye. He put his pencil and notebook down, took a handkerchief from his coat pocket and blew his nose. It was so loud it made Alderman Hanaford look up to see from where the interruption had come. Polly's potential rival seemed unfazed. He picked up his pencil with a yawn and jotted down no more than three or four words, she calculated. *This guy doesn't know who McCartney is...there's not a flicker of recognition*, she silently reasoned, suppressing the urge to smile.

*What a story! What incredibly good luck! What sensational timing!* Her mind was racing with images of the *Express* front page, with a bold *Polly Jordan* by-line and the word *exclusive* blazoned everywhere. She reasoned the other reporter would be from a local Wallasey paper, but that was a long way out of the *Express* circulation area, so to all intents and purposes, she had a scoop.

She quickly rose, bowed again to the bench and made her way out with as much dignified haste as court protocol allowed. Having quickly ascertained the magistrate's name and checked the spelling, she feverishly looked around and weaved through the gathering of people in the corridor to find McCartney.

Headlines were running through her head. *Beatle banned. No mercy across the Mersey.*

For Polly it was all too perfect. This lucky break was just what she needed to mend the bridge with her news editor nemesis, Jocelyn Duckworth.

In the meantime, Beatle McCartney had vanished. She had his address in Forthlin Road, Allerton, but had no idea how to get there. However, she had enough information for a great story. After a quick chat with the prosecuting officer, Inspector Harrison, she was satisfied it was *the* Paul McCartney and she mentally began to compose to her story as she ran back to her car.

"You're back sooner than I thought you'd be," Bill said with surprise. "They obviously haven't jailed you. Why were you running?"

"Eight quid fine, but don't worry about that. I've got a cracking story," Polly told him, panting for breath. "Paul McCartney, you know, the Beatle, the good-looking one that every girl wants to...well never mind...*he* was there...in court, in person. He's been banned from driving."

"Is that a big deal?" Bill asked innocently.

"Are you kidding?" Polly said incredulously. "A Beatle in the same court I was in? It's the scoop of the year. There was only me and another local reporter in court. I have to find a phone, pronto. Quick, give me the car keys. Let's get moving."

She couldn't contain her elation as she fired up the Spitfire, crunched the gears into first and swung out into the traffic. "I can't believe the major papers have let this slip under the radar." She scanned the street from side to side like someone watching a tennis match. "Phone, phone, phone, where are you? There's never a bloody phone-box around when you want them. They're like coppers. When you want them, they're not there, when you don't, they're on every street corner. There, there! Over there, on the other side of the road. Phone-box. Hang on!" With a cursory glance in her rear-view mirror, Polly swung the Spitfire round with a squeal of tyres. She stopped abruptly and yanked on the handbrake.

"Won't be long, wait here," and she slammed the car door.

Polly yanked open the door of the newly painted red phone box. She fumbled to feed coins into the handset slot and dialled the *Express*. She had a dial tone. It seemed an eternity before someone answered.

"Hello, *Cardwell Express*, how may I help you?"

Polly recognised the voice and the Scottish accent. "Hello, Fiona, it's Polly Jordan. Can you put me through to the copytakers urgently, please? I've got a cracking story and I'm in a phone-box in Wallasey. I haven't much change."

"Right away, Polly."

The phone clicked.

Polly panicked. *Don't tell me I've been cut off!*

The phone clicked again. "Hello, copy, Alison speaking!"

"Ally, Ally, I've got a massive yarn. I'll be ad-libbing so tell the sub-editors they might have to polish it."

"Fire away, Polly."

"Okay, here we go…

*Mop-topped Paul McCartney, heartthrob member of the Beatles, who sings the hit song "Please, Please Me," has not pleased the law.*

*McCartney appeared in a Wallasey court today, and pleaded guilty to speeding along Seabank Road on June 14th, this year.*

*The offence took place following The Beatles' appearance at a Mersey Beat Showcase in the Tower Ballroom, New Brighton.*

*The twenty-one-year-old pop sensation, who lives at 20 Forthlin Drive, Allerton, was hit with a fine of twenty-five pounds.*

*McCartney, who had two previous convictions for speeding this year, was told by Alderman W.O. Hanford presiding: "It is time you were taught a lesson."*

*But for the cute and popular member of the Beatles, who also have a hit song "Misery," it could be a miserable time ahead.*

*Alderman Hanaford banned him from driving for a year.*

*But there was more misery to come and, if Alderman Hanaford were to say, "Ask Me Why," he would tell you it was because McCartney twice failed to produce his driving licence and his certificate of insurance within five days of being asked to do so by a police officer.*

*McCartney told the court he did not comply because he was on tour.*

*He was fined a further three pounds for each of those offences.*

"Okay, Ally, that's the end of message. Can you put a note on for the news desk and the sub-editors, please? *Tried to interview McCartney, but he'd gone. No time to follow to home address. Get photos from picture library and maybe pad out the story with Beatles background stuff.* Thanks, Ally, Polly signing off, but I'll give you the phone box number in case of subs' queries. I'll be on this number for...say...ten minutes. Cheers. See you later."

Polly emerged beaming. She pumped both fists into the air.

"Done it. By-line, here we come. Front page. It has to be. The world is Beatle crazy. Can't wait to see tonight's front page. I'm so excited."

"Good job you were able to find a phone," said Flint.

"Sure was. I was lucky. Sometimes the phone boxes are damaged or in use. Minutes count when you have a deadline. Do you mind if we hang on here for about ten minutes in case there are any queries?"

"So how can that work?" Bill said, puzzled. "If anybody rings back, how can you guarantee nobody jumps in and wants to make a ten-or fifteenminute call?"

"Oh, the phone's out of order now. There's a note on it."

Bill was gobsmacked. He scratched his head and stared at Polly. "How can it be out of order when you just made a call?"

Polly rummaged in her handbag and produced a flat metal disc about two inches in diameter. "See this?" Polly smirked. "It's called the diaphragm. All phones have them. You unscrew the cap at the earpiece end and slip it out, then screw the cap back on. The diaphragm controls air-pressure vibrations and converts them to sound...speech...in your ear. Without that, there's no audio. To the uninitiated, the phone line is dead. They know that no dial tone, no call. Simple! I learned this little party-piece from one of the blokes on the *Daily Express* in Manchester. We were covering the same story and he showed me the DDD, the 'dastardly diaphragm disabling'. It's priceless! You can disable any phone box and only you can use it."

Bill's brow became furrowed. "Isn't that illegal?"

"I suppose it is. It's probably against some obscure telegraph act law, or something that nobody has read for years. Anyway, who cares? It's not like I was vandalising the phone. If I do it, I'm always careful to replace the diaphragm afterwards. It's just a way of guaranteeing I have a phone to file my stories. Tricks of the trade, Bill. I'm sure you've got plenty of those up your sleeve."

Bill shook his head. Despite the afternoon shadows, his face seemed to light up with a knowing smile. "You're full of surprises, Miss Jordan," he said and put his arm around her shoulders. "What now?"

"In the aforementioned ten minutes, we'll drive back, call in at my place for a quick..."

"Yes?"

"...cup of tea," Polly joked.

"You teaser. Okay, I'll count every minute until we hit the road and there's one thing to remember."

Polly cocked her head like a curious kitten. "What's to remember?"

"I'll spell it out," Bill said deliberately, slowly in determined voice. "Do not exceed the speed limit or you might end up like your Beatle pal and find yourself walking for a year."

Polly looked shocked. "Crikey, I couldn't stand that. I'd be totally lost without Spittie."

Although Bill had known Polly for only a short time, he had never seen her so happy and, for once, she was sticking carefully to the speed limit. He gazed at her smiling face, her long blonde hair, smooth round cheeks and cupid-bow lips.

"I can feel you looking at me," Polly said with a grin. "What are you looking at?"

"You. Just you. I think you're the most gorgeous woman I've ever seen."

"Think? Only think?" she giggled. "You do too much thinking, Mr Flint. Life's too short for thinking. Just get on with it."

Bill thought about what she had said. *The more I get to know her, the further away I am from figuring out what makes this girl with the looks of an angel tick.*

# *Eight*

"**S**hall I drive you to Manchester airport the day after tomorrow?"

"I'd love it," Bill said, "But you'd better not take any more time off, otherwise your news editor Jocelyn Duckbill will be having a go at you again."

"Duckworth, not Duckbill. She's a lot of things, but she's not a platypus. You've spent too long in Australia," Polly joked. "You can't get to Ringway airport on your own, Bill. You'd have to take about four buses, or two trains. A taxi from here would cost you a bank loan. In any case, Duckworth should be so thrilled with my scoop even she couldn't deny me the afternoon off to say my goodbyes."

"You know best," Bill replied. "What time does the first edition come out?"

"It'll be on the streets now, but the second edition is the big seller. They'll probably hold my story back for that. Holding it back means it will be too late for freelances at the local news agency to pick it up and sell it to the national papers in Manchester. The agencies already make a decent living picking the eyes out of our stories. This time they'll miss out." She glanced at her watch. "Right, come on, let's go the newsagent's round the corner and see how the *Express* has run it. I haven't been this excited about a story for ages." Without warning, she grabbed Flint's hand as they strolled out of the block of flats which Polly had called home for the past two years.

The newsagent's shop door opened with a *doy-ing* as a lever activated a funny little bell mounted above the lintel. Newly delivered copies of the *Express* were stacked neatly on the floor. Polly grabbed the top copy and dropped a two-shilling coin onto the counter just as the newsagent emerged through a heavy curtain from the back room.

"They can keep the change, it'll be worth two bob," Polly said jauntily. She scanned then re-scanned the front page in astonishment. Where was her story? Her mind was in a whirl. *Perhaps it's inside; maybe they've decided to give it more space and run pictures.* She scoured the paper from front to back, back to front. Nothing. The only mention of the Beatles was a two-paragraph filler on page fourteen to say the group had performed in Blackpool on Sunday.

Polly was aghast. "I can't believe it. Where the hell is my story?" She folded the paper, slipped it under her left arm and gently shoved Flint towards the door. "C'mon. I have to find out what's gone wrong. This is the biggest scoop of my career and it's not in." With Flint by her side, she walked almost at a trot back to her flat. After fumbling for the door key, she threw the paper onto a chair and grabbed the phone. Her fingers trembled as she dialled the *Express*.

"Hello, who's that? Oh, hi Jenny, it's Polly Jordan here. Can you put me through to Duckworth, please, urgently?" She gently bit her lip and hopped from foot to foot as she waited for a response from the news editor's secretary. "What do you mean she's not available? Go and find her...this is an emergency."

"Hello, Polly," Jenny said after a few minutes' silence. "Miss Duckworth's gone home for the day."

Polly seethed. Her face was flushed with anger. She slammed down the phone. "Bloody cow! Gone home? She's bloody hiding."

Bill sensed Polly's rage and decided the best way to support her was to stay silent and just speak when spoken to. "Are you going to be all right, or do you want me to stay overnight with you?" Bill asked as he took Polly's face in his hands and gently brushed away a tear from each eye.

"No, not tonight," Polly apologised. "I won't be good company. I'll either smash every bit of crockery in the house, or get paralytic drunk...or both. After this bullshit day, trust me, I won't be nice to know."

Bill kissed her gently, let go of her hands and brushed hair from her damp cheeks. "I'll see you tomorrow...won't I?"

"Yes, but don't call or come round until midday. Are you okay to walk home?"

He nodded and smiled, blew a kiss from the door and went quietly down the concrete staircase of her apartment building. He stuck his hands in his pockets and silently told himself, *Yes, I'll be fine. The walk will do me good.*

~ * ~

Polly was up early next morning. In the bathroom, she showered and brushed her teeth for at least five minutes, staring at herself in the mirror like someone in a trance. She got dressed and brushed her hair until it shone. She finished the drawn-out ritual by carefully applying lipstick and powdering the end of her nose. "Duckworth, you'd better have a bloody good reason for not running my story, or you will bleed, I promise you," she said to her reflection in the mirror and at the same time, checked her teeth for lipstick overload.

For the next fifteen minutes, she walked back and forth in the lounge, taking sips of black coffee as she paced, then in a loud confident voice she rallied herself. "Okay, Polly, this is it. This is where you and Duckworth sort it out, no holds barred." Slipping on a warm coat, she closed her door with a bang and stomped down the stairs.

"Good morning," Polly said to Jenny and marched straight past the secretary's desk.

"Hang on, Polly," Jenny stammered, "you can't go in there, Jocelyn is..."

The advice was ignored. Polly shoved open Duckworth's door and slammed it behind her.

"What the hell, Polly?" Duckworth protested. Her faced paled. "Just settle down. I can see you are angry." She looked directly at the irate reporter. "How can I help you, Polly?" she asked nervously.

"Help! Help? You've helped me to lose the biggest fucking scoop of my career. Don't talk to me about help, you arsehole."

"Calm down, Polly...and there's absolutely no call for obscenities."

"Obscenities?" Polly yelled, "I haven't even started yet. What happened to my Paul McCartney story? It's a massive story and it's not had a run. What the hell is going on? I expected it to be front-page news."

"It's a court story about some small-time musician fined for speeding. So what?" Duckworth argued.

Polly listened red-faced, hands on hips in an aggressive pose as Duckworth meekly tried to put up the defence that happenings in Wallasey were too far away and out of the *Express* circulation area."

"Are you fucking kidding? Do you think our readers care that it happened in bloody Wallasey? Do you think they're too bloody parochial to read about Paul McCartney landing in the shit? Circulation area? What a joke. Cardwell has more than eighty thousand people. Do you think they're all blind to what goes on in the outside world?" Polly was beside herself with rage and allowed the rougher side of her journo character to show. "If President Kennedy was killed in a plane crash in Outer Mongolia, would you ignore it because it's out of our circulation area?" she spluttered. "It's a bloody national scoop, a world scoop. Do you have the slightest fucking idea who the Beatles are?" She paused and looked up at the ceiling in disgust. "Probably not, because as a news editor you're rubbish. They're taking the world by storm, you imbecile, and we've missed a massive exclusive. He's a Beatle, for god's sake!"

Polly's face was scarlet. She gasped for breath and tried to calm down. "There were two reporters in that bloody courtroom, me and a bloke from some piddling local rag who didn't seem to know what planet he's on, never mind who McCartney is."

"You have to see it from my point of—" Duckworth tried to explain before being cut short yet again.

"This is personal, Jocelyn. You didn't run the story because you have it in for me. You're an arsehole. No, you're even bloody worse. You're a useless fat bitch and you wouldn't know a good story if it bit you on your enormous flabby tits. I'll bet you didn't even show the story to the editor, did you? Ronnie Day would have run it big, so I know it never crossed his desk. You never even showed it to him, and don't deny it. You know damn well he'd have gone to town on it...big headline, pictures, quotes from the music industry, from driving safety groups...the whole box and dice, and with my by-line on it—*Exclusive by Polly Jordan.*"

Duckworth sprang to her feet and pointed to the door. "That's enough, Jordan! Get out! Get out of my office! Get out of the building! You're fired, Jordan. Get out and don't come back. You've dug your own grave this time, you stupid girl," Duckworth barked.

"Horseshit! You can't fire me," Polly yelled. "Only the editor can fire me. You're just a shit-shovelling lacky who preys on young girls. You're an absolute disgrace. I've a good mind to ring the national papers myself and sell the story right from under your bloody nose which, I might add, is well shaped for sticking up the editor's arse and not for sniffing out news."

With that Polly stomped out of Duckworth's office and slammed the door so hard the noise brought the entire newsroom to a startled halt.

~ * ~

Bill had taken a taxi to Polly's apartment to be there when she arrived home and he tried his best to comfort her, but knew tension was high and her fuse was short. His response was measured and cautious. Eventually, he put his arms around her gently and led her over to the loungeroom settee. Seconds later she was practically inconsolable.

"I have just committed career suicide," she wailed.

"Shhhh! C'mon sit down. It'll be all right. It'll blow over. I think you have every right to be upset, though."

Polly snivelled and wiped tears from her cheeks with the sleeve of her blouse. "My career's gone. I've just blown my future," she whimpered. "Even if that fat cow hasn't the power to fire me, she'll have been straight into Ronnie Day's office sticking the knife in my back. I wish I hadn't threatened to sell the story. That was so spectacularly stupid. I was a total idiot. Apart from calling her every foul name I could think of, that threat alone was enough to get me fired for breach of workplace loyalty." She grabbed a cushion and hugged it tightly. "I've ruined everything I have worked towards and the biggest story I have ever had didn't even see the light of day. What a bloody mess. What am I going to do, Bill?" she sobbed, throwing the cushion to the floor. "Duckworth knew what she was doing. She set a trap and I walked right into it."

"Well for a start, you can cheer up. You're young, talented and drop-dead gorgeous. The world's your oyster."

Polly tried to stem the tears and blew her nose on a tissue. Her eyes were reddened and her cheeks smeared with black streaks of mascara. "I called her some terrible names. Perhaps if I turn lesbian, I can get my job back at the *Express*," she said, still sobbing, but managing an unconvincing laugh.

"Please, please don't do that," Bill grinned. His eyes seemed to shine in the fading afternoon light. "That would be a tragedy the world could not cope with. Especially me."

Just as Bill put his arm round Polly to give her a hug, the doorbell rang. She slowly got to her feet, glanced in the mirror over the fireplace, dabbed her eyes with a tissue and opened the door.

"What the feck has that queer gobshite done to you now?"

It was a voice Bill had not heard before. Doc walked in with a bouquet of a dozen long-stemmed roses. "Me and some of the lads and lassies at the *Express* threw in a few quid and bought you these. We thought you might need cheering up. Oh, you might notice they have no thorns on 'em, unlike that tyrannical tart of a news editor."

The joke and Doc's visit made Polly smile. " Good lord, Doc, they're beautiful," she said, taking the flowers from the visitor and disappearing into the kitchen. "I'll put them in a vase straight away. Long-stemmed roses...they must have cost a fortune."

Doc shrugged, his expression of *don't know, don't care* clear.

"How did you know about my disaster?" Polly quizzed.

"Bloody hell, just about everybody at Malthouse Lane knows about it. It's a travesty."

"Oh, sorry, introductions first," said Polly flustered. "Bill, this is Gerry Docherty, the best photographer I've ever worked with. In fact, the best colleague ever." She paused and took a deep breath. "The operative word now is *worked*...past tense. Doc, meet Bill Flint, a new chum who's over from Australia for his mother's funeral."

The two men shook hands with firm but friendly grips, and Polly was quick to notice they were about the same age, height and build. They had many physical similarities except Doc's hair was the length many a girl would envy.

"Pleased to meet you, Bill. I'm sorry to hear of your loss. Was it sudden?" Doc asked with obvious sincerity.

"Yes and no," Bill said. "She wasn't really that old, but it seems her heart had been on the way out for some time. I don't think she suffered."

"Well, that's truly a blessing, sure it is," Doc sympathised.

After a short silence Doc began again. "That Duckworth is one poisonous whore. The whole office is talking about how she withheld your story to trap you into flying off the handle." He paused as if he were withholding something.

"Go on, Doc," Polly prompted.

"The news isn't good, babe. Ronnie Day resigned this afternoon. He's taken early retirement."

Polly suspected there was more to come.

"The really bad news is they've bumped Duckworth up to assistant editor and she's in the chair until the board can meet and appoint a new editor. How does that make you feel, because it makes me feel sick in the guts? What's more, the entire editorial staff is on the verge of calling a stop-work meeting to protest."

"I just feel like getting drunk," Polly moaned, "but, one, I haven't got any booze in the house and, two, Bill has to pack his suitcases tonight for the trip back tomorrow, so the pub's out."

"Well, now, let me see." Doc cogitated as he flicked his hair back and away from his neck. "I don't carry drink around with me, only chemicals in the car, as you know, babe, but I have something that might help you unwind in the absence of whiskey...that's the real whiskey, with an *e*." He fished in the pocket of his leather jacket and pulled out a cigarette packet. "It says Sweet Afton, but you won't be finding any of Dundalk's finest tobacco in this wee packet. I'll leave them here. You can use them or you can lose them, it's up to youse. But don't get caught with them. Don't leave them lying around. If you don't want them, flush them down the lavvy. Okay?"

"Doc, you know I don't use that junk," Polly said gratefully but firmly. "Where do you get this stuff from, anyway?"

"Well now, my old mother, God rest her soul, said ask no questions and you'll be told no lies. Wouldn't you agree, Bill?"

Bill nodded politely. "That's what they say."

"To be truthful, you know press photographers have lots of contacts and get asked to undertake all sorts of jobs and wee favours."

"Quiet little jobs people just mumble about," Polly said knowingly.

"Precisely," Doc agreed, and tapped his nose twice with his right forefinger. "Well, I just happen to know a certain magazine publisher. He asks me to develop and print pictures that any decent individual would be too embarrassed to hand in at the local pharmacy's forty-eight-hour photo processing service, if you follow my drift."

"Trust you," Polly said with a knowing look. "And of course, in exchange you get given something green that, when introduced to fire, gives off a soothing smoke."

"And how in God's name did you arrive at that conclusion? And here's me thinking all along you were just some young and innocent lassie."

All three joined in the lighthearted moment before Doc took his leave. "Don't forget, babe, use or lose. That's the watchword. Hey, hope to see you back at the *Express* before the end of the week."

"Don't think so, Doc. I've crossed the Rubicon."

Doc clapped his hands and applauded. "Not only is she absolutely gorgeous, but she does poetry too. Safe journey back to 'Stralia, Bill. Might see you again one day."

"Thanks, Gerry, I hope so. Good to meet you. Stay well."

As Doc's footsteps grew fainter as he descended the stark concrete stairs of Polly's apartment block, she closed the door gently and engaged the lock.

The street lights were on and the daylight was as good as dead. Polly picked up the cigarette packet Doc had left, then threw it onto the coffee table. "Sweet Afton. What a rogue that man is, but you have to love him."

Bill shrugged in silence. Her use of the word *love* had him fazed.

Polly picked up the packet again and tipped its contents on the glass table top. Four hand-rolled cigarettes fell out, along with tiny specs of dried green plant material. "I can't believe I'm even doing this without flushing it straight down the loo," she said with overtones of guilt. "I've only ever smoked a cigarette once or twice. Well, maybe a bit more than that, but I have never been what you'd call a smoker. I might as well be. It seems just about every other person at the *Express* smokes. If you have to go into the sub-editors' office, you almost need to wear a gas mask."

"I could always go out and find an off-licence to buy alcohol, if you like," Bill volunteered.

"Come and sit over here," Polly purred. "Next to me on the settee."

As he settled in next to her, she used a finger to touch and tap one of the joints across the coffee table towards him.

"What are you doing, Polly?"

"Shall we? I've never tried it."

"Jeez, I really don't know. I have to say I'm reluctant."

"What the hell? I can't get drunk, so I may as well get high," Polly concluded. "It's the sixties," she proclaimed, echoing what Doc had said when they went to interview Lizzie Flint. "Pot is the new beer. Haven't been there. Might like it, might not. It could be the very thing I need. Doc's always raving about the benefits."

"You really shouldn't," Bill cautioned.

"I know I shouldn't, Bill, but bugger it, I'm going to. I want to forget today. Forget Wallasey, forget the Beatles, forget work, forget bloody Duckworth, forget everything."

"Me included?" Bill teased.

"Of course," Polly parried with a half-smile. "Sorry, that's a typo, a printing error. It should read of course *not*. You're quite special, Mr Flint. I'm going to miss you like crazy."

Polly licked one end of a joint and put it to her lips. "Have we got any matches? Oh, I might have some in the kitchen. I usually keep a couple of candles handy in case of a power failure so there *should* be matches." She returned from the kitchen with a box of Swan Vesta matches. "Bingo! Let's trip."

The first mouthful of smoke made her gasp and splutter. "Shit, that's strong," she said. Her voice sounded as if she were choking.

"Smells a bit sweet," Bill observed as he put a match to his joint and drew in heavily.

"Mmm, this is good stuff. Smooth...not too bitter, not too hot," he assessed with a wide smile that signalled pleasure.

"How come you are such an expert all of a sudden?" Polly teased, stifling the urge to cough.

"I never said I hadn't smoked pot. I don't remember you asking me if I had."

"You cunning devil. What else haven't you told me?"

"I suppose there's lots, but it'll have to wait."

"For what?"

"Next time." He drew in another mouthful of smoke and held it in for a good twenty seconds before letting it out slowly with a deep sigh of satisfaction. Little wisps of bluish smoke spilled from his nostrils.

Polly tried to emulate it and after several bouts of coughing and gagging, she seemed to get the hang of things. "Phew, this stuff is so strong," she said, with her eyes half-closed. "What am I supposed to feel? Am I going to see psychedelic sea monsters crawling up the wall or chairs and tables floating?"

"It's all subjective, Polly," Bill advised. "Seeing weird creatures sounds more like dropping acid to me. Not that I've done that, I might add. Just relax, let it all waft over you and go with whatever happens. Sometimes it's nothing, sometimes you get the most amazing feeling of wellbeing and calm...a tranquil state alcohol can't give you. Plus you won't get a hangover."

"Well, that *has* to be a plus," Polly reasoned, taking another deeper drag on the joint.

"Hey, Bill," she giggled. "I think it's working. It feels like my head has just become detached from my body and it's rolling upside down across the ceiling. Whoa...this is cool. Definitely weird, but cool." She slipped off her shoes and sprawled across the settee, her head resting on Bill's lap. "I can see my favourite cloud now," she said with a childlike laugh. She waved her arms around and pointed. "It's up there, look, above the bedroom door. It's sort of purple, now it's green...no yellow. It's changing shape all the time."

"You must have got the super weed there,' Bill joked. "I don' think I've seen anyone react so quickly."

"Hey you, how come you know so much about cabbanis?"

"Cannabis," Bill corrected her.

"'S'wat I said. Hey, you didn't tell me you were a doctor of dope."

"A couple of years after I opened my art gallery in Melbourne, I went up to the Northern Territory to look at Aboriginal bark paintings. There was a big demand for indigenous artefacts developing in the southern states and overseas, particularly in North America. A local tribe invited me to live with them for about a week and learn some of the tribal customs and how customs and the Outback environment influenced their art. It was an eye-opening experience. There's not a plant growing in the Outback these people don't know about, whether it's food or medicine, or for recreational enjoyment. Do you know they have leaves they can drop into a billabong that will anaesthetise fish in about thirty seconds? All they have to do is scoop them off the water and cook them. Brilliant. They secretly laugh at the white folk who go fishing with a rod and line."

"That's what I used to think about my ex-boyfriend," Polly chimed in. "He and his pals went fishing for stuff they couldn't even eat. They put back anything they caught. How stupid is that?"

Bill resumed what he was saying. "Don't think they don't know how and where to find marijuana. When the gold rush was on in Australia midway through the nineteenth century, Chinese immigrant workers took cannabis from Asia, mainly India. Now it grows wild in hundreds of places. The local tribes know all about it and many of the elders, the menfolk, smoke it at corroborees...they're sort of tribal get-togethers, pow-wows." He looked to see if Polly was still awake and listening. Seeing her eyes still open, he continued. "One of the tribal elders told me about the time he watched a herd of water buffalo chomp into a patch of weed with healthy flower heads. Ten minutes later, they were all lying down in a trance. He said their eyes were wide open like full moons."

"Water buffalo?" Polly asked incredulously. "Don't they live in Asia? Australia has kangaroos not buffalo, you silly billy. Ha, ha, ha, Billy! I called you silly!"

"No, that's where you're wrong. You don't know everything, Miss Jordan."

"I know my head is spinning out of control and I feel weirder than I've ever felt before. It's all about feeling, Bill, isn't it? You know, life. All about feeling and feelings."

He chose to ignore her ramblings.

"As I was saying, Australia has big wild mobs of buffalo at the Top End, the north. There are crocodiles, too. You have to be careful wandering about up there."

"Up where? Where were you?"

"Well, the tribe I was with was in the region around Humpty Doo, east of Darwin."

This made Polly laugh hysterically. She laughed so much she rolled off the settee. "Humpty what? You're making this up. Humpty Dumpty Doo. Oh, look at that...I accidentally blew a smoke ring. Check it out. Look at my smoke ring. That's another favourite clown...I mean cloud."

Unfazed, Bill continued. "It's a huge honour for a white man to be asked to join the men at a corroboree. I went twice and I smoked with them both times. I can't remember the Aboriginal name they have for it, but they take the mature flower heads and crush them with a few leaves and stuff them into hand-made pipes they roll up from some sort of tree bark. Then they light them up just as you do with a joint. The bark reacts with the dope and makes it even richer, so they said."

"Totally fascinating," Polly said sardonically and with one last, long draw on her joint announced, "I'm out. Where are the other joints?"

"Don't you think one's enough for tonight?" Bill cautioned, with a glance at his watch.

"No, no, no, I want to be totally out there, man. I wanna be cool, daddy-o. I feel like I wanna feel a totally new...feeling."

"Up to you, but don't say I didn't try to stop you."

"You know today..."

"Yes, I know today..."

"I fantasized about you. In the dock, of all places. When the magistrate was telling me off. It was like being back at school."

"I don't know where this is going, Polly, but you're beginning to worry me." He sucked hard on the cigarette and swallowed a mouthful of smoke. "Tell me you're not expecting me to play the headmistress. You're stoned, totally zonked."

"Well...perhaps you're more suited to being the headmaster, Mr Flint."

Polly slowly and unsteadily got to her feet and disappeared into the kitchen. Bill could hear a snipping noise. When Polly emerged, she had the long-stemmed roses tied in a bunch, with their heads hacked off. She swished the bundle. "Wanna use this, headmaster?" Polly burbled. "Or d'you wanna play a game of Isle of Man justice instead?"

Bill reeled and sprang from the settee. "Are you crazy? There's no way I'll play such silly games. What's got into you, Polly? Are you telling me you're kinky?"

"Just a thought," she said dismissively.

"You're in la la land, Polly. In the morning you'll wake up and realise how ridiculous this whole scenario is. You're a grown woman, although I will say you deserve a smacked bottom for butchering those lovely, very expensive roses Doc bought for you," Bill said angrily. "No, wait, I take that back, totally. Absolutely the wrong choice of words. Forget this nonsense and grow up. Now!"

"Boo-hoo! What a disappointment. I figured you to be more red-blooded than that. Man or mouse? Which are you, Bill?"

"I'm sensible."

Polly threw herself sulkily onto the settee next to Bill. She covered her face with her hands and remained silent for a moment. With a shake of her head, which sent waves though her long blonde hair, she whispered, "I'm sorry, Mr Flint. I let the dope cloud my judgement. If I'm bringing clouds into the mix, I certainly can't call it my favourite cloud, but on the other hand, maybe I could."

"You're the dope," Bill said, unable to hide a smile. "A beautiful, enigmatic, complicated dope, but please, no more talk about smoke, or clouds, or ruined roses."

# *Nine*

Bill Flint stared out through the window and watched the rain dance and streak across it. In less than thirty seconds, his plane nosed up off the runway and Manchester disappeared into a thick blanket of cloud. In seconds, the rivulets of rain were sucked away into the night. His mind was preoccupied with thoughts of the woman he had left weeping at Ringway airport and how his life, in a matter of days, been turned upside down. He could think of nothing else but Polly Jordan and the incredible events of the past few days. Soon he would be back home in Australia and he would certainly ask himself if the whirlwind life he had just led could be gone like the Manchester rain, or would he be forever changed?

~ * ~

Back in Cardwell, Polly sat in her bathtub. Feeling miserable, she gently waved her hands through the layer of bubbles and let salty tears roll down her cheeks and drop into the foam that had clung to her body. Even before she had taken Bill to the airport that afternoon, she knew she would be a mess of tears saying goodbye. She had kissed him and clung to him until the last moment and even decided to tell him she loved him. But he had put his finger to her lips and said, "Sshh, Polly. Don't say anything more. I have to go. I'll come back. I promise."

She wanted to believe him, but thought about how many movies she had seen and how many loves had disappeared into the clouds. She smiled as she dreamily relived Bill's crazy story about his favourite cloud. A knock at the door snapped her out of her lassitude.

She climbed out of the tub, pulled the plug and wrapped herself in a huge pink bath towel before throwing on a white towelling robe. She pushed her damp feet into sheepskin slippers and shuffled to the front door. "Who's there?"

There was no answer. She opened the door and peeped out to see a tall figure with flowing hair disappear down the flight of stairs. "Doc! Doc, come back!"

"Oh, there you are. Just came to check on you."

"What, no roses?"

Doc quickly saw the joke. "Still got the ones I brought you?"

"Er, no, the petals came off so I threw them out this morning," she fibbed, her cheeks flushed.

"Jeez! I thought they would have lasted longer than that. They cost an arm and a leg and I had to go to about a thousand florists to find any roses this time of year. Can I come in?"

"Sure, Doc. Sit down. Give me a couple of minutes while I throw on some clothes."

"You don't have to get dressed. I like you better without your gear."

"You never give up, do you? That's one thing I can guarantee about you, Mr Docherty. Consistency. Consistency and persistency. You're a bloody rogue, but I love you..." She stopped herself from revealing her thoughts. "Well...don't get any ideas."

"You were going to say like a sister, weren't you?" Doc groaned. "Even worse, like a daughter." The bedroom door was closed so he assumed his comments had been unobserved.

Polly reappeared from her bedroom in jeans and the sweater she had worn for the trip to Wallasey.

"Is your man gone?" Doc asked.

She nodded with a sigh. "It's been a hell of a week, Doc. Meeting Bill, going to court, going to war with Duckworth and talking myself out of a job."

Doc shrugged. "What can you do? The *Express* is the only game in town unless you up sticks and go to Manchester."

"I'm going to be struggling. My car needs money spent on the gearbox, I've the rent on this place and too many clothes bought on hire purchase I knew I was making a mistake taking up the store's easy-pay offer. I don't know how I'll pay it off."

"Sounds like you're in a paper boat sailing the seven seas of shite," Doc said, with the wisdom of Job's comforter. "I can give you some to tide you over but..."

"No, Doc. Thanks but no thanks. This is my mess and I have to figure out a way to get through it."

"You know," Doc mused, "I might just have a solution. No promises, mind, but give me a few hours to speak to a contact or two. It won't be reporting, you understand, but needs must when the devil drives and all that stuff."

"I'll look at just about anything, Doc, but my ultimate aim is to get my job back or at least get back into reporting. It's my life."

As soon as Doc left, Polly thumbed through her contacts book and found her mechanic's number. With the Spitfire's gearbox sounding sick, she knew she must call him in the morning. Her mind raced with thoughts of Bill and where he would be on his journey home. Already she was missing him and hoping to get a phone call to say he had made it back to Melbourne safely. It was going to be a sleepless night.

First thing next day, Polly parked her Spitfire on the oil-spattered drive at Joe Wright's garage then tutted as she realised she had not checked the boot to see if there was anything in it she might need if she had to leave the car for repairs. She lifted the boot lid. *Oh, bloody hell! I don't believe it! Oh, no!* There in a corner, next to a flashlight and a tartan blanket she always carried was the blue cube-shaped box she had carefully put in there the day before. She and Bill had been so engrossed in each other they had forgotten about his mother's ashes. The discovery was bittersweet. She knew Bill would be devastated when he got home and realised his mistake, yet she allowed herself the hope that this embarrassing oversight would mean a reunion with him in the very near future.

Joe Wright picked his gearbox specialist, Frankie, to examine the Spitfire and to Polly's horror, he told her it was beyond repair. Several cogs were stripped and a new or reconditioned box was the only solution.

"If you don't get it fixed, the gearbox could fail any minute, maybe next week, maybe by the time you get to the end of the street," Wright said bluntly.

"And the cost?"

"Four hundred and ninety pounds for a new one, fitted and tested or two hundred and ninety-nine for a reconditioned one, fitted and tested," Joe said apologetically. "Can't do it for anything less I'm afraid, Polly."

A bill like that was the last thing she needed. "You'd better install a re-co," Polly said gloomily. "I can't survive without my Spittie."

It was a long, five-hour wait. She drank several cups of tea from a chipped mug, tried to ignore the saucy pin-up-girl calendars and worried whether she could rustle up enough money to pay the bill, or whether she would have to ask for time to pay. Wright's garage had not moved with the times. It was cash only or a cheque. Either way she was in trouble. "Look, Joe," she told the proprietor as he handed her the keys and wiped his hands on an oily rag, "I can give you about fifty quid now and owe you the rest until the weekend. You know I'm good for it. I always come to you."

"Gee, I don't know...that's a lot to be owing me," Joe replied. "Two hundred and forty-nine quid, Polly." The grey-haired mechanic peered over grubby spectacles. "If you can make it a hundred, I'll wait for the rest."

Polly fished in her handbag. She had a compartment in which she kept fifty pounds for emergencies. She undid a tiny zip and stuck her fingers in. "Here you are, Joe. That's literally all the money I have on me."

"All right, love," Wright said and shoved it in the top pocket of his overalls. "I'll overlook the rest for two weeks. Is that OK?"

"That's great," Polly said, with a confidence that belied her state of panic. Her thoughts were in turmoil. *I know I can't find almost two hundred pounds in the next four days and pay my rent and buy food and petrol. I'll just have to bank on receiving pay plus the three weeks' holidays I'm owed by the* Express, *but that could take too long to come through.* She grimaced. *Why, why, why have I spent so much on kinky boots, as Doc aptly described them, and other trendy clothing?*

At least now her car was repaired. She slipped it smoothly and silently into gear for the short drive home and thanked her lucky stars Joe Wright had no idea she was unemployed.

The immediate future looked bleak, and the man who made her pulse race was so far away. He could not help or comfort her. Just where *was* Bill? Was he home? She willed her phone to ring, but it remained silent as the rest of the day slipped away. Eventually, she cried herself to sleep.

## *Ten*

"Top of the morning, as they say south of the border. To be honest, that's a bit of a myth. I've hardly ever heard another Irishman say that. It's just what the comedians and lousy actors trot out." Doc was at Polly's front door by eight-thirty.

The bleary-eyed ex-reporter in her pink towelling bathrobe let him in.

"Polly, I have some news for you, part good, part well, I'm not sure you'll jump up and down with joy."

She plonked herself down on the settee. "Am I going to like this or have I to throw you out at knifepoint?"

"Well lassie, last night I had a few drinks with one of my many contacts."

"Go...on," Polly said hesitantly.

"Lenny Horowitz is looking for new talent."

"And who on earth might Lenny Horowitz be?"

Doc paused, clasped his hands together, then confided almost apologetically. "Well, Lennie Horowitz is the guy behind *Raunch* and *Spy*, and a couple of other..."

"Dirty magazines," Polly interrupted. "Are you frigging serious? You expect me to strip and pose for a bunch of bloody perverts?"

"I know it sounds dodgy, I know, but Lennie is well thought of in the magazine publishing world. He's got a pretty sound reputation."

"You've lost your marbles, Doc. I'm sorry. No way. Discussion over, finito, final. Thanks, Doc, I know you mean well but..."

"Up to a hundred quid a day...cash."

Polly gasped and put her hands on her flushed cheeks. "How much?"

"One hundred pretty pictures of our noble queen a day, the folding stuff, and you'd be working with Lennie's wife, Karen. She used to be a model, but is, er, a bit past it now, so she looks after the girls. Lennie hardly gets involved. He just collects the cash and takes care of the publishing. Karen runs the day-to-day stuff. In her day, she was known as Maxine. She's been on loads of covers and has been a centrefold girl umpteen times."

"I'm flabbergasted," Polly confessed. "That's almost more in a day than I got at the *Express* in a bloody month. Are you for real?"

"You know, Polly, I'm many things, but I wouldn't string you along with blarney. All you have to do is ring Karen. I'll jot down her number, and let her see what you've got. In my opinion you've got exactly what they're after."

Polly tried to keep a serious face, but the thought of so much money was going to be a temptation she knew would be hard to ignore.

"You said pictures...*of the queen*...banknotes?" She didn't require an answer. "I'd be a useless novice."

"Well, you might not be on top dollar to start, but I'll make sure Karen pays you well. I've done heaps for her."

"I don't know, Doc, stripping isn't my thing. I'd be too shy," Polly argued.

"Darkroom!" was all Doc chose to say.

"That was different. I was off my face, you know that."

"Talk to Karen; think it over," Doc said as he prepared to leave. "No-one will ever see you, apart from those in the studio. You'll be a girl guys admire and have a fake name. Easy!"

"Maybe I will think it over. Maybe I will consider it."

~ * ~

The Sunset Strip sign was easy enough to find, once Polly had threaded her Spitfire through the maze-like industrial estate in Ashton, a small neighbouring mill town on Cardwell's western outskirts. It had taken her only twenty minutes to drive there, but she felt she'd be far enough away from home to feel comfortable. Karen Horowitz had sounded friendly on the phone and she had used her reporter's guile to ascertain as much information as she could before agreeing to be interviewed. It was an eerie role reversal for the reporter—someone asking *her* the questions.

Polly had a hard job politely turning down Karen's offer of a glass of champagne, but it was only ten-thirty in the morning. Karen escorted her into a small office lined with framed glamour photos of dozens of models, some partly clothed, some naked—blondes, brunettes, redheads. She settled into a comfortable armchair and faced her inquisitor who looked to be in her early forties. She had ear-length sandy hair, piercing green eyes and shiny red lips. Although she was dressed in business attire, Polly clearly saw she possessed a trim figure, and struck the young journalist as the sort of woman who would be at home among any gathering of company directors.

"Tell me about yourself, Polly," Karen invited. Her quiet soothing voice put Polly at ease. "I want to know all about you and if you have what it takes to be a model for us. I know you're a good friend of Gerry Docherty and he's put in a good word for you, but we still like to go through the formalities."

"Okay," Polly agreed nervously and set out to convince Karen she would, indeed, make a good model, all the time thinking, *Who am I trying to convince—Karen or myself?*

After a friendly half-hour chat, Karen rose from the armchair and politely asked the recruit to follow her. They walked along several corridors in the former cotton warehouse and through what seemed like dozens of doors.

Polly couldn't help thinking if she had to leave in an emergency, she would never find a way out without help. Finally, they went into a small, white-walled room, absolutely bare of furniture.

"All right, Polly, undress, please."

Polly hesitated. Fear took over. Then she began to remove her clothing as slowly but seductively as she could. There was nobody in the room except for Karen, yet she felt totally inhibited. Her face flushed with embarrassment.

"You don't have to peel them off like that," Karen said, with almost parental guidance. "We're not hiring a stripper. Just yank 'em all off and let's see what you have under all those autumn clothes."

In all her naked glory, Polly stood with her hands on her hips and tried to pose like a professional.

"Wow, yes, I see what Doc meant when he described you as a hot chick. You have a great body...and those boobies! They're to die for. I wish I'd had those when I started out in this industry. I notice you don't wear a bra. Don't let them get saggy, Polly, they're your best assets. Men live for boobs."

*Mmmm, I like the compliments. Not just a pretty face, but I mustn't seem smug.*

Karen continued, her manner businesslike. "Turn around, darling, slowly, slowly."

Trying to move like a professional model, Polly asked sheepishly, "Do I have the goods?"

"You sure do, my love. You're hired."

Polly wanted to hug Karen, but thought it would be too familiar a gesture.

"We do have a tiny problem," Karen continued.

Polly's expression clearly showed her apprehension.

"It's okay, it's surmountable."

"What is it?"

"You've shaved and it's growing back stubbly."

"Oh, er, yes, I read about Mary Quant and..."

"Frankly, Polly, most of our readers like muff. We have a selection of wigs you can have a look at."

"Wigs?" Polly exclaimed in disbelief. "Pubic wigs?"

She wanted to laugh at the absurd theatre prop, but managed to keep a straight face.

"We think of everything here. Come next door."

Polly dressed quickly and with her shoes still in her hand, followed Karen. The boss went to a cupboard and took out a box. Polly looked inside. It was half full of hairy objects in sealed cellophane packets.

"They're brand new. Nobody gets second-hand. It's just a matter of size and shape. You get to pick your own. They stick on with theatrical gum."

"But they're all brown or black," Polly observed as she rummaged through the contents. "I'm blonde."

"It makes no difference. Most men like to see dark hair. Anyway, half the blondes walking around these days are dark...*there*," Karen said. "Besides, under the studio lights, blonde pubes tend to look wishy-washy or disappear altogether on camera."

"You're the boss."

"Come back to the office and fill in some forms."

Back in Karen's office, she handed Polly a brown envelope. "Here's an advance. Can you start tomorrow? Nine-thirty sharp?"

"Why are you paying me before I do anything?" Polly asked with a hint of suspicion.

"Two reasons. First, if we pay you, we can almost *guarantee* you'll come back."

Polly was pensive. *Is this a veiled threat, like if you take our money and don't come back, it will be theft...*

"Second, Doc told me you were a bit short of readies. There's two hundred quid in there. That's four days' work you owe me. You'll get more with more experience. "Don't forget, I know where you live," she joked.

*It's half the amount Doc mentioned, but still a small fortune.* Polly's face beamed with pleasure and relief. She readily took the envelope and shook hands with her new employer. "Nine-thirty, sharp, I'll be here," she said jauntily and left.

By the time she reached her apartment, all sorts of images were fuelling Polly's vivid imagination. *What have I really let myself in for? Maybe I could do it just long enough to scrape together the money to get out of my financial jam, then try to get back into journalism. On the other hand, will I have the courage to show up at nine-thirty tomorrow and become the object of men's lust?* Suddenly her thoughts went to Bill. *How would Bill react if he knew?*

She parked her prized Spitfire in the small car park of her apartment block and strolled towards the stairs. Suddenly she stopped and retraced her steps. *What am I doing? I can't leave Lizzie Flint's ashes in the boot again.*

Once inside her flat, Polly gently placed the box of Lizzie's remains on the coffee table. Carefully she slid off the sleeve-style lid and surveyed the contents. A bag made of thick transparent plastic held what looked like grey gritty material that was speckled with black grains. *So this is what people look like when they're cremated.* She replaced the sleeve and placed the box under a pile of blankets in her kitchen linen cupboard. "Lizzie, it looks as if you'll be living here with me for a while until Bill comes for you." In the absence of anything alcoholic in the flat, Polly brewed a cup of tea and toasted Lizzie. "If it hadn't been for you," she whispered, "I wouldn't have met Bill. God bless!"

# *Eleven*

Polly put her latest paperback on the bedside table and was just about to turn off the light and go to sleep when the phone rang. She checked her watch. *Almost eleven o'clock. Who could be calling me at this time of night?*

"Hello," she said cautiously. Then she let of a shriek of delight. "Bill? Bill, is that you? Oh, thank the Lord. I was worried about you. How are you? Are you at home?"

"Slow down, Polly."

Her questions almost overwhelmed the man she had farewelled more than forty-eight hours earlier. There was a time delay on the long-distance link so Polly had to slow her rate of questions, otherwise she found herself talking over Bill's answers. As a journalist, she was used to phoning people, but it was the first time she'd had a conversation with anybody so far away.

"I've tried to call you umpteen times," Bill assured her, "but every time I rang, I was told all lines to the United Kingdom were busy."

"I'm missing you like crazy," Polly said and sniffed as she blinked back happy tears. "You know you forgot to take—"

Flint cut in. "I know. I can't believe I was so incredibly stupid. Have you got them safe?"

"Yes, they're here in the house. I just brought them in from the car."

They talked for an eternity. Polly could not contain her excitement and laughed and giggled at anything remotely funny Bill said. She was in two minds whether or not to tell him about her new 'career' move, but decided silently, *it might give him the wrong impression. In any case, I haven't yet whole-heartedly decided to take the* Sunset Strip *work.*

Finally, Bill said he would have to go, but promised to ring again in a matter of days.

As she said goodbye, Polly blurted excitedly, "I love you."

"I know you do," Bill chirped back.

It wasn't exactly what Polly wanted to hear in reply, but put it down to Bill's being busy back in Melbourne and it was not the clearest of phone lines.

Still in a happy mood following the late-night phone call, Polly arrived promptly at nine-thirty for her debut session at Sunset Strip. The small car park was almost full but she found a space next to a powerful-looking Norton motorcycle. She went inside and asked a girl who looked no more than sixteen where she could find Karen Horowitz.

"Not in today, love," the girl told her, "but follow the main corridor to a door with a sign that says *Shoot in Progress* and ask for Trish or Terri."

Despite being bamboozled by all the doors and corridors on her interview, Polly found the room quickly. She knocked and entered. "I'm looking for Trish or Terri," she told a woman who was directing a photographer. In progress was a set involving a shapely teenaged model wearing a schoolgirl outfit that consisted of a white shirt, blue-striped tie, long white socks, black patent leather shoes and the shortest, skimpiest, grey gymslip imaginable.

"I'm Terri," the woman replied curtly. "And you are...?"

"Polly Jordan. Karen hired me yesterday."

'Oh, right. Well, you're not on yet, so just hang around and watch and learn. There's nothing to it really. Just do as you're directed and look sexy and desirable. Imagine every hunky guy in the world is looking at you and...you know..."

"Okay...watch and learn."

"Phillipe," Terri yelled. "Come on. You're needed."

A curtain in one corner of the room parted and Phillipe, a short, stocky man, emerged dressed in a grey suit over which was draped a headmaster's gown. He carefully placed a mortarboard hat on his balding head and said, "Ready, Freddie."

"Okay, it's Phillipe spanking naughty schoolgirl Chantelle," Terri called out.

Phillipe took up a wooden ruler that had been placed on a padded chair on the set. He arranged his gown. After straightening his mortarboard, he gently lowered the pretend schoolgirl across his lap.

Polly watched in stunned silence as the lights were switched on and the shoot began. As a journalist, she had by no means led a sheltered life and had seen her fair share of pornography, but never close up. Photographer Desmond took pictures from every angle possible against a school classroom backdrop two handymen had just wheeled in. Phillipe raised the ruler.

"Pretend it's hurting, Chantelle, for god's sake, love. You're not supposed to be enjoying it. I'm after a grimace, not a grin," Terri grumbled. She turned to Polly and rolled her eyes. "She's just out of school, you'd think she'd know."

Polly laughed nervously. Her mind raced.

"Are you okay with S and M and bondage and all that stuff?" Terri asked as she put a piece of chewing gum into her mouth.

Polly fell silent. Her cheeks were flushed and when she spoke, she sounded perplexed. "I don't really know. I sort of…"

Terri struggled with the ambiguity then quickly changed the subject. "You just have to clear your mind and think of something that turns *you* on and forget the scenario you're in. It's not rocket science."

Without warning Polly blurted, "Gotta just pay a quick visit," and shuffled out of the door. She had no idea where the toilets were, but chose the nearest corridor to escape. Within seconds she encountered two other girls whose skimpy costumes left little to prospective readers' imagination. "Sorry, girls, which is the way out?" Polly asked with urgency and she walked quickly in the direction given. Back in daylight, she breathed in deeply. *What the hell am I doing*? And she drove towards Joe Wright's garage as fast as she dared. After kissing the envelope from Karen, she ripped it open. *Yes, here it is… two hundred pounds in five-pound notes. Four days' work, paid in advance, thanks to Doc.*

Without hesitation, she paid off her debt. Afterwards, she sat in her car in guilty silence. *What have I done? I'll be hunted. What will I tell Doc? He vouched for me and I've dropped him in it.*

# *Twelve*

With the little money Polly had left after paying Wright, she called at the off-licence close to her apartment and bought a bottle of scotch. She sat on her settee and stared into the glass containing her third drink and wondered how she would break the news to Doc that she had taken Karen Horowitz's money and fled.

There was a knock on the front door. She gingerly opened it and was pleased to see it was Doc looking very *avant garde* in a cream-coloured trench coat.

"Oh, shit," said Polly, "You'd better come in, Doc."

They both flopped onto the settee.

"Go on, let me have it. Slap me if it'll make you feel better. I'm truly sorry, Doc. I couldn't do it and now I've fucked you up and I owe Karen two hundred quid."

"I *should* spank your backside, sure enough," Doc joked, "for being so silly. D'you think I'd let you drop me in it over money? Karen called me and told me you'd bolted. Do you think you're the first girl to get cold feet? Karen and me, we go back a long way, Polly. I just stumped up the two hundred and we had a good laugh – at your expense, to be honest."

"At *your* expense, more like it, Doc."

"Shit, don't worry about the two hundred quid. I'll make that and more with my next moonlighting job."

"Was Karen angry? Should I be scared?"

"The Horowitzes are not the Mafia, Polly. There's no contract on you," he joked "and she says if you change your mind, the deal is still on. She likes you and says you've got massive potential."

"I'm a potential disaster."

"To be honest," Doc confessed, "Karen and I were both eighty per cent sure you wouldn't go through with it. I knew you'd be too stubborn and proud to accept money as a gift, so we hatched this little plan."

"You bastards," Polly said with a hearty laugh, "you cunning, wonderful, generous bastards. There's just one thing I don't get," she confided as she took another sip of her drink. "If you make so much money on the side, why do you still work at the *Express*?"

"Good question. I'm like you. I love the newspaper game. It's a rush. Every time I see one of my photos in print, I tell myself I've made a little bit of history. When I'm dead and gone, there'll be a record of me. If I get a picture by-line, my name will live on for a while. I suppose it's nothing but bloody vanity at the end of the day."

"Blimey, Doc, you sound almost philosophical. I never looked at it that way."

"Well, you've a damn sight more years left in you than I have, so leaving something behind is more important to someone like me." Doc swept back his hair. "Hey, pour me a scotch and I'll tell you the real news," he blurted. "How much would you love and respect me if I told you I have Duckworth by the balls?"

"Tell me later, Doc. I just want a good drink and forget about today and forget about Duckworth. Cheers, Doc! And thanks for bailing me out."

"You don't have to thank me. You know I'd do anything for you. Just tell me you love me ...."

Polly looked nervously at the floor, then stared up into Doc's kind, albeit it rugged, face. Drinking in what she saw was an expression of total sincerity and want, she slid across the settee. Her small fingers pulled his face towards her and she planted a soft, warm and lingering kiss on his lips. "You're the best, Doc. In a different world, I could fall for you."

"That's always the problem, Polly. Different worlds; different times." He finished his drink then stood up to leave. He stroked her hair tenderly.

She stood and took his hand in hers. She squeezed it once and let go.

"Polly...I..."

"Shhhh...don't spoil it, Doc. Just leave it like this."

"See you soon," Doc whispered hoarsely. He closed the apartment door so gently it barely made a click.

~ * ~

Polly spent the next few days alone in her apartment, killing time reading paperbacks. She had no further contact with Bill and no visits from Doc. The seclusion didn't bother her, but her emotions made her restless. According to Lizzie Flint's clock propped up in a corner of her lounge, it was ten-thirty at night, but several urgent raps on the door put paid her plan to go to bed early.

"Doc, what's wrong? It's late for a visit."

"It's not late for this news, Polly. Wait till I tell you..." He took off his coat and threw himself onto Polly's settee. "You'll never believe this—"

"I won't if you never get round to telling me," Polly grumbled.

"Duckworth's gone...dead!"

"Christ! Did somebody kill her?" Polly gasped. "I hated her, but I didn't want her dead."

"Not dead, like really dead. She's been pushed sideways. A good journalist friend of mine in Sheffield just phoned me. He's been appointed editor of the *Express* and he's bringing his deputy as assistant editor. Duckworth's going to a local paper as editor-in-chief. Weekly stuff. Duckworth is a dead duck," he continued, beaming with self-satisfaction, and coughing a deep, gravelly cough as he enjoyed his own joke.

"Are you okay, Doc? That cough sounds serious."

"Yeah, no cause for concern, Polly. I'm just a bit winded running up your stairs."

"Wow, there *is* justice in the world. Where does that leave me?"

"You're back, Polly. Reinstated. Brooky—Steve Brooks—swore me to secrecy. It's not been made public yet. You're not supposed to know, so stay cool. Not a word."

"Yahoo!" Polly shrieked. "Happy days return. Let's celebrate, Doc, I've got scotch."

"Not this time, babe, I still have work to finish."

"Oi! You called me *babe*, again, my friend," pointing a forefinger at Doc, "and tonight I just don't care. Thanks, Doc. Has this anything to do with what you were about to tell me about Duckworth the other day?"

"Can't remember saying anything, Polly. No bells ringing."

"I can tell you're lying, Doc, but I guess it doesn't matter now. I'm back. Whoopeeee! I should reward you for the inside information."

"You reward me every time I feast my eyes on you, Polly, my love."

"You old Belfast smoothie."

"Carrickfergus!" Doc sighed.

Polly slipped into her bedroom and emerged in her bathrobe.

Doc's face wore a frown, "Hello...what's this?" he asked.

Polly flung open the robe. "It's what you really want, Doc, isn't it?"

Her naked form took him aback. The photographer gulped. The sight of her large, perfect breasts fighting to be free of the pink towelling robe was torture. "You can't be drunk this time, miss, so what's all this about?"

"Your reward, I told you."

"What about Bill?"

"Ouch! I don't know. I haven't heard from him. For all I know, he could be thinking we were a temporary cure for our blues. I don't know when he'll be back. I think he'll come. He has to pick up his mother's ashes, which are here in the flat. We both forgot they were in the boot of the Spitfire." She slid over to Doc who was on the couch and sat on his knee. "So, in the words of the Bard, don't sweat it."

He fumbled for words. "Babe, you know I—"

A rat-a-tat-tat at the door stopped him mid-sentence.

Polly shot up and hurriedly wrapped the robe around her. She fumbled for the ties and fastened them tightly around her waist. "Who the hell can this be at this time of night? Coming!" she yelled.

A small, slim man sporting a black motorcycle helmet and leather gloves stood waiting on the landing. "Mrs Polly Jordan?"

"*Miss*," she insisted.

"Telegram, miss." She took the pale pink envelope and ripped at it.

"Will there be a reply, Miss?" the messenger asked.

"Oh, my god, it's Bill. He's on his way. He's in London and will get here tomorrow evening." She turned to the young man. "No, no reply," she said and clapped her hands with obvious delight. "Doc, Bill's coming. Bill from Australia."

Doc looked crestfallen. "I'd best be off," he said wistfully as the playful mood evaporated. "That's good news, babe. I'm happy for you." Once again Doc said good night and quietly let himself out.

~ * ~

Tears of joy seeped through Polly's mascara as she threw her arms around Bill at Manchester airport.

"My, God, it's been so long."

"It's only been a couple of weeks," he said, smiling. "Polly, I can only stay for a few days. I have to be back in Melbourne for a really important meeting with Asian buyers that could end in a deal worth hundreds of thousands, perhaps millions."

"That's a bummer," Polly said with disappointment. "I was hoping to keep you for at least a couple of weeks. Anyway, let's make the most of it, and this time don't go home without your mum. So much has happened, Bill. I don't know where to start."

On the drive to Cardwell, Polly told him everything, except her indiscreet offer to reward Gerry Docherty. It had misfired, she reasoned, so why muddy the water? The rest, however, she laid on the line. Bill was shocked at the thought of her even thinking about posing naked for men's magazines and told her so in his characteristic quiet, firm and very sensible manner. "Polly, I could have sent you money. My art business has money pouring in. That's the only reason I'm able to come to and from Australia. The fares cost a fortune, but I can afford them."

Sunset Strip shocked Bill. It was the first time he had shown any sign of displeasure and for the first few hours of his return to her apartment the atmosphere was chilly and tense. It was only after Polly had enticed Bill into her bedroom and made love to him industriously that the mood improved.

"Wow, you were like a tigress," Bill remarked. "What have they been teaching you at Sunset Strip?"

"You complaining, Mr Flint?"

"No way! Hell, I've missed you, missed that incredible, hot body on top of me."

"Well, you would go away, wouldn't you? It's entirely your fault."

They laughed together and rolled across the bed. "More?" Polly asked saucily.

"Yes, please," Bill answered huskily.

"You're not fit, Mr Flint," she scolded. "I'll have to whip you into shape."

"Oh, no—anything but that," Flint whimpered jokingly. They roared with laughter and embraced again.

For the best part of three days, Polly and Bill stayed in the apartment and engaged in a love binge neither had thought possible.

"We'd better slow down, catch our breath and eat some proper food," Bill suggested. "We've been living on sex and snacks and there's almost nothing left in the larder."

"Is that a euphemism?" Polly joked.

"Be serious!" Bill countered.

# *Thirteen*

In the Nag's Head the following afternoon, barmaid Annie Campbell brought over two drinks. "Scotch for you, Polly, and a beer for your handsome friend, wasn't it?"

"Thanks, Annie. Have you seen Doc today?"

"No, I haven't, hen, in fact I don't remember him being in for a few days now."

"Okay, thanks, Annie. If you see him, tell him I was asking, would you?"

Bill sipped his beer and said, "What now?"

"What now, how?" Polly replied.

"Well, with Duckworth, for starters and your job? When are you going back to work?"

"The new boss hasn't started yet, so I'm in limbo for a while."

"Write a book."

"You're the one who should write a book. What about all your war exploits and your heroism rescuing those troops."

Bill looked out towards the bar in contemplation. With reluctance in his voice, he said, "Polly, I have something to get off my chest."

"God, don't tell me you're married; married with kids. I couldn't stand it."

"No, nothing like that. It's just that, yes, I did rescue two soldiers from the sea at Dunkirk, but I wasn't in the army and I didn't get any medals."

"But you were a hero who—"

"Hang on, Polly, let me finish.

"By the time I was fifteen or thereabouts, I'd gone to live with my father in Ramsgate. He and Mum were living apart because he inherited a part-ownership of a small fishing boat from a cousin. He had also developed a lung illness in Cardwell and the doctor advised him to get sea air. I suppose you couldn't beat being a sea fisherman for breathing in good clean air." He paused. "Then the war with Germany started and the emergency appeal came from the Churchill government to help with the Dunkirk evacuation. Dad wanted to help and do his bit for his country. He insisted on sailing across the English Channel and refused to let the army commandeer the boat.

"I was seventeen then and had seen little of life. I went, too, and we accomplished our mission. We managed to bring back two English Tommies and a Polish guy. We had a French corporal on board, but he was shot dead by machine gun fire from a German fighter plane. My mother always assumed I was serving in the forces and I didn't want to disillusion her. She hero-worshipped me. I get quite emotional when I think I deceived her all those years." He paused again to regain his composure.

"It was several years before I managed to get back home via the Isle of Man. They said I suffered some type of amnesia brought on from being shot at and dive-bombed by the Luftwaffe."

"Did you spend much time in the Isle of Man?" Polly asked, with an obvious interest about her birthplace.

"Yes, I suppose I did," Bill replied hesitantly. "I recuperated in a place called Abbey Tower."

"Do you mean Abbey House?"

"No, it was Tower. I saw it on the sign in the garden."

"Are you sure, Bill? Abbey House used to be an asylum, but it was closed down in the 1860s."

"Oh, that's right. Sorry, I forgot you were from the Isle of Man. I'm obviously mistaken. I was a bit out of it and unable to think clearly for many months. So I must have heard mention of Abbey Tower and got confused. They reckoned the trauma might have screwed up my memory."

"That's understandable. An easy mistake to make in the circumstances," Polly conceded, but it was a strange mistake. The only reason Polly knew about Abbey House was because she had researched historical Manx places of interest for a feature she wrote when she was a trainee journalist on the island's biggest newspaper, *The Examiner*. "It's no big deal. We all make mistakes," Polly said and tried to ignore Bill's explanation. "Forget the memory thing," she added, amused by her accidental play on words. "You were brilliant, a hero."

"Actually, I sort of have another, even bigger confession."

"What?"

"I think I want to take you Down Under."

"Down under?" she giggled and slapped his right hand playfully. "Naughty boy!"

"I mean Australia, you saucy minx. I swear sometimes that's all you think about."

Polly went deep in thought, like a poker player with everything at stake. "That's a dilemma. I've just been told I can get my job back at the *Express*." She looked Bill in the eye. "Wow, going to Australia? That's a major life-changer, Bill. I don't know. It's not that I'm saying no...it's just massive."

Bill drew close. "It could be arranged, but we'd have many loose ends to tie up here first. You could get an assisted passage for ten quid," he said excitedly.

'You're joking! Ten pounds? Obviously you've made enquiries, Mr Flint."

"Yes, tentatively."

"I'm torn in two with guilt. I want to go and I want to stay and follow my career path."

"It's a huge decision, Polly, I agree. Just say you'll think about it."

Three days later as Polly waved Bill off at the airport, he looked back at her through the huge glass wall of the departure lounge. Like a seasoned mime artist, he pointed a finger to his right temple then pointed it to the floor.

*Yes, Bill, I'll think about Down Under*, Polly pledged silently.

## *Fourteen*

One week later, Polly was finally back in the *Express* reporters' room at eight o'clock sharp.

"Welcome home, Polly," greeted Rachel Myers, secretary to the new editor, Steve Brooks.

No sooner had she sat at her desk than Rachel flitted over to her and said, "Steve wants to see you in his office."

Polly teased her hair as she walked through the rows of desks. Her knock on the editor's open door was met with, "Come in, Polly, sit down."

The voice belonged to a man in his early forties with a tired-looking face and a head of premature grey hair. He remained seated. "I'm Steven Brooks, Ronnie Day's, replacement. Nice to meet you."

Polly smiled. *Keep your wits about you, Pol. Don't give any hint that you know what's coming.* "Good to meet you, sir. Welcome to Cardwell."

"No need for airs and graces, Polly. Steve will do just fine. The reason I've sent for you is that a little bird has told me about your previous troubles and differences with a former senior member of staff."

Polly knew the little bird he was talking about was Doc, but pretended to be surprised.

"Whatever happened before is the past, the slate's wiped clean and we start again and I hope your career at the *Express* will be long and happy. I see a very bright future for you here."

"Thank you, sir...Steve, thank you," Polly managed to say, almost getting tongue-tied with nerves.

"I hear you're good friends and work well with photographer Gerry Docherty."

"Well..." she started.

"That's great. Gerry's 's a damn fine photo-journalist and I'd like to keep the partnership going, if you agree."

"Absolutely, Steve. I enjoy working with Doc, that's Gerry..."

"It's okay, we all know him as Doc. That's it then, Polly. Go and see our news editor, Isla Cassidy. I've brought her from Sheffield as part of my team and she'll find you an assignment. See you later and good luck," Steve added, holding out a hand towards his door.

Polly walked briskly to the news editor's desk.

"Hello, Polly, I'm Isla Cassidy. I'd like you and Doc to get a spread about the circus that just arrived back in town. I know we probably have a circus story every other year, but I'd like to explore some different angle, not just the juggling clowns and trapeze flyers. I've heard about Doc's elephant scoop, so maybe you two can come up with something similar or even better. Steve would be really impressed if you could come back with a front-page story and pictures."

"I'm onto it, thanks, Isla. I'll get Doc's engine revved up."

"I'd love it for tonight's second edition, if you could do it. No pressure though," Isla added.

~ * ~

The big top was up and a small army of workers was putting the finishing touches to the network of sturdy guy ropes anchoring the canvas dome to the ground at Cardwell Recreation Reserve.

"Geez, Doc, I can't remember the last time I was at the circus. When I was a kid, I used to get butterflies in my stomach when I went into the big top. I think I might get them today."

"It's just excitement being back working with me," Doc chimed. "We've got to make a big impression on the new editor. Scout around and find us a story while I hunt down Harry Bingham, the animal trainer. He's always good for an idea or two."

They separated and weaved through the acrobats and clowns rehearsing their acts for the evening's opening performance, due to start in about seven hours. Polly could hardly believe she was 'backstage' at one of Britain's most prestigious circuses and chatted to as many people as she could in search of an angle. Less than fifteen minutes had passed when Doc returned. "You'll never guess what Harry told me."

"Er, no. My psychic powers are a bit feeble today."

"Harry's daughter Miriam has trained as a lion tamer and tonight's her debut. How's that for a story. Plus she's nineteen and a real stunning -looking lassie."

"Trust you to find a chick, you horny old sod. But I'll grant you, it sounds like a top yarn. Is she happy to be in it?"

"Of course. It's publicity. Not only that, but I've got her to agree to pose in her bikini with a couple of lions. Wow, wow, wow! Pure gold. Roar!"

Polly was happy to see Doc in his element. He thrived on being a newspaper man, but she sensed he was not as bright and bubbly as usual and looked pale. "You feeling all right, Doc? You look a bit off colour."

"I've been off colour all my life," Doc replied with a half-smile. "I'm just a bit winded with all the rushing to get here."

Polly thought his reason, being winded, sounded familiar, but let it go. Moments later, Harry Bingham found her and Doc and led them to the entrance of the huge red and white canvas tent.

"OK, let's go in," Harry casually invited.

The smell of animals and sawdust and not a little sweat greeted them. Harry shouted to someone to flick on the lights and there, taking up most of the circus ring, stood the lions' cage in the middle of which were two extra-large wooden stools. He walked the pair over to a sturdy steel-barred door.

"What! Do you expect me to go in there?" Polly shrieked. "With lions? I thought we'd be staying outside the cage."

"Think how much better your story will sound," Doc told her. "Think of the headline: *Fearless reporter faces roaring lions.*"

"Fearless?" Polly said with sarcasm. "You have to be joking. Can you hear that sound? My knees are knocking now and I'm *outside* the cage."

"Don't be scared," he reassured her. "Harry's fed them and they always have a little something added to their meat before an appearance."

"What do you mean, like a drug?"

"Sort of," Doc replied. "They'll be calm and placid. Harry has guaranteed it."

"OK, but I'm going to be standing right behind the two of you," Harry reassured them.

Polly and Doc slowly followed Harry into the twelve-feet high cage which, she noticed, was crowned with a sturdy rope-net roof suspended on a chain from somewhere high in the tent's apex.

"Look around, Polly. It's all safe. Nothing can go wrong," Doc assured her.

"Here's my lovely daughter, Miriam," Harry announced as a tall, attractive young woman wearing a small shiny blue bikini, high heels and a top hat, let herself in by a cage door opposite. She had a long trainer's whip in her hand.

Doc looked around for the best angle to shoot from and weighed up the scene with a handheld light meter. "Might have to use the flash, Harry. Will that be all right?"

"Shouldn't be a problem," said Harry matter-of-factly. "What do you reckon, Miriam?"

The young lady smiled. "They're pretty docile today, they'll be all right."

Polly looked over to Doc and said, "That's got to be good news. I've got to say, I'm so scared, my bum cheeks are just about welded together." Her joke had all four of them laughing, which went a long way to relieving the tension.

"Right, let's have Atlas and Titan in. Fasten the gates. Tell Zelda to let them out of the pen and make sure she closes the trap door behind them," Miriam shouted confidently. "Do *NOT* forget that trap door!"

"Okay, done," said a voice from beyond the curtain-draped entrance to the arena.

Seconds later, two huge male lions with massive black manes charged through the tunnel, then into the cage. There was a clang as an assistant lowered the tunnel's trap door with a rope pulley. The two huge cats ran around the perimeter of the cage then on command from Miriam jumped smartly onto the stools. They pawed the air and bared their teeth silently as if on cue. Miriam raised her whip and gave it a little crack. Atlas and Titan gave her their full attention.

"How would you like us?" Miriam asked helpfully.

Doc quickly replied. "If you could get between them and tousle their manes, that would be good."

Miriam obliged with a huge smile. Both lions seemed relaxed and happy at sharing the cage with strangers.

Polly looked frozen. There was fear in her eyes and she kept them locked on the beasts. "Shit, they're enormous," she whispered to Harry. "They'd eat me in one mouthful."

"Captive lions always look bigger," Harry explained. "They don't have to hunt, or fight for food like their relatives in Africa do. And they get well fed every day."

"How close can I get safely?" Doc asked.

"No closer than arm's length," said Miriam, still smiling.

"Miriam, er, can I ask you a bit of a delicate question?" the cameraman enquired.

"You want to know if I'm married?" she joked.

"Well, apart from that," Doc replied with a grin. "Could you sort of pull your arms in closer to your, er, chest?"

"Oh, right. Why didn't you just say you wanted a cleavage shot? No probs. I know what you snappers like. How's that?" she volunteered, accentuating her breasts.

"Marvellous," said a happy Doc and he took more shots.

As he took his photos and the flash went off several times, the two lions opened their mouths and almost closed their eyes.

"Oh, look, so cute, they're laughing," Polly said innocently. "Oh jeez, look at the size of those teeth!"

"That's not a laugh," Harry replied with a hint of concern. "That's what they call the Flehmen grimace. They do that when they smell lionesses that are, er, how shall I put it, in season."

"Miriam, I think we should call it day. Have you got all your shots, Doc?" Harry said. His voice was beginning to signal urgency. At that moment, there was a second clang then a series of loud growls from outside the arena. Before anyone could blink, two lionesses had run into the cage's access tunnel and were clawing and biting each other. Their roars sounded angry and

Polly was rooted to the spot as the ground seemed to shake beneath her feet.

"How the bloody hell did they get out?" Harry yelled with panic in his voice. "Somebody get those lionesses back in the pen, for god's sake. Right now!"

"What idiot left number one trap door open?" Miriam screamed.

In the blink of an eye, Atlas and Titan were roaring too, clearly disturbed by the females' condition and the fighting.

Atlas bolted and charged towards the lionesses, clawing wildly at the tunnel bars and roaring as if he wanted to tear them open. Titan kept his place on the stool, but he was baring his teeth with a low, deep growl. His fiery, amber eyes were wide with menace.

Polly looked at Titan's long, yellow canines and in a trembling voice said, "Doc, be careful. Just back away slowly. Please don't make any sudden movements."

As Doc tried to withdraw calmly to keep himself and his camera out of harm's way, Titan lurched forward towards Polly, who screamed, terrified. In a trice, Doc threw down his camera and instinctively jumped in front of Polly, pushing her to the ground for safety. As he did so, Titan slashed a paw in a wild arc and struck Doc across the neck and throat. The two-inch claws ripped into his Doc's flesh. The impact flung the unfortunate man backwards and he collapsed to the sawdust-strewn cage floor.

Blood spurted immediately from the wounds. There were no moans or cries, just gurgling noises as Doc clutched at his throat.

Harry Bingham yelled, "Lion attack, lion attack. Get the guns. Somebody get the bloody guns." There was a weird air of calm as Harry took charge. "We need help over here. There's a man down," he bellowed at the top of his voice. "We need an ambulance, and get a doctor."

Miriam ran over to the tunnel as the two huge males squared up to each other. With the trap door raised by its pulley, she punched and kicked Titan and Atlas out of the cage and into the tunnel, still snarling and biting at each other, the lionesses having retreated from the tunnel as if they sensed the danger themselves.

Polly was screaming and had fallen to her knees to tend to Doc. "Oh, my god, Harry! Look at him! Look at these wounds!" Gently she put her arm under Doc's head and tried to raise him, but he was big and too heavy for her to move. She stroked his blood-soaked hair away from his face.

Hysterically she screamed again. "Christ, get a doctor! Get an ambulance! Somebody help! He's in a bad way! Help us!"

Within seconds, a sense of calm returned as she tried to comfort Doc. "It's Polly. I'm here, Doc. It's all right, you'll be fine. I'm here for you."

As the minutes ticked by, Doc had all but lost consciousness. The gurgling was slowing and becoming fainter. Polly began screaming again. "Doc, don't go to sleep. Open your eyes! Look at me, Doc, please! Listen to my voice!" She took his face in her hands. "Doc, listen to me. It's going to be all right. I'm here. Look at me, Doc, look into my eyes," she pleaded. Tears streamed down her face and made tiny tracks in the blood covering her suede jacket. She took it off and used it to try and stem the blood. She bent lower and whispered "I love you, Doc. Stay awake. Don't go to sleep. Open your eyes."

She watched a tear trickle from Doc's right eye. For a fleeting moment, his eyelids flickered. Polly saw a flash of that familiar green, but the lustre was gone. Slowly his eyes closed. She gently wiped his tear away. His skin felt cold to her touch. In the glare of the banks of big-top spotlights, Doc's face had paled. He looked at peace, but all his colour had ebbed to a ghostly, waxy, yellowy white.

"Get him to hospital, *please*," she implored. Don't let him die. Don't let my Doc die." She looked around at the people who had gathered in the big top. "Where's the goddamned ambulance? Please God, make them hurry."

Her dress was a mass of scarlet, like the sawdust all about them. She stood, then fell again to the ground, taking the seemingly lifeless body in her arms. "Doc, Doc, please. C'mon, Doc. Talk to me, talk to me. It's Polly. I love you, Doc. Don't die, I love you! I love you, can you hear me?" There was no response. She rose again and could clearly see the deep bubbling lacerations across Doc's throat.

Harry was standing behind her. He took Polly by the shoulders and slowly managed to peel her away from her stricken colleague. He gently covered Doc's limp body with a fire blanket. "Polly, love, come away now. The ambulance crew is here. They'll take good care of Doc."

With that he led her gently from the cage. "Why did they attack us?" Polly sobbed. "They'll save Doc, won't they?"

At the door, she turned to see the medics placing Doc on a stretcher.

"He'll be in Cardwell Infirmary in no time," Harry said, putting his arm round her shoulders "He's in good hands." He guided Polly to the caravan that doubled as the circus headquarters. Very soon, circus security personnel and police from Cardwell crowded into the caravan.

Miriam knocked on the door and climbed in. "We might have to shoot them, Dad, before they tear one another to pieces. All four of them are going berserk."

"Wait. Don't do anything just yet," cautioned Harry. "How the hell did those lionesses get out?"

"I don't know," Miriam said, sobbing as the situation enveloped her. "One is definitely coming into season. That's why they were having a go at each other. Naturally, the males would know this. Titan was grimacing earlier, but I didn't detect anything from the girls. What a mess, what a god-awful mess." She covered her face with her hands and wept. "That poor man was here to help us and..." Before she could finish, her tears overwhelmed her. "I can't go on tonight, Dad. I don't know if I'll be able to set foot in that cage again."

"There'll be no show tonight," Harry said quietly. "I'll cancel the whole week. There's a lot of questions to be answered."

"Where have they taken Doc?" Polly asked again.

A friendly policeman offered the information. "He'll be in Cardwell Royal Infirmary by now. It's a teaching hospital so they'll have plenty of top surgeons there. If anyone can save the gentleman, they can."

"I'll give it about ten minutes then phone," Harry said, his voice shaky and choked with emotion.

The mood in the caravan was sombre. Even the police were respectfully reticent to ask questions. Fifteen or so minutes elapsed before Harry Bingham slowly got up from his seat. "I'll phone the infirmary."

"We can do that. I'll radio in," said one of the police officers, his name, Sergeant Gordon Ashworth, clearly displayed on his badge.

"Thanks, Gordy," said Harry. "It's good to know we can rely on old friends.

Ashworth nodded and smiled before he went outside to a police vehicle. Time seemed to stand still inside the caravan until the door creaked open and Sergeant Ashworth climbed back in. All eyes were on his face. He stood silent for a moment and swallowed hard.

"How is he?" Polly asked frantically. "Is Doc all right?"

The sergeant's face seemed to pale. "I'm sorry to have to tell you—"

Before he could finish the sentence, Polly let out a harrowing scream. "No! No! You can't be right. Don't you dare tell me Doc's dead. Don't you dare. You can't do that to me."

"I'm sorry, miss. By the time they got him to hospital, he had lost too much blood."

Polly wailed and rocked back and forth. Her hair tumbled over her face and she started to gag as though she were about to throw up. Harry gently put his arm around her shoulders, but there was little else he could do to console her.

"This isn't happening. They can't just take Doc away from me like that. It's got to be a mistake. Tell me it's a mistake." She sobbed bitterly. "I loved that man. I loved that man. He can't leave me."

Sergeant Ashworth dabbed a tear away from his right eye and Miriam cried into a handkerchief, shaking her head pitifully.

Gaining his composure, Ashworth said, "There was a vascular surgeon on hand and he tried everything to save Doc, an infirmary spokesman said, but he'd slipped away by the time the ambulance reached the emergency department. Doc's arteries or veins, I'm not sure which, were so badly torn nothing could be done. He'd lost too much blood. He passed away before the doctors had a chance to do anything."

Polly rose, ashen-faced, and walked to the door. Below each eye were smudges of mascara mixed with blood, dreadful and morbid evidence of what had just happened.

The sergeant vainly tried to persuade her to stay.

"Let me out. I need some fresh air. I have to be outside for when Doc comes back. He'll never find me in here."

No one tried to reason with her. She was clearly in deep shock. Sergeant Ashworth could only ask a constable to stay close to the young reporter and make sure she was all right.

They heard Polly's voice fading as she wandered the circus grounds. "Doc, Doc, where are you, mate? Doc, come on, don't play bloody games. You know how pissed off I can get."

The people in Harry's caravan were at a loss for words and shook their heads in disbelief. Sergeant Ashworth drew back a curtain and looked through a caravan window. "That young lady is going to be a mess. God help her."

# *Fifteen*

The afternoon was still. Polly Jordan stared through a large plate glass window into a garden where numerous birds busily foraged for seeds in a bird feeder.

In the background were bushes and a stand of pine trees, and sturdy bare-branched beeches. A red squirrel flitted here and there before scurrying up a tree. In a trice it disappeared into a hole almost hidden by the canopy of pine needles.

Cranbourne House had been a stately home, now serving as a two hundred pounds-a-day country retreat for the assessment and treatment of psychological disorders among Britain's top professional people.

"What do you see, Polly?" a warm, gentle voice enquired.

"Nature. I see nature."

"And what does that nature mean to you?"

"Life. Raw life. Life like the one I had with Doc before..."

"Are you still hurting?"

The questions were from a middle-aged woman. Today was Polly's assessment by her. For the past five weeks, Polly's carers, Gordon, Caroline, Alice, and Thomas had gently asked her questions in their day-to-day activities. This new person's voice had a calm, precise monotone. She wore a shining white laboratory coat over a grey trouser suit. An array of framed certificates on the wall of this plush, secluded office identified her as a therapist. In fact, Dr Helen Crawley was more than a therapist; she was a consultant psychiatrist commissioned by the *Cardwell Express* to help Polly Jordan deal with the unimaginable trauma of Gerry Docherty's horrific death. She questioned Polly in her permanent office at Cranbourne, which she visited just once a week. "Do you remember being brought to Cranbourne House, Polly?"

"No nothing. I was in the lions' cage with Doc, then *it happened*. After that everything's a blur. I woke up one morning and Caroline, one of my carers, was opening the curtains in my room."

"And you cannot recall anything in between?" Dr Crawley continued.

"Nothing, it's just blackness," Polly said sadly.

"Had the length of your memory loss been shorter, I would probably have diagnosed it as global transient amnesia. GTA is quite a short-term blank which patients, try as they may, can never fill in. All memory from that period is gone for ever. In your case, I think your blank is self-imposed due to trauma. For want of a better description, it's a nervous breakdown. In military terms it would be called shell-shock."

"Oh, bugger, I don't like the sound of that," Polly moaned.

"Well, the good news is your memory seems to be returning. I think you have turned a corner. What do you think, Polly?"

"Me? I'm having a hard time thinking of anything but death."

Dr Crawley rephrased her previous question. "Does your life hurt?"

"The whole fucking world hurts, Doctor. I can't see anything that is good. Nothing can ever be as good as knowing that incredible man. I miss him so much. That's the hurt. It's a pain I didn't know could exist." She paused. "Sorry about the swearing, by the way."

"That's all right. Swear as much as you like if it helps you feel the depth of your emotion towards him. Have you had any thoughts of leaving this life, of joining Mr Docherty?"

Polly stared back in disbelief. "What? Kill myself? No way. I could never do that. I wouldn't have the guts even if I wanted to. But I'll miss him. I'll never forget him."

"I've read and reread your case notes and I've been appraised of the tragic circumstances that led you to us."

Polly felt at ease. "I didn't realise just how much I liked him...loved him. It's not everyone who can love *and* like a person. Sometimes it's one or the other. I know that sounds a strange thing to say, but with Doc, it was both. It was so different."

"Your case notes say you are, or were, in love with a man in Australia, a Mr Flint. How do you reconcile those feelings with your feelings for Mr Docherty?"

"I haven't come to terms with it yet. All I feel, now that you have said Bill Flint's name, is total guilt. Bill was the centre of my universe at the time. It's a crazy thing, Doctor. I didn't realise until now I was in love with two men at the same time. Like my heart and my soul were divided into halves and totally separate. It's been like living two different lives at one time."

"That's an interesting concept, Polly. Did you feel that was always the case, or just since Mr Docherty's passing? Was it a case of loving someone or being in love with them?"

The questions fell on deaf ears.

"I never got to tell him," Polly sobbed. "He never knew. We nearly always butted heads or had a go at each other, in a friendly way. He was always pretending to want me...you know…sexually. Maybe he wasn't pretending. But when it came to the crunch, he was an absolute gentleman, a true friend and a brilliant colleague." She wrapped her arms around herself as though she were holding herself together. "I was so conceited that an older man should find me alluring. I fed on the attention and felt like some sort of trophy, a toy perhaps." She shook her head slowly. "Why couldn't I let Doc in? I trusted that man with my life. In fact, he died saving my life and I never let him love me the way he wanted to. I'm such a bitch. A selfish, stupid bitch who couldn't see genuine…" Polly's hands dabbed at her eyes.

"Is how you felt when Mr Docherty passed away similar to how you felt when your father passed away?"

Polly folded her arms and gently bit her top lip as she dwelt on the question. "Doctor Crawley, my father died. Doc died. They didn't pass away. Why do people say *passed away*?" She was becoming irritated, almost angry. "If a battery chicken gets its neck wrung for somebody's dinner, it doesn't pass away. It dies a violent death. If a cow goes to the abattoir, it doesn't pass away. Somebody addles its brain with a stick after shooting a bolt between its eyes. It doesn't fucking pass away. It dies a brutal death."

Dr Crawley sat quietly and listened intently.

"Dad died from a heart attack. Doc died because some creature that weighed as much as his Mini Cooper tore his fucking throat out. They didn't just pass away like the end of some boring day. They died…died! Please…everybody…don't use soppy euphemisms for death. Say die! If we can say *born* then we can say *died*." She inhaled deeply and blew out a long, slow breath. "I'm sorry, Doctor Crawley. That rant was uncalled for and I'm sorry about the bad language again."

"That was good, Polly. You showed flashes of anger. Your reasoning was sound. I'm very pleased. That was externalisation at its best and with a lot of passion. Were your feelings for the two men you admired most in your life similar?"

"No, definitely not. I see where you're going with this. You think I lost my father then I latched on to Doc as some replacement father figure. Bollocks! My feelings for Doc were in no way some sort of crazy mixed-up reversed Oedipus complex. I wasn't looking for a father figure, so don't go analysing me down that path."

"Wow, that's good again, Polly. Your perception is sharp and, dare I say, so is your tongue. I'm impressed."

Polly's eyes filled with tears again. "There'll never be another Gerry Docherty. That loving rogue would have done anything for me."

Dr Crawley slowly inched a box of tissues across her desk towards Polly, who ignored the doctor's action. The doctor had been taking notes, but replaced her fountain pen on the antique writing desk she chose to sit next to, rather than behind. She let Polly cry herself dry then she looked into the young face. "You've been here for five weeks and according to what I hear from your carers that's the first time you have really unbuttoned your thought pocket. It's good you are able to self-analyse this way, Polly. Do you reckon you're strong enough to face work, or shall we carry on these sessions for a few more weeks?'

"Helen, may I call you Helen?" Despite her highly emotional state, Polly had seen the doctor's name on the walled certificates.

The doctor nodded her approval.

"I can't see myself ever being ready for work again, certainly not at the *Express*. Perhaps nowhere. I know you've been so kind and helpful, and I appreciate the *Express* has gone out of its way to do right by me, but the soul has been torn out of me, just as it was torn out of Gerry. I know my boyfriend in Australia has been asking about me. One of my carers told me a few days ago. I won't say which one, in case they weren't supposed to divulge that information."

"That's all right. I know about it," Dr Crawley replied pointedly.

"I should phone him soon and let him know I've not gone stark raving mad," Polly said, "although at times, I'm not convinced I haven't." She leaned forward and rested her elbows on her knees. "You know, I dream about Doc almost every night."

"That's a very interesting development. Can you tell me more?"

"He phones me and asks me to meet him in the photographers' darkroom at the *Express*. I go in to find him, but he's never there...there's just his voice."

"Is there something significant about the darkroom?"

"Definitely, Helen, but there's no way I can tell you. It was a crazy interlude involving too much drink, but in all honesty, it was one of Doc's finest hours. Other than that, my lips must remain sealed, sorry."

"That's okay, you must only discuss what you are comfortable with. Can I ask what you dream about on other nights?"

"Nothing, really. Nothing I can ever remember."

"I think you are showing the beginnings of being able to come to terms with things, but I'm not convinced you are well enough to go home, if I'm being perfectly honest. You are here voluntarily, therefore you are the only person who can determine when you leave. However, I should caution that in my experience, people who have endured such trauma sometimes bury intense memories and feelings and may even become emotionally numb.

"There's still much research work being done, especially to help people traumatised by wartime experiences. Just be prepared, Polly. At some stage you might be overwhelmed by newly-evolved emotions and maybe you cannot cope. If that should occur and you are able to recognise it, feel free to contact me."

"Thanks, Helen, I'll take that onboard, but I think I have to leave the nest and fly on my own. It might turn out to be hell, but I'll never know sitting here, going over and over what happened. You good people have done all you can, it's down to me now. I'm going home."

"As I've said, you can discharge yourself whenever you choose, Polly, we can't keep you here against your will."

Polly held out her hand and Dr Crawley hesitantly shook it. "Are you absolutely sure you can manage?"

"Thanks, Doc." She gasped audibly. "Shit, I've said it! I swore to myself I'd never say that word again in honour of Gerry."

"It's okay. If he were able to, I'm sure he'd say it was okay."

"Do you think he's here?"

"If you want him to be," Doctor Crawley said. "What form do you think he would take, Polly?"

Polly closed her eyes tight as she answered. "Maybe he's a cloud that disperses, then re-forms and comes round again?"

"Is that how you imagine death?" quizzed Doctor Crawley, showing a renewed clinical interest. "A never-ending cycle?"

"That's how some people see clouds," Polly said in a measured tone. "I used to think they were here and gone in a flash. Changed for ever. Now, maybe they *do* have a life that goes on. I'd love to believe it."

"It's another interesting concept, Polly, and one that you should hang on to if it brings you comfort."

Polly sensed a measure of condescension. "Are you humouring me, Helen? That look on your face is telling me you think what's happened to Doc has driven me over the edge. I'm not a crackpot, Doctor. Really, I'm not. Don't take any notice of my ramblings about bloody clouds. It's just something Bill and I joked about once ages ago. It's just rubbish...maybe I should say it's pie in the sky."

"It's good that you're playing with words again."

"It's my job, Helen. Or at least it *was*."

"Will you return to journalism?"

"I can't say for sure. Probably not."

"If it's *not*, what will you do?"

"I'll survive, Helen. Survive."

"I really would recommend staying for another few weeks. I don't think you're fully equipped to go home."

"Helen, I'll survive or I won't. I won't know unless I walk out of here, so I'm going. I need to survive and I will."

"I hope you will, but keep my phone number handy and if ever you have trouble, call me immediately. Good luck!"

With that, Polly left Doctor Crawley to ponder the cloud concept.

As she crossed the car park, Polly silently started to process the interview. *I can't believe I talked about that stupid cloud stuff. And to top it all, Helen genuinely thinks I've lost the plot."*

Despite an initial spluttering from its engine, her Spitfire fired into life after standing idle for five weeks on the grounds of Cranbourne House. "Goodbye, Cranbourne," Polly whispered and revved Spittie. Its rear wheels spun on the loose gravel driveway before gaining traction on the tarmac highway as Polly pointed her pride and joy in the direction of Cardwell for the thirty-minute journey back home.

~ * ~

While Polly had been in isolation at Cranbourne House, most of England had been bombarded with sensational headlines about the circus tragedy. However, the medical staff at Cranbourne had managed to keep Polly shielded from it all.

At the inquest into Doc's death, the county coroner had arrived at a verdict of misadventure and had ordered an official inquiry into safety issues, particularly at the circus. There could have been engineering flaws concerning the lions' enclosure.

Despite Polly's being a material witness, Sergeant Ashworth, who was in attendance when news of Doc's death was received at the circus, had managed to get her excused from having to attend and give evidence. The officer had argued that to do so would have been a cruel revisitation of the trauma and would possibly have undone any good accomplished during her rehabilitation at Cranbourne House.

It would take Polly almost a week to analyse the media publicity and get herself back on an emotional keel, although her thoughts were often about Doc. *It's a relief to be able to remember Doc without the nightmarish details. I'm proud of myself for no longer needing alcohol to cope and I think Doc would be proud of me too.*

# *Sixteen*

Nineteen-sixty-three had only a couple of weeks left as Polly phoned Australia. At this time of year, demand was heavy on phone connections and it was almost one hour of failed attempts and seemingly endless recorded messages saying *all lines to Australia are currently busy* before a familiar welcoming click put her through. "Bill, it's me, Polly."

"Thank the lord. Are you all right? Gerry's awful death was all over the news here in Australia. I can't imagine what you have gone through. That would have sent me round the bend. Did your therapy help you? I contacted the *Express* and they told me you were resting at Cranbourne House. I only met Gerry briefly, but I found him a lovely man, an attractive man—attractive in its literal sense. He commanded your attention. He drew you to him."

His questions came thick and fast, like a hailstorm, and Polly was hard pressed to answer cohesively, but her excitement at hearing Bill's voice was overwhelming. "Bill, I've got something to tell you."

"Yes, I'm listening.

"I've decided to give up everything here and come out to Australia to be with you."

There was a stunned silence. When Flint composed himself, his voice was weak and trembling. "I can't believe it. Tell me I'm dreaming. My god, you don't know how much I've longed to hear you say that."

"Are you crying?" Polly asked gently.

"Crying? No." He took a deep breath. "Sorry, yes, I am. I have a few tears rolling down my cheeks. It's the wind, it's a bit blowy today. No, that's bulldust...it's not the breeze," Bill said. "It's all lies. I'm weeping like a baby. I've missed you. I've lain awake night after night worrying about you and whether the trauma of Gerry and the job would take its toll, and maybe even wreck everything we have going for us."

"No way, Bill. I want to be with you and I want us to spend our lives together. I want to put all the crap of the past months behind us and be together in Melbourne, or wherever life takes us. I'm coming, Bill. I think I'm finding happiness again. You know I'll never forget Doc, but I want to be over there with you."

"Brilliant, magic, phenomenal. I can't find enough words to—"

"Leave the words to me, Mr Flint. You do the art."

They laughed and made hurried plans.

"I've already been to the consulate in Manchester and my paperwork is in. I should know in about two weeks."

"Blimey, that's going to be just after Christmas. It's as well you're not applying here. Just about everything closes down for the Christmas and new year holiday period."

"Let's hope I hear soon then." Her words echoed back at her from the long-distance phone line and she smiled with satisfaction. "Gotta go now, Bill, I need to write a resignation letter. The *Express* has been marvellous with me, but I need to cut the ties." She almost replaced the receiver on its cradle. "Oh, Bill I have to tell you one last thing. How could I forget? The coroner has at last released the body and it's Doc's funeral the day after tomorrow and I *have* to go. I *must* go. It's at Overdale, then there's to be a wake at the Nag's Head. I'm just letting you know because I might become a gibbering heap for a while, so be patient with me if I don't get in touch. When I left Cranbourne, I felt stronger and able to cope, but the funeral is a dark cave I'm going in and I don't know how I'll come out."

"Don't worry," Bill reassured her, "I'm here for you. You have my support and I'll wait for you for ever if I have to."

~ * ~

After the lengthy procedure of the inquest, Doc's funeral took place on the morning of Monday, January sixth, 1964. The morning was sunny yet cold. Polly eased her car into low gear and began to brake for the turn into Overdale Crematorium's driveway. She looked for a place to park. Already assembled was a huge collection of cars of many different brands, shapes and sizes. *If all these people have come to farewell Doc, he must have been way more popular than I ever imagined*, Polly thought, with a sense of pride. Parking space was at a premium and she was thankful to be able to squeeze Spittie onto a patch of lawn between a silver Mercedes-Benz and an ex-US Army World War Two Willis Jeep. There was hardly enough clearance to open her driver's door and escape, but Polly, being slight, wriggled out.

She straightened her clothing and walked slowly towards the chapel. She glanced at the sky. On such a cold winter day it should, by the rules, be clear. Yet there were clouds, grey and still, as if awaiting direction. *Quite right, too*, Polly thought. *The whole world should be grey and stop to farewell Doc.*

Outside the chapel there were small groups of mourners in dark attire. They smoked and talked in hushed tones. As Polly began to climb the seven steps to the chapel door, some stopped talking and proffered hushed hellos. All eyes were on her and she felt self-conscious. Her mind was in turmoil. *Stop looking at me,* she urged silently.

She had deliberately chosen her funeral clothes with care, not wanting to attract unnecessary attention. It seemed she had failed. She looked stunning. The black dress she had bought from Cardwell's Style Emporium was knee-length and fitted her figure like a glove. To accompany the dress, which she had reasoned she could shorten later, were light grey nylon stockings, and a small black hat comprising delicate black feathers on a black velvet cap. This in turn had a short black lace veil that stopped at her eyes. In her gloved left hand, she carried a small silver clutch bag. Around her shoulders, she had draped a stylish black fashion shawl to ward off the cold. Perhaps the shawl had failed too, because by the time she reached the large marble doorstep, her body was shaking. She told herself it was due to the icy cold, not raw nerves. To complete the picture, her angelic face was like porcelain and her hair shone like polished platinum.

A grey-haired doorman in black opened the large smoked-glass outer door with a muted "Good morning, miss." On the left lapel of his suit was a badge that read *McCabe Funerals.*

As she nervously walked towards elaborate inner doors, she saw row after row of people to the right and to the left of a dark blue carpet. It led to a small area of polished wooden floor upon which was a stand bearing the coffin. People were talking in respectful, hushed tones, but there were so many that the chapel echoed with a sound reminiscent of the hum of bees. Despite all the funerals she had attended at Overdale as a reporter, today Polly felt lost. Strange feelings she had discussed with Helen Crawley were in play. She was just a lost entity intruding at a deeply private ceremony. She was not really there. All these people were strangers who would be unaware of her presence. She felt herself starting to sob and her shoulders began to rise and fall involuntarily.

All at once a voice said, "Good day to you. Am I right in thinking you might be Miss Polly Jordan?"

She turned to her right to find a tall, handsome man with an engaging smile. He held out his right hand. "I'm Conor. Mr Docherty is my father."

Polly could hardly manage a reply. Her mouth was so dry with trepidation, her tongue felt like a worn, withered sponge, but she managed to return a gentle smile and was heartened that Conor had said *is* my father, not *was*.

"I'd like it if you would come and sit next to me at the front," he said. His request was both polite and persuasive.

"How did you know who I am?" she quizzed the young man.

"You may be surprised to know I have known about you for quite a while. Now if you'll allow me, I'll guide you to our seats. If you choose to sit elsewhere, it's okay. Even so, I'd like to talk to you later if you don't mind."

Polly could not refuse the invitation. "I'd love to...to do both."

"Okay, I'll walk you to your seat and join you when I've greeted the last of the mourners."

Within minutes a clergyman in a white robe climbed into the pulpit and the hub-bub ceased. Polly picked up an order of service. She ran her fingers over the gold embossing bearing Doc's name: Gerrard Gilbraith Laughlin Docherty. *That's one hell of a big name and Doc was one hell of a man*, Polly told herself. Suddenly she recalled the time she had called him Sir Gerald. It was soon after the darkroom incident and she immediately reprimanded herself for getting it wrong. He was Gerrard not Gerald and she felt ashamed. For a reporter to get someone's name wrong was a cardinal sin. In this case, it was unforgiveable.

Where she had been asked to sit by Conor was only feet away from the coffin. On it stood a framed picture of a very youthful Doc in army uniform. Next to the photograph was a military cap with a silver badge she thought resembled half angel, half harp.

She allowed herself to look around cautiously and caught sight of the new *Express* editor, Steve Brooks, and a contingent of senior editorial staff. She gave a nervous little wave in return for polite nods. Turning further, as unobtrusively as she dared, she saw, on the left of the blue carpet, rows of uniformed men and women: police officers, firefighters, members of the army forces and others she could not identify. Many more wore suits of dark grey or black.

To Polly it was clear Gerrard Docherty had lived a life in which he had made a huge and lasting impression on countless others. She dabbed away a tear from the corner of each eye. Until it was drawing to a close, Polly felt a helpless numbness during the service. She wanted to pray, something she had not done since Sunday School as a child. She knelt and kissed Doc's name on the order of service. *I miss you Doc, my love. If there IS an afterlife, I hope I find you, Doc, and we...*She didn't get to finish. Everyone suddenly stood. She jumped up to join them just as the velvet curtain began to close, silently ushering Doc to his eternal rest.

A woman on Polly's left was the first to weep, then another somewhere behind her. Men were coughing in an attempt to choke back emotion. Polly, herself, could keep it in no more. She wailed and wept like she had never cried before. She felt an unfamiliar pain in her heart. Doc was gone.

A strong arm around her shoulder brought comfort and she let herself be pulled to Conor's side. It was only when he escorted her out into the cold January air that Polly composed herself. "I didn't know I had so many tears in me," she told him.

"It's a mystery where they come from, sure it is," Conor responded graciously.

She was quick to notice his speech pattern and accent were just like Doc's.

"Will you be coming to the wake?" he asked. "I've organised it at the Nag's Head. Most of Dad's colleagues will know it."

"Thanks, Conor, but I'm emotionally exhausted. Would you mind if I just passed?"

"Not at all. I've found it all taxing too. Look, don't get me wrong when I ask this, but can I see you again? No strings...I have a lot to tell you about Dad and stuff he would have wanted you to know."

"I can't believe you knew about me and I knew nothing of you," Polly said with surprise. "You two talked about me?"

"Yes, but in a good way, Polly. I think a chat would be of benefit...maybe to me as much as you."

Polly's eyes darted up and down this handsome stranger. "Okay, where and when?"

"Perhaps not tonight. An Irish wake is a drinking marathon. There'll be casualties. Maybe me...particularly me." He shrugged as he spoke. "Actually, I hope I don't drink too much. I would hate to let Dad down. I'm staying at the Crowne Hotel. If you can be in the lobby by six tomorrow evening, I'll meet you there."

"The Crowne? Good choice, but expensive I hear. Sounds good, see you tomorrow," Polly said. She drove home, removed her smudged makeup, had a long shower and a welcome early night.

## Seventeen

When Conor Docherty appeared from the elevator, he found Polly already seated in the lobby. A tall standard lamp behind her chair cast a sheen on her hair.

"Wow, you're already here. Have I kept you waiting?"

"Nope. Professional trick...always get there before your interview target."

"Oh, yes, I'd forgotten you were a reporter."

"I was. Or maybe that should be I'm transitioning."

"Don't you like your career?" he asked. "Sorry to push it, but Dad...Doc...often said you were a dedicated newshound. Let's adjourn to the lounge. It's quieter and more comfortable in there."

They found a vacant table and sank down onto plush fabric-covered armchairs. Polly took a sip of the soft drink she had ordered earlier from the bar and thought about an answer. Finally she said, "Things change, Conor. I've changed. After the past few months of my crazy life, I've become a grown-up, no longer a silly girl. What about you? What line are you in?"

"I graduated from the University of St Andrews School of Medicine six months ago."

"Wow, a doctor. What field?"

"A regular MD, but I want to specialise. I'm thinking of tropical diseases as there'll be lots of travel involved and many parts of the world are still struggling with disease such as malaria, still the world's biggest killer."

"Can I get you a drink?" Polly said.

"Er, not right now."

"Don't tell me you overdid it at Doc's wake."

"Not really. I don't drink much usually, apart from tea and coffee, perhaps the occasional glass of white wine."

"Your dad loved a whisky."

"I know. He drank way too much scotch. I remember one time when I told him he should stop drinking. Typically, Dad's reply was 'But I stop every time my glass is empty.'"

"He smoked heavily too and not just tobacco," Polly added with sad resignation.

Without warning and with her eyes welling up, Polly declared, "I loved him, Conor. I loved your dad, but I never got to tell him. I loved him not as a father, or a brother or even a colleague. I loved him in a crazy soul-mate way. It's as if we were meant to go through life knowing each other." She composed herself and continued. "Doc was always calm, always cheerful and, I have to admit, always loving. I never heard him say an unkind word about anybody. Oh, wait, that's not quite true. He couldn't stand our former news editor, Jocelyn Duckworth, and he said some very unflattering things about her, but she's the only one he bad-mouthed. Am I talking too much?"

Connor smiled. "No, please go on."

Polly held up her hand as a sign of gratitude. "Yes, I realise now I was in love with him." She paused again. "I'm sorry, Conor, I *am* running off at the mouth. It's something I tend to do now and then. You were saying..."

"Because I was studying for so long, I didn't see Dad often in later years, but about three months ago, I drove down from

Edinburgh for a fortnight's break, so we could get to know each other again. Of course, Dad was busy doing all sorts of jobs, but we did get one night when we talked for hours and he opened up."

Polly made herself comfortable and fondly recalled how Doc was, indeed, always busy doing something.

"Polly, he believed you loved him, or could learn to love him. He certainly loved you, but didn't know how to tell you because of the age difference. I heard him refer to you once as the little Manx kitten. Then he divulged there was Bill from Australia on the scene."

"But what about his fiancée, Lesley?"

"Some say Dad was occasionally a bit of a rogue, but I'd be surprised to hear he played with people's emotions. He told Lesley about his feelings for you months ago. They mutually agreed to call the engagement off and Lesley left for Canada."

The tears were flowing again as Polly declared, "I'll live the rest of my life punishing myself for not telling Doc how I felt. I was always flirty and flighty, but never honest. We could have been so..."

Conor fell silent for a moment and twirled a drinks coaster on the table as he gathered his thoughts. "You know what? I think I will have that drink. How about you?"

"Okay," Polly said. "I'll have whatever you choose."

Conor strode across the lounge and ordered two large gin and tonics. "No ice, just a slice of lemon," he told the waiter.

There was momentary silence as the waiter placed the drinks on the table.

"Polly, I need to tell you something before you say anything else. During my visit, which turned out to be the last time I would see Dad, he was very croaky. I'm sure you noticed his husky voice. It wasn't always like that. I persuaded him to let me give him a quick unofficial check-up. Of course, Dad being Dad, said he'd rather forget about it and have a drink. He was reluctant and I suspect he knew his health was failing.

"I didn't tell him, but I was fairly sure he had throat cancer. I just knew. After Dad's post-mortem examination which the coroner ordered, I read the pathologist's notes and discovered I was right. The cancer had spread to his lungs, plus his liver was damaged beyond repair with the booze."

Polly gasped.

"I'm afraid Dad would have had little more than one year to live, perhaps even less. I'd guess this was why he never revealed his true feelings. He knew he was on borrowed time. If you had given yourself to him, you would have ended up heartbroken."

"Oh, my god, I had no idea. He was always so lively and healthy-looking...except he did look a bit ill on that...last day." Polly began to weep again and Conor offered her his handkerchief to dab at her tears.

Several minutes passed before Polly could continue. "I'm heartbroken now, but I'm glad you've told me."

"I just felt you should know," Conor explained. "I don't think Dad would mind that I have told you his secrets."

"He was an incredibly attractive man," Polly said quietly. "I don't mean he was a Clark Gable or William Holden, yet he was handsome. A man who attracted your attention. I secretly loved his long hair. He wasn't so much a Beatnik as a loveable Bohemian, a real cool cat. His personality and charm drew me to him, right from the word go. I loved working with him. I loved being with him. It could have been the Irishness, if that's a word. I just miss him. Doc not being around has left a huge wound and it will never heal. I'm certain of that. There's a voice inside my head that tells me I will never forget him." She paused while she took a sip of her gin and tonic. "I feel so stupid and useless that I didn't read the signals, and now it's all too late." She paused again and took her time to say what came next. "I never slept with him, Conor. I want you to know that, though there were times..."

"Dad was many things, but always discreet. He never revealed any personal details about the *people* in his life, and, yes, there have been a few. He swore that since you appeared on the scene, he was scrupulous."

Polly shut her eyes tightly and looked up as if she were trying to see the ceiling. When she lowered her face to look at Conor, her eyes were red and bleary with tears. She again went silent as she reflected on what Conor had said. "Did Doc always want to be a photographer?"

Conor unbuttoned the jacket of his suit, loosened his tie and sat forward in his chair. "You ask about his photography? That's a story in itself and a long one."

"I have time," Polly said gently and focused on Conor's handsome features. She was struck by his eyes, emerald green just like Doc's. "Please tell me."

"Polly, much of this was unknown to me until my visit to Dad in Cardwell. With hindsight, it was almost as if he was mustering facts for his own obituary. When Dad...okay I'll stop there. Let's both call him Doc, that's what he got called most of his life."

"I'd rather hear Doc than Dad," Polly agreed.

"When Doc was about eighteen, he joined the Royal Ulster Rifles. It was early in 1942, not long after the attack on Pearl Harbour which pulled the Americans into the war in Europe."

"I knew it! Polly shrieked. In her excitement she threw her arms wide then clapped her hands. Had it not been for Conor's quick reflexes, she would have knocked her drink off the table. "Yes! I asked him once if he'd served in the war and, in typical Doc fashion, he evaded the question. Hah, right," Polly exclaimed, "that explains the military cap and badge on Doc's coffin."

"Yep," Conor conceded, "he spent time training in Scotland. Then D-Day came and he was in the first wave of troops to land at Sword Beach in Normandy with the Ulstermen."

Polly nodded. "I'm following you. I recently edited a huge special supplement for *The Cardwell Express* about the start of World War Two, so my war history is not too bad."

"Great," Connor said. "Mine wasn't good at all until about eight years ago when Doc mentioned it briefly. I think it was the first time he'd talked about it with anyone other than ex-comrades whom he saw once in a while. Just before the invasion, he had secretly stowed a small camera in his kit and was taking snapshots at and around the landing area in France. His company commander threatened to have him court martialled for dereliction of duty."

"Oh heck," Polly interjected.

"Doc being Doc, he talked his way out of trouble, but as punishment, he was designated assistant official regimental photographer. That was a dangerous job, often right on the front line. As the Allies advanced, bullets and shells were flying everywhere, but the only shots Doc fired were from cameras. After the Normandy landings, he never even carried a firearm. Later he was transferred to an airborne reconnaissance unit taking photographs of strategic targets such as bridges and dams. After that, he was transferred to RAF bombers and flew over Germany doing the same thing. Talk about the luck of the Irish. He used to joke about the only wounds he got were from shaving with blunt razor blades!"

"Wow, that's incredible," Polly said with total admiration.

"There's more, but they were mostly missions he hated and refused to discuss for years. It was like getting blood out of a stone. He had stints with British regiments and the Yanks towards the end of the war."

"It's hard to believe he never talked about it," Polly pondered.

"It is, but eventually Doc revealed he was assigned to take photographic evidence at three massive concentration camps in Poland. He said his pictures showed horrible atrocities. Thousands of prisoners had been slaughtered in the most obscene ways, and others were walking skeletons. They were all but dead from starvation, wandering through piles of corpses. Just horrible. The Allies realised that if no photographic evidence was taken, later generations would forget the horror or even deny it ever happened."

"We all know about that. I bet Doc was affected by it more than others. He would have seen the horror at first hand," Polly said sadly.

"Apparently he endured nightmares and mental anguish for years. He played down the repercussions and said it had been work that had to be done, if only for the history books."

"I'm only now realising there was so much more to Doc than met the eye," Polly acknowledged. "I would never have guessed he was hiding so much pain when he came home all those years ago."

"He joked about not being wounded, Polly, but he *was* wounded. Deep inside his soul, he felt the hurt," Conor said. "Despite the trauma, he volunteered his photographic services in the hunt for SS officers who were wanted for war crimes. His commanding officer refused. He said Doc had done enough, and sanctioned an honourable discharge from the army. That's when he returned to Ireland and was shocked to find me, aged nearly three, waiting for him."

Polly leaned back in her chair and stretched her arms about her head "Wow," she whispered. "Who knew?"

"Are you sure you want to hear all this?" Conor asked. "Like I said, it's a long story."

Polly nodded eagerly. "You can't stop now. Even if we are here until tomorrow, I have to hear the rest."

"Okay, here we go then. Early in 1943, Doc had been granted leave from his unit in Scotland and met Nancy Lowry in his home town..."

"Carrickfergus! Not Belfast!" Polly pitched in enthusiastically.

"That's it, yes. She became my mother. Apparently, he had no idea when he went into battle he had become a father. Mum wrote to him, but the mail never caught up with him. He was always on the move. They never married, but had a great, if unconventional, relationship, thanks in part to Doc's roaming around after the war seeking work as a photographer. He wasn't what you'd call a regular dad and there were times when I didn't see him for many months on end, but I know he loved and cherished me. Mum died from heart failure when I was about thirteen, so I was sent to live with her parents in Donaghadee. It was a beautiful, peaceful seaside town and I was loved and looked after, but I missed Mum so much. Her death had already sparked a longing in me to become a doctor. It was Doc who paid for my upkeep all those years and then paid my fees all through medical school."

Conor thoughtfully sipped at his gin and tonic. "That's enough about me. I'm supposed to be telling you about Doc."

"Don't apologise," Polly said gently. "Whatever you tell me is so...so healing. I want to know everything about Doc, and about you, Conor," she added and reached across the table to pat his knee.

"Well, where was I? That's about all there is. The war was over and Doc went back to Northern Ireland and, as we know, eventually became a press photographer."

"You're so fortunate to have had Doc for a father."

"I know. He was the best," Conor said wistfully.

"And I'm so lucky he touched my life, too," Polly added. "He was the kindest, most trustworthy, chivalrous, loving man I have ever known. God bless you, Doc," Polly said as she threw back her head and downed the rest of her gin and tonic. "In a different world, Doc and I would have…"

"I should go now," Conor said, "It's nine-thirty already and I have a pile of jobs and appointments to get through tomorrow. They're mostly legal, to do with Doc's estate and his will, and insurance issues tied in with the *Express* and the circus management. It all sounds complicated for a doctor, but there could be compensation awarded to his estate, so it's important stuff. My head's in the clouds when it comes to legal matters. Give me simple medical stuff every day."

"Simple?" Polly said. "I can't see medicine being simple, or it wouldn't take years of study to perfect. Anyway, I have stuff to do too, so I'll say goodnight and thank you for letting me in on Doc's secret world. There have been times when losing Doc has brought me to my knees. Tonight has been cathartic, like medicine, soothing balm. You don't know just what a difference tonight has made to my life. All at once I feel I have a new connection with Doc. It's brilliant. I'm so happy."

"It's been my absolute pleasure," Conor said, with a beaming smile.

"I'll give you my phone number," Polly offered, "just in case there's anything else you think I might like to know."

"I'll definitely try to think of something," Conor replied with a grin and held out his hand.

Polly felt the warmth of his palm on hers and moved closer. She thought she saw his eyes twinkle just that bit brighter. Standing on tiptoes, she grabbed the lapels of his coat and pulled him down to her level. "Thank you for tonight," she whispered and gently kissed him on the cheek.

Polly silently stared at him, trying to read his face.

"What are you looking at?" Conor asked with a smile that suggested apprehension.

"Your smile. It's a Doc smile. A perfect copy. Good night, Doctor Docherty."

"See you soon, Polly," Conor said. There was anticipation in his voice.

They paused for a moment. Their eyes met and neither seemed to want to make the first move to part. Then, as if by some unseen signal, they turned and slowly walked in opposite directions.

~ * ~

Despite going to bed earlier than usual, Polly couldn't sleep. Her thoughts were on Doc's funeral and what Conor Docherty had revealed about his father. Amid this maelstrom, she found herself envisioning life in Australia. Although it had only been three days since Polly and Bill had spoken by phone, but she was puzzled as to why he had not contacted her, especially as she had indicated the funeral might pose emotional problems.

She had deliberately not wound the chiming mechanism of Lizzie's clock. As the fingers indicated three in the morning, it whirred falteringly as if to strike just as Polly went into her lounge and turned on the television. There was just the usual test pattern the BBC screened between broadcasts. Within seconds that faded to black. She had read all the paperbacks she owned, so she turned off the light and sat in the darkness.

As the weak wintery sun backlit the closed curtains, Polly sleepily glanced at the clock. It was nine o'clock and she had slept sitting up for hours. Her back and legs ached and she felt cold. *Wish I were in Australia. Wish I were with Bill.* She was daydreaming. "Brrr, I'm so cold," she said out loud and headed for the shower to get warm. As welcoming water coursed through her hair and soothed her body, she shook both fists in celebration. *It won't be long before I'm in Oz...and it will be warm. Warm, warm, warm!*

She had not felt so happy and uplifted since she had landed the Paul McCartney scoop, the very thing that was the start of her world being turned upside.

~ * ~

Polly busied herself for the next few days preparing to leave for Australia. Her application for assisted passage had been approved, she had passed the Australian government's rigorous health assessment, and had a visa and a time and place for embarkation. She had sold her much-loved Spitfire to Joe Wright, the mechanic, wound up the lease on her apartment, and said goodbye to friends and former colleagues at the *Express*. She had met with Conor twice at the Crowne and they had developed a firm friendship. However, she had told him she was emigrating to Australia and had given him Bill's business phone number and address in case he should ever want to contact her.

Finally the big day arrived. Polly had taken a taxi to Cardwell railway station. There she began the journey that, after two changes of train, would take her to Southampton. In what seemed like very little time, she stood on the docks looking up at the magnificent ship *SS Manxman* that was waiting to take her and just over six hundred others to a new life in Australia.

"I can't believe it," she said to a middle-aged woman standing on the quayside. "Look at the name. *Manxman*. I was born on the Isle of Man. That *has* to be a good omen."

"That's nice," said the woman, who was trying to control two obviously excited children aged about five. "These two rascals have never been on anything bigger than a wooden rowing boat, so they're driving me mad. Their dad will be along soon, so he'll calm them down."

Finally, when the crew had undertaken last-minute preparations, passengers were allowed to embark. It was a slow process of checking identification and exchanging papers, but almost an hour later, Polly found her cabin and made herself known to the other female passenger with whom she would share the accommodation for the best part of a month. Her cabin mate, Pamela Partington, was a single woman, whom Polly estimated was about forty. "Where are you heading?" she inquired.

"Melbourne," Polly answered cheerily. "I'm going out to live with my boyfriend. And you?"

"I want to get to Sydney. I was there four years ago then went back to Preston. Biggest mistake I ever made, going back. You realise what a different lifestyle it is in Australia. I had to repay the entire fare because I hadn't stayed the two years you agree to when you get the ten-pound passage. Cost me over one hundred and twenty quid."

"Blimey, that's a lot," Polly said, trying to empathise. She had read the terms of the agreement time and time again and was well aware of the pitfalls... and the benefits.

~ * ~

For the most part, the long journey to Australia was uneventful. Some activities were organised to relieve boredom among passengers and crew, and children especially enjoyed the daily games of hide and seek, deck quoits and hopscotch. Mostly, Polly stayed close to her cabin. The third person meant to share the cabin did not sail, so Polly and Pamela had more room and more privacy than they had anticipated.

Polly kept clear of the activities and contented herself by lounging in a deckchair and reading books from the ship's library. Occasionally, she stared at the passing sky and wrote in her diary. The thing that preoccupied her thoughts was contemplation of her life with Bill Flint. There was one day, however, when the weather turned villain and had Polly fearful. In her diary she wrote: *Today we had a violent storm. It was the day after a party the crew organised when the Manxman crossed the equator. Battleship grey clouds gathered on the horizon directly in the ship's path. Within five minutes, the clouds were almost black and the ocean turned the colour of ink. Bolts of lightning hit the ocean and flashed seemingly parallel to the water. The claps of thunder were as loud as any naval gun and hurt my ears. I've never seen clouds so menacing, so evil. I was reminded of Lizzie Flint's story about her Land Army friend who was kicked to death by a horse during a freak storm. I've never been so scared by weather. This was a total weather freak. Those changing cloud formations did nothing to inspire me. No clouds worth remembering today.*

# Eighteen

It was just after lunchtime when the *Manxman* slipped slowly into Port Phillip Bay through The Heads, a narrow but relatively shallow stretch of water that acts like the neck of a bottle for shipping in and out of Melbourne's busy port complex. The *Manxman* had rested at anchor for several hours awaiting a favourable tide and now the final leg of her voyage, and that of Polly Jordan, was underway. Passengers clambered onto the main and upper decks and rushed to the bow to catch a glimpse of the land that held the key to a new life for so many of them. Children squealed and chattered excitedly as they caught sight of a pod of grey bottlenose dolphins riding the ship's bow waves.

Polly joined the crush, but soon determined the cabin was the most comfortable place to wait out the final half hour or so until the *Manxman* docked. Somewhere in the eager crowd was her cabin friend, Pamela, with whom she had shared the voyage and more than a few stories of her career as a journalist. Polly learned that Pamela would be one of the first called to disembark and they would not see each other again.

Once she was down the gangway and on the quayside, any thoughts of goodbyes were gone. Now, all she could think of was throwing her arms around Bill Flint. She had called him by ship's radio phone from somewhere in the Australian Bight after rounding the southern tip of Western Australia. Everything was arranged. He would be waiting beyond the security barriers if the tide enabled the ship to put in by the estimated arrival time of eleven to eleven-thirty in the morning.

Clearing immigration checks and customs was tedious and time-consuming. When Polly was finally free to travel into Melbourne, having formally turned down the need for migrant accommodation and transport, it was three in the afternoon.

*Where is Bill?* She worried. *Surely he should be here by now.* All she had was a letter from him giving the address of his art gallery in the Melbourne city suburb of Malvern and the address of the rented apartment in inner-city Prahran. Bill had told her he had chosen it for her in case she felt she needed to be closer to the central business district. Right then, the suburb names meant nothing; the entire city was a maze waiting to be explored.

*Where is Prahran? How do I get there? How far away is Malvern?* Her mind swam with questions. All the while, her eyes darted here and there hoping to see Bill's friendly face and warm smile. After waiting in vain for close to an hour, she decided to venture alone into Melbourne. She grabbed her two heavy suitcases and bulging shoulder bag and trudged to a taxi rank. The Silver Top driver beckoned her in. "G'day, love. Where ya off to?" He whistled cheerily as he heaved her luggage into the car boot. "I reckon from here it's gotta be Prahran, love."

She read out the address and they set off, stopping and starting in the city traffic and accelerating when he could to pass trams as they rattled along their steel tracks.

"Do you always overtake trams on the inside?" she observed.

"Yep, you gotta put up with the old red rattlers," he joked, "And when the tram stops, so do the cars. It usually means a passenger is getting off or on, and they have right of way. It's a crazy city for transport, but it works. Well, most of the time. Here we are, love, number fifty-nine Porter Street. You're pretty well in the thick of it here. Chapel Street's not far off and there's a cracking market, great pubs and loads of shops around here. Good luck."

He took her fare and Polly was relieved it was in pounds and pence, and not some strange currency she couldn't fathom.

Number 59 was a small grey block of apartments and once inside she saw a man who looked like he worked there.

"Hi, I've just come from England and I'm to meet Bill Flint. But he didn't show up at the docks and, well, not to put too fine a point on it I'm stuffed unless I can get into my accommodation," Polly said. She was fatigued and her tone advertised that fact.

"You don't have to tell me where you're from, darl, I can tell by the accent," the jolly looking man with a slight stoop and suntanned face told her. "I'm Larry Simpson. Simmo to most people. Bill called a couple of weeks ago and told me to expect you. He left the key. I'm sort of caretaker here. I live in a ground-floor flat and do all the odd jobs and cleaning. Haven't seen him for a while, but here's the key. Your place is on the third floor, the top floor actually. There's no lift, so it's a bit of climb. If you leave your bags, I'll bring them up in five or ten minutes."

"Simmo, that would be great, thanks. I'm so tired after the journey. I just want to sleep for about a week."

She threw open the door and half expected Bill to be there with a bottle of champagne and a massive hug. Disappointment hit her in one fell swoop. She was mistaken. She was alone, but the long and, for the most part, tedious journey from Cardwell had taken its toll on her. As soon as Simmo brought her luggage into the apartment and left, she fell onto her bed and it was almost ten o'clock next morning when she woke. From her third-floor bedroom window, Polly looked out on the bustling suburb of Prahran with its busy streets and shops that fused easily with dozens of single-storey houses with corrugated metal roofs. She took it all in, watching people come and go and trams trundling along, shaking her bedroom window as they went by.

She wandered slowly from the bedroom to the loungeroom and was about to sit at a table with two chairs when suddenly there was a loud noise at the door and before she could react or even say anything, a suntanned man in khaki shorts and rolled-sleeve shirt barged in. Polly imagined he had just stepped out of the pages of an Edgar Rice Burroughs explorer novel.

"Oh, sorry love. You must be Polly, right?"

She was so taken aback she couldn't reply. She grabbed a tartan rug from the sofa and fumbled to hide the flimsy nightdress that barely covered her.

"I'm Norman, Norm...Norm Flint, Bill's brother. Obviously caught you at a bit of a bad time, eh!"

Polly was shaken by the intrusion.

"I guess I should say pleased to meet you, Norm, but you came in unannounced. What would have happened if I'd just stepped out of the shower and was in the nude?"

"I'd have looked away, love."

*That's not what your brother would have done,* Polly mused.

"I promise. I wouldn't deliberately embarrass you. Sorry if I made you jump, and sorry I didn't knock."

"It's all right. No damage done...this time," she said. "I didn't know Bill had a brother. He never mentioned you," Polly replied warily.

"Well, strictly speaking, we're half-brothers. Same dad, different mothers. It's complicated."

"Right," she said cautiously. She was weighing him up. For half-brothers, they looked totally dissimilar. Norm was short and stocky with olive skin, whereas Bill was a little tanned, but tall and of a medium build. She wondered what the complication had been. "Did Bill say anything about where he is and why I'm here?" she asked.

"Not a thing."

Polly was upset that Bill had not been there to greet her and she tried to hide her disappointment from Norm. "But we had arranged that he'd pick me up at the docks..."

"Good old Bill," said Norm with a wry smile. "When he gets a sped in mind, he forgets just about everything else."

"What's a sped?" Polly said tentatively.

"Oh, Bill's shorthand for an expedition, a trip into the Outback to acquire more Abo art. Sorry I shouldn't say that word. Aboriginal art, I mean. These people have been doing paintings on bark and bits and bobs for ever, and now in the past few years, people all over the world are buying them as fast as the Ab, sorry, Indigenous artists can turn them out. Can't get enough of them and Bill's trading in them."

"Wow, that's fantastic."

"I wouldn't say that exactly. I can't make head nor tail of some of them. They're mostly colourful dots and squiggles to me, but the punters pay huge money for them, for the genuine article. When Bill gets really swamped, he calls on me to help him out. I love it, because it usually means a long drive north and getting out of chilly Melbourne for a couple of weeks."

"Chilly?" Polly said incredulously.

"Whoops, dropped a clanger. Did Bill tell you summer was all sunshine and lollipops? We have hot days, but we can have wind, rain, or hail at the drop of a hat. Four seasons in one day, they say about Melbourne's weather."

"Oh, yes, of course," Polly chimed, "it's summer here and it's still pretty damned cold and wintery back in Cardwell."

"Had breakfast, or should I say lunch?"

"No, I haven't had a chance, I just got up," Polly said, stifling a yawn.

"Well, if you want to get dressed and come with me, I'll take you to a great little diner close by and I'll fill you in on Bill's business. I've arranged to ring him in Katherine tomorrow night at seven, so if we can get a phone line through, you can speak to him. The phones here aren't like in Pommie land," Norm explained. "Katherine is in the Territory, the Northern Territory. That's a zillion miles from Melbourne."

"Zillion?" Polly asked.

"That's a number too big for Aussies to count, so we say zillion. I'm no expert on phones, but someone said your call goes to Darwin, then is re-routed south to Katherine."

Polly detected some uneasiness in his explanation. Her already flagging spirits took another hit as she realised it would be yet another twenty-four hours before she could talk to Bill...if the phone lines permitted. "Norm, look, I'll pass on the diner, thanks," Polly said with as much gratitude as she could muster after the let-downs. "Why don't you come over tomorrow and we can figure out where to contact him?"

"Yep, no worries. How about I meet you, buy you dinner and then we can go back to the gallery and call Bill from there."

"That sounds really great," Polly agreed unenthusiastically.

Norm jotted down the restaurant's address and directions to find it. After a short and awkward interlude, Norm nodded, and with a little comical salute went home, leaving Polly to anticipate another lonely night. After about an hour of gazing out of her bedroom window, her thoughts were confused. *This is not really what I expected. I thought Bill would be here and as excited to see me as I would be to see him. Ah well, I'll have a shower and then go and explore this place...she sighed...alone.*

Once outside, she was amazed by how warm the air felt and how the light seemed much more intense than in England. All the colours of the shops, the cars and even the people seemed more vivid. Polly thought of Cardwell and how cold it must be in early March at the opposite side of the world. She desperately wanted to call Bill, but the apartment had no phone. She strolled along Chapel Street and came across a store selling alcohol. "Can I buy a bottle of Johnnie Walker scotch?" she asked the young man behind the counter. He had dark eyes and smouldering good looks. She assessed him as coming from somewhere around the Mediterranean.

"Can I see some ID first?" he asked. "You don't look old enough to buy grog."

Polly tutted and began to rummage through her handbag for her passport.

"Just kidding, babe. Just a little joke to make you laugh."

Polly was slightly irritated. "Do I look as if I need a laugh?"

"To be honest, you don't. I'm sorry. I've had a slow day and you look like the kind of chick I can have a giggle with."

*God, even ten thousand miles away from Cardwell, I can't escape being called babe,* Polly muttered under her breath. Then she smiled as remembered scolding Doc endlessly for the same crime. She paid for whisky and was about leave.

"You from London?" the young man asked.

"No, farther north. Near Manchester. What about you, where are you from?"

"Born here in Melbourne, but my folks are Greek, from Thessaloniki."

"Are they many Greeks in Australia?"

"Hell, yeah. Melbourne's Greek population is massive."

"That's nice," said Polly and closed the door on the way out. Outside she remonstrated with herself. *Polly that was rude and dismissive. The poor lad just wanted to talk, or at least chat you up. Bill Flint, you'd better watch your back if this is an example of red-bloodied Aussie youth.*

Back in her apartment, she ate the sausage rolls and chips she had bought, poured a large scotch and added a little water. As she enjoyed that first sip, she thought about the Greek lad and smiled at his attempted humour.

As the effects of her second scotch hit home, his banter was forgotten and the focus of Polly's longing and desire returned with youthful urgency, to Bill Flint in far-flung Katherine. A cocktail of fatigue and alcohol helped her to have the best night's, dreamless, sleep she had enjoyed for many months.

# *Nineteen*

Norm was already waiting in the restaurant when Polly arrived. It was just an easy two-minute stroll from the apartment to Greville Street and the evening was still and balmy. Polly was refreshed after a very long, whisky enhanced sleep and felt re-energised.

"Hiya, Norm, thanks for picking somewhere close to my accommodation, although it's such a lovely evening, I would have enjoyed seeing more of Prahran."

"Prahran's all right, but the city centre is where the real nightlife is." Norm informed her.

"Why do they call this place Steak Diana, when the name of the steak dish is 'Steak Diane'?" Polly asked.

"Well... Steak Diane, the meal, is named after British high society member Lady Diana Cooper."

She quickly realised she might have underestimated Norm. "Wow, I didn't know that," Polly said with obvious surprise.

"In other words, you're thinking, how could he possibly know that. Am I right?" Norm joked.

Polly blushed and had to admit her gaffe.

"Plus, the restaurant owner's wife is called Diana and they're good friends of Bill."

"Ha-ha!...so you had inside information," Polly said with a laugh.

From that potentially awkward start, Polly and Norm quickly established a friendly rapport and after they enjoyed a very welcome, hearty dinner, he drove her to Malvern. On the drive Norm asked, "How did you enjoy your steak?"

"Blimey, it was beautiful. So tender and juicy. I could eat that for ever, thank you," Polly gushed.

"It was kangaroo," Norm revealed.

"You're kidding, right? Kangaroo? Never!"

"Yep, Diana's is known all over Melbourne for the kangaroo medallions."

"Bloody hell, I can't believe I've eaten one of those cute hopping creatures. Isn't there a law against it?"

"No, not at all. Out in the bush, the farmers are glad to get rid of them. They're in plague proportions."

"Is all steak kangaroo here?"

"No, not at all. Diana's is the only eatery I know around here that sells it and it brings customers from miles to try it."

"I don't know how I feel about eating kangaroo, but I have to concede, it was bloody good."

"Here we are in Malvern," Norm said, pulling on the handbrake of his Holden car. "Over the road is Bill's gallery."

The large double display windows on either side of a glass door were brightly lit and immediately commanded Polly's attention. Melbourne's inky black star-studded sky added extra glitz to the light show. "It's gorgeous," she exclaimed. "I'm very impressed. The gallery looks fabulous. All the lights and all that colour on display. Wow!" She screwed up her face in deep thought. "Who is Artovoz?" she questioned. "It sounds Polish or Russian." She stopped mid-thought. "Oh, wait. I get it...Art of Oz, Australia. How stupid of me not getting it the first time." She giggled at her own foolishness.

"Bill goes to a lot of trouble to display his art stock and there's always a fast turnover. But I shouldn't be saying this. I think it's Bill's place to fill you in on the nitty-gritty."

"Can't wait," Polly blurted.

"C'mon, let's go in and call the man."

Norm guided Polly through a shadowy alleyway and to a sturdy door at the rear of the building. He fumbled for a switch on the wall and a large paved courtyard was illuminated by a bank of six spotlights. "Are all these vehicles Bill's?" Polly asked as she scanned a collection of windowless vans and a large truck painted in black and white stripes, reminiscent of zebra hide.

"That's only some of them," Norm replied. Once inside, he led Polly up two flights of stairs and through a door that was treble locked for security, and into a large room. When he switched on the lights, an opulently decorated loungeroom was revealed. Four enormous velvet settees surrounded an equally large and elaborately carved coffee table. Norm was eager to tell Polly it was fashioned from rare and incredibly expensive Huon pine from Tasmania.

"That wood's probably two or three hundred years old. Huon pine takes an eternity to grow and only grows in Tassie."

"God, it's magnificent!" Polly marvelled.

"Bill would kill me if I told you what it cost," Norm muttered.

Two sparkling chandeliers lit the area and there were numerous small lights and standard lights in many parts of the room, enhancing the luxurious décor. The huge stone fireplace with a large mirror above it caught Polly's eye.

"That's fantastic. Does Bill use the fireplace much?"

"It can get cold some days in Melbourne, so it's nice to sit back with a log fire and a glass of something or other." He paused before he added, "Actually, if you pull on the right-hand edge of the mirror, it will open and you'll find Bill's secret stash of booze...just about anything you'd want."

"Ooh! The secret's out now," Polly said mischievously. She struggled for words to sum up her admiration as she took it all in. The one she chose was *success* and thinking, *Bill Flint, you've come a long way from Pitt Street.* She looked at her watch. It was almost seven-thirty. "Oh, hell's teeth, Norm, we were supposed to ring Bill at seven. I can't believe we've stuffed up."

"Relax, Polly. Katherine time in summer is an hour and a half behind Melbourne time.

"Oh, blimey! I'd forgotten about being upside down with the seasons and being in a country with time zones. Britain is tiny in comparison. It's the same time no matter where you are."

Norm dialled and waited for a reply. The seconds passed and Polly was on tenterhooks.

"Come on, Bill...where are you?" she said in a loud voice that displayed a mix of anxiety and frustration.

Norm held up his left hand, palm towards Polly. "Ssshhhh! It's still ringing."

After what seemed to Polly like an eternity, Norm said "Hello, is that you Bill?"

Immediately Polly was at his side and took the phone from Norm's hand.

"Hello, Bill, it's Polly...I'm here in Melbourne." Suddenly her face fell. On the line was a woman who sounded as though she'd had too much to drink. "Who are you? Where's Bill Flint?" Polly demanded.

Whatever the woman said, it upset Polly so much, she slammed the receiver down and burst into tears.

Norm was at a loss as to what had happened and what to say. "Sorry, Polly, I don't know who that was or where Bill has got to. There has to be some logical explanation."

"I've come all this way to Australia and Bill has…"

"Trust me, there'll be a reason. I know my brother and he wouldn't knowingly or willingly let something like that happen."

Just at that moment the phone rang. It startled Polly. "You answer it," she nervously urged Norm.

"Hello? Yeah, mate. Yes, she's here. What the hell happened before? OK, you tell her yourself." He handed the phone to Polly.

With trembling hands, she took the receiver. "Hello, Bill. It's so good to hear your voice. Who the hell was that drunken woman who answered the phone?"

"I'm sorry, Polly. I've no idea who she was. Just some woman passing the phone. I'm in a hotel in Katherine and the phone's on a wall near the bar."

Polly's worried expression changed to one of relief and smiles. "What happened, Bill? Why weren't you there to meet me on the dock?"

"Polly, listen, the phone connections out here are dodgy, to say the least, and it's noisy in here, so I'll make this quick. I'm due back there in two, maybe three days at the most. I'm sorry I wasn't on the docks, but I'll explain everything to you when I'm home. I had a business crisis I had to sort out. I contacted the *Manxman* by ship-to-shore at least two hours before it was due to berth. I left a message and I stressed it was absolutely vital that you received it."

"Obviously something went wrong," Polly said miserably.

"So sorry, my dear. Sorry, too, that I have to go now. Try to relax and settle in. In fact, tell Norm to give you a set of keys for the gallery apartment and stay there. At least you'll be in a lovely part of town and have a phone handy."

"Okay, thanks, Bill. I'm so happy I've spoken to you," Polly said with tears trickling down her cheeks. "I can't wait till you're here." There was a click and the phone reverted to a dial tone.

Norm had already fished out some apartment keys from his pocket. He held them out to Polly. For a moment, she wondered why Norm seemed to know about the keys, but dismissed it as her mind began to race with the prospect of being with Bill.

"I'm betting Bill told you to stay here," Norm said.

"Yes, he did. How did you know?"

"Just a hunch," he added, with a shrug. "I would have expected nothing less of my brother. Anyway, I'm off, Polly. I'm going home now. I checked the fridge while you were on the phone. There's loads of food, milk and dairy stuff, and if you run short of anything, the street we're on has any numbers of shops for everything you could need or want."

*Not everything*, Polly thought.

"Oh, yes, I almost forgot, there are two bedrooms and two bathrooms up the little flight of stairs in the corner and you know about the mirror over the fireplace. Okay, that's it, the end of the two-bob tour. I'll say good night and see you...well, next time, whenever that might be."

"Good night, Norm and thanks," said Polly and threw herself onto one of the large, velvet settees. Five minutes later, she decided to check out the bedrooms. The main one was quite big and plushly furnished. It had a king-sized bed with no less than eight pillows and burgundy satin bedsheets. The other bedroom also was well furnished with an apricot décor, but did not contain a bed.

Polly puzzled for a moment then returned to the room in which she clearly would spend the night. She slowly slid open one mirrored door of a long wardrobe. There, on a brass pole, hung a collection of suits, numbering about twenty, although she did not count them.

In a built-in set of drawers were numerous immaculately pressed shirts. She slid open another door to find more shirts and shorts on hangers. Below them on the floor, were four pairs of sturdy lace-up work boots. Curiosity satisfied, Polly returned to the loungeroom. She snuggled back between two huge cushions and was close to falling asleep when she jumped up. *Dammit, I've let Norm go and I should have asked him to drop me back in Prahran to pick up my belongings. Stuff it, I'll wait until tomorrow and call a taxi.* She sank back between the cushions again and minutes later she was fast asleep.

Next morning Polly was up, showered and out exploring the shops of Malvern by nine o'clock. She found a baker's shop that offered an alluring collection of cakes and pastries. Blueberry pancakes and cream, followed by a sweet, creamy coffee were just what Polly needed to kick-start her day. For the first time, she felt comfortable in Melbourne. It was a warm morning and she was surprised how many people had said *G'day* to her as they strolled in the sunshine. *Yessss! I think I'm going to enjoy this lifestyle after all.*

When she paid for her brunch and passed several customers still seated, she noticed one reading Melbourne's morning newspaper, *The Sun*. A headline on the front page heralded the June arrival of The Beatles. The Liverpool band were scheduled to visit Australia as part of their world tour and Melbourne was one of the few stops on the itinerary. Her mind wandered back to her Paul McCartney scoop that, thanks to Polly's nemesis Jocelyn Duckworth, never saw the light of day. *Bloody Duckworth! What a cow! But without her vindictive actions, I might still be in Cardwell. You'll never know it, Paul McCartney, but you've done me a big, life-changing favour.*

It was almost four o'clock when Polly, tired from her explorations, climbed the stairs to the gallery apartment. She put on the kettle and was ready to make a cup of tea when the phone rang. She quickly turned off the kettle and dashed over to the phone. "Hello, Bill?"

"No. Is that Polly Jordan?"

Hesitantly she affirmed.

"It's Conor. Conor Docherty!"

"Oh, my goodness," Polly shrieked excitedly. "How are you? Where are you? In England or Scotland?"

"I'm in Australia, in Darwin."

"Oh, brilliant! What a surprise! Now I've homed in on your Irish accent. Oh, Conor it's so good to hear from you. What are you doing in Darwin? That's way north of here, isn't it? Almost in south Asia, if my map memory serves me well."

"It is. I'm working at Royal Darwin Hospital. Do you remember I said I would like to specialise in tropical diseases?"

"Vaguely," Polly confessed. "We talked about so much that night and the other times we met. Most of my attention was focused on what you told me about Doc."

"I started to make enquiries and discovered a chap I was at med school with was working over here. I contacted him and he said I'd be a welcome addition to a team that's just been set up to study Aboriginal health issues and tropical medicine," Conor explained, the undisguisable enthusiasm in his tone evident in every word. "I couldn't wait to say yes and come over. I'm in a place called Tiwi. It's a northern suburb of Darwin. If you've got a pen and paper, I'll give you my phone number and address."

"Conor, have you forgotten I'm a journalist? I always have a notebook handy." And she scribbled down Conor's details. They talked for about twenty minutes before he said he had to get back to work. "Don't forget, Polly if you ever get up this way, look me up."

"And likewise, you look me up if you're in Melbourne. It's been great catching up, Doctor," Polly giggled. "You've made my day. My week! Hey, before you hang up, guess what I ate last night?"

"No idea. I give in," Conor chortled.

"Kangaroo."

"What, a whole one?"

Polly laughed so hard she could hardly speak. "No, you silly...a steak. A beautiful kangaroo steak. So tender, so tasty. And, this afternoon I went to a fish and chip shop. The fish tasted great and when I asked what it was, they said flake. It was shark! I've only been here five minutes and already I've scoffed kangaroo and shark."

"You'd better stop," Conor wisecracked, "or there'll be no fauna left in Australia. Up here crocodile is on the menu," he said with a swagger. "Real man's food."

"Don't tell me you went into a café and said *crocodile sandwich, and make it snappy*," Polly fired back.

"Boy, you are *so* good with words, Polly."

"Sorry to disillusion you, but that's an old corny joke. It sounds like something Groucho Marx would have come up with."

"They reckon there are more crocs in the Northern Territory than people. Some are massive and could swallow you whole," Conor went on. "Hunters risk their lives trapping them."

"Well, you can keep them all there, thank you," Polly asserted. "Keep the terror in the Territory."

Conor took a little time to reply. He quickly put the receiver down on the desk. He rubbed his sweaty palms across his pale blue shirt before resuming. "I'm probably way out of line saying this and it's going to sound crazy...but I'm missing you. There, I've said it.

"Doctor Docherty!" Polly said, feigning shock. "And here's me thinking I was unmissable," she laughed.

"There you go again. You're just too good with words, Miss Jordan. Doc did warn me. I'll quit while I'm behind."

"Didn't figure you for a quitter. Anyway, you're probably surrounded by loads of nurses who flutter around like butterflies trying to attract your attention."

"A few, but they haven't got your...well...your personality."

"That's one hell of a way to charm a girl. Wow! You don't have a fantastic figure, no! Fantastic hair...no! Great legs, no! Beautiful complexion, no! Outstanding personality...yes! Gee, thanks."

"I know we've only met twice, but I feel like I've known you for years." Conor admitted.

"Same here," Polly sighed, "but..."

"I know. I'm sorry. I haven't even asked how things are with you and Bill," Conor said thoughtfully.

"Yeah, things are okay," Polly replied quietly.

"Mmmm, I think that's my cue to sign off. Stay well and say hello to Bill, even though we haven't met."

Polly put the phone down and dropped onto the closest settee to mull over the conversation with Conor. She had poured a whisky before the phone call; it was untouched. She pushed the glass away on the coffee table. *He's just being friendly, Polly. He's just being a guy, just like the lad in the Prahran bottle shop. Or was he flirting? Maybe I was flirting back? Stop it, NOW!*

After the past few days of living in confusion, and not a little doubt, Polly's thoughts were positive. *I simply have to wear my confidence hat just now. I mustn't allow myself to get too emotional if I am going to survive in this strange place...well strange to me. Onwards and upwards.*

At eleven o'clock the next morning, she let out an almighty shriek and jumped for joy as Bill Flint slowly pushed open the door to the apartment.

"Thank the good lord you're back in one piece," Polly blurted happily.

"Sorry, Polly. If I hadn't gone to the Top End, I'd have lost two important agents. There's a new rival mob trying to muscle in on the native art game and steal our business. They're trying to recruit our best people. Losing them and their Aboriginal contacts could cost our business hundreds of thousands of dollars and lose us hundreds of regular buyers if art stock dries up."

"I'm so happy you're home," Polly purred. "I've tried to settle in, but it's seemed like years since I've seen you and I got scared when you didn't pick me up. Then there was that weird woman on the phone..."

"Polly," Bill interrupted gently, "I'm absolutely knackered after driving back from Katherine. It's more than two thousand miles, much of it on roads only fit for camels."

"It's okay, Bill, we can go straight to bed and..."

"Sleep," Bill grunted. "Anything else is out for tonight. I'm sorry, I can hardly keep my eyes open."

This was a new facet to the man Polly had come to adore. She had anticipated long bouts of strenuous love-making, not what she initially felt...rejection. She was seeing Bill dishevelled and looking much older than his almost thirty-nine years.

"Okay, Bill. Maybe I should sleep in the other bedroom tonight while you get your rest."

"No, Polly, please...you can't do that. I'll have a shower and we can lie together, but I will fall asleep the second my head hits the pillow. I guarantee it."

~ * ~

Next morning was dull and overcast. Polly was up before eight o'clock, but Bill emerged from the bedroom a few minutes before noon.

"Do you want me to make you some breakfast, or should I say lunch?" Polly asked.

"I'd like a big mug of strong coffee and then I think I'll go back to bed."

Her face was a picture of despondency. She turned away from Bill before he added, "And you, Miss Jordan, are coming with me. We have a lot of catching up to do."

Polly spun round and ran straight at Bill, jumping up on him so hard she knocked him off his feet and they both fell, locked in an embrace, onto a settee.

Polly smothered him in kisses and Bill responded in kind.

"Hey, forget the coffee. Let's just stay here on the couch."

"What if Norm barges in?

"He won't...he knows better than to—"

Bill stopped himself from saying more. Polly picked up on it, but the mood was too tempestuous to get bogged down in words.

"Oh, speaking of Norm, are those his work clothes in your wardrobe or are they yours? I can't envisage you as a workman getting dirt under those manicured fingernails."

Bill was quick to respond and seemed defensive. "Oh, they're Norm's. He sometimes stays over if we get back late from a long trip."

"But there's no bed in the second bedroom," Polly said with a measure of suspicion.

"Oh, that's right, no need for one. Norm just bunks down on one of the settees. When he's tired, he can just about sleep standing up."

Slowly the mood changed and more than four hours passed before they emerged from the main bedroom. Then they showered together and went out on the town.

~ * ~

Next day Bill invited Norm to the apartment for Sunday lunch. A large dining table at the opposite end of the loungeroom from the fireplace was laid out for three. Royal Doulton crockery, silver cutlery and silver serving dishes, flanked by Waterford crystal wine glasses added to an ambience of opulence. The occasion was made complete with a private cook Bill hired from Steak Diana to prepare lunch.

They feasted well on pan-tossed garlic king prawns, roast chicken, steak, and ham, accompanied by a selection of seasonal vegetables. The digestion and the discussions were lubricated to everyone's satisfaction by, Polly counted, four bottles of South Australian vintage red wine. After a dessert of cheese and biscuits, rounded off with a glass of smooth rich port, Polly was feeling relaxed. Her attention flitted back and forth like a spectator's head at tennis match as the brothers traded views on Indigenous art and their business plans, politics, history, and religion. She was tempted to add her opinions to the mix, but chose to mainly listen and learn.

The dinner table chat swung to Australian Rules football, a sport the majority of Melburnians look upon as an alternative religion, such is its popularity. Polly was left agog as club names such as the Tigers, Lions, Cats, Saints, and Demons were bandied about. The brothers' obvious division of team loyalties wandered dangerously close to a quarrel.

"Shall I make us coffees?" Polly interjected as she folded her napkin and placed it carefully on the table.

"Nah, not for me, thanks," said Norm as he wiped his mouth on one of the serviettes. "I've gotta be going. I'm driving up to Humpty Doo tomorrow. If I'm lucky, it'll be just about a four-or five-day trip."

"Four days?" Polly said with surprise. "That seems quite quick."

"Nope, Polly, it's four or five days there and the same back. That's as long as the roads up north are not flooded. The Top End is in a monsoon and cyclone belt, so the weather can stuff you up big time. I went up one time and was away for nearly three weeks."

"Can't you fly up?" asked Polly.

"That would be a hell of a lot more convenient, but I have to take the big truck and bring back a huge load of artworks, plus on the way up, I have to stop off and pick up more..."

Bill quickly butted in, his voice raised slightly. "Shut up, Norm. I'm sure Polly doesn't want to know all the boring details about your trip," he snapped.

"Oh, yes, I'd love to know more..."

"Trust me, Polly, when Norm gets going, he'd bore a crocodile into volunteering to be a handbag. I'll see you out, Norm," Bill insisted, shoving his chair forcefully from the table.

"Bloody hell, Bill, I've been here often enough to..."

"Norm!" Bill scolded. "Enough!"

The brothers left the room and Polly could hear raised voices, but could not make out what was being said. It was the first time she had heard Bill lose his temper.

"Sorry, Polly," Bill said sheepishly as he came back and gently closed the door. "Sometimes my brother doesn't know when to shut up."

"No worries," Polly replied. "Hey, Bill, I said something Australian. I'm becoming an Aussie."

"You sure are," Bill said impassively.

"That was a bit condescending," Polly told him, a little peeved.

"Sorry, it's just sometimes...I...oh, never mind."

After loosening his tie, Bill casually draped it over the back of an adjacent dining chair and stretched his arms in the air with a noisy yawn.

Polly's mind was busy assessing the last few minutes and trying to weigh up Bill's mood. *I know you're humouring me, Bill, and I know Norm has put his foot in it somehow.*

In an instant Bill's demeanour changed. The innocent expression and apparent vulnerability that first endeared him to Polly returned. "Let's sit and unwind after all that chit-chat," Bill said and gently took Polly's hand. The warmth of his soft palm and the faint whiff of Old Spice after-shave sent her pulse racing.

*At last, I have Bill back...the Bill I fell for.*

"You look radiant in this light," Bill whispered as he planted a kiss on her left cheek. "That was some meal."

"What about clearing the table and washing the dishes?' Polly sighed.

"No sweat...we can do them together tomorrow."

"Okay, if you're sure," Polly replied with a yawn. "Tired? A bit, but I'd love you to tell me about Norm. He said on that first day when I arrived, his story was complicated."

"It is, but I'll try and untangle it for you. First I'll pour us an unwinder. What do you fancy?"

Polly shot a knowing glance at Bill and winked.

"Not that. I shouldn't have said fancy."

"I'll have whatever you drink."

Bill stood and went to the fireplace. He slipped his right hand behind the frame of the mirror and opened the cache of alcohol. He glanced quickly over his shoulder before taking a bottle and two shot glasses over to the coffee table. Like an expert barman, he served up two shots from a bottle of opaque glass. "Let it rest for a minute at room temperature then gulp it back."

Polly dutifully waited for a short time then lifted the glass to her lips. Bill followed suit.

She was just about to take a drink when spirit fumes found their way into her nostrils. "God, that's smells strong. What is it?"

"For want of a better word, it's vodka."

Polly's senses reeled. She jerked her head to one side and away from the glass as if she had smelled acid. "Fumes went up my nose. What is it?" *It smells worse than the stuff Doc gave me the night of my embarrassing striptease in the Express darkroom.* She had never recounted the darkroom story to Bill, and was determined it would remain a secret. "I can't drink that. It's too strong," she said with an expression that wrinkled her nose.

"How do you know—you haven't tried it."

"Sorry, Bill, the smell of it is making me gag."

"I didn't know it had a smell. Perhaps I'm used to it. No problems," Bill said. "How about a gin and tonic instead?"

Polly nodded and rubbed her nose vigorously as if she were trying to exorcise both the smell and the memories.

"It won't be wasted. I'll drink yours. It's good stuff, a special blend of top Russian and Polish spirits."

"I reckon it would blow my head off."

Bill smiled as he gulped down Polly's drink, then his own in quick succession.

Polly was shocked, yet at the same time impressed. "How could you belt those back? You should be unconscious. Are you trying to prove what a macho man you are, Bill Flint? You don't have to...I already know that."

"And you are an incorrigible little minx. Have I ever told you that?"

"No," Polly chortled. "Do you think so, sir?"

Bill conjured a little growl. "Miss Polly Jordan..."

~ * ~

It was five-thirty in the evening when they woke from post-lovemaking slumber. As they roused and sat up in bed, Polly said, "Now what about the Norm story? No more naughties until you tell all, and I mean everything."

"What's the fascination with Norm?"

"Well, he *is* your brother, or half-brother, so I'm interested, or at least half-interested."

Once again Polly's word-play replaced a look of concern on Bill's face with one of joy.

"Okay, but first of all, pull the sheets up over your boobs, or I'll never be able to concentrate."

Polly leaned over and managed to reach her flimsy nighty from the carpet on her side of the bed. She slipped it over her shoulders and adjusted it.

She groaned. "Get on with the story or it will be bedtime. Okay, I know, we're already in bed. Midnight then!"

"All right, you win," he acknowledged with a grin. "It *is* complicated, so I'll try to get things in the right order." He pushed back into the pillows and put his hands behind his head.

Polly copied and they had a playful little elbow joust.

"Okay..." Bill began. "Norm was born in Bolton, that's in Lancashire..."

"Yes, I know where Bolton is," Polly interrupted.

"Mum, Lizzie, was only fifteen. For a young unmarried girl to have a baby back then was almost worse than a crime."

"Did she live in Bolton?" Polly asked.

"Let me get things straight," Bill cautioned. "I knew your reporter's instincts would kick in, so just..."

"Shut up, is what you want to tell me," Polly conceded with a grin. She riddled her feet under the sheet. "My lips are sealed."

"Polly!" Bill groaned, exasperated. "Please! Stop! Or I won't carry on." He sighed with dramatic effect. "There was a young African American lad called Benjamin Cotton. He was about seventeen or eighteen when he met Lizzie. He had been drafted into the U.S. Army towards the end of World War One. He spent two years training for action and was sent to France. I think it was France. Anyway, that bit doesn't matter.

"Luckily for him, the Armistice was signed before he was required to fight. He was disappointed after all the training he had gone through, especially as he had to endure all sorts of racial abuse. All Black soldiers were segregated from the whites and there was a lot of tension between the two groups. He told Lizzie he was sick of fighting his own countrymen and not the enemy.

"Three days after the war stopped, he deserted and managed to get across the English Channel. It's thought he stowed away on a cargo ship, but no one is really sure. He found his way to Cardwell and met Lizzie and they had a one-night stand, or a very brief fling. A few days later he was captured and sent back to the U.S.A. He was court martialled and sent to a military prison."

Polly sat up and hugged her knees. "Go on," she said. "Don't mind me. I need to get into a good listening position."

"That was the last thing Lizzie heard about him. Of course, nine months later, Lizzie had a half-coloured baby boy. She was desperate. She had no support, no money, no prospects, and basically no idea how she was going to cope.

"Her baby was born about September 1919, but there's no record of a date, so nobody is sure. In fact, there was never a record of any kind. Technically, the baby didn't exist. Lizzie used to say he was a beautiful baby. You wouldn't think so to look at the big lump now," Bill said laughing.

"So what happened next?" Polly quizzed.

"Lizzie had an older cousin, Ada Sharp, living in Bolton and secretly went to stay with her during the pregnancy. Ada desperately wanted children, but her husband, Wilfred, fought in the trenches during the war and was poisoned with mustard gas."

"Heard about that," Polly said confidently. "If you were gassed, it was an almost certain bet you'd end up sterile."

"Spot on, Polly. You've done your homework."

The throwaway compliment brought a brief smile of pride to Polly's face.

"So..." Bill continued, "Norm was unofficially adopted by Ada and Wilfred. I'm not even sure he had a name back then."

Polly frowned in puzzlement.

"About a month later, Lizzie heard they had emigrated to Australia. Wilfred had heard about a need for farmers and stockmen, so they packed up and caught a ride on a steamship. Nothing was heard for about four years until one morning, Lizzie received a letter from Ada giving her the news that they were all right, had settled on farmland east of Melbourne and that Norm was now called Norman...Norm."

"Did nobody question why a white couple had a brown baby?"

"Apparently everybody thought he was a young half-Aboriginal kid the Sharps had adopted. His brown skin was from Ben Cotton. Norm's half African American, but it's obviously fooled everybody Down Under."

"So how did your dad get to know about Norm?"

"That's a typical reporter's question. Straight to the bull's-eye." Bill slipped his right arm around Polly and drew her closer to him. "He didn't. Lizzie never told him. Why she bothered to tell me, I don't know, but she did."

"That's all a bit mysterious, don't you think?"

"I suppose it is. Because he's my half-brother, she thought I should know. She swore me to secrecy. Apart from us two, there's only one other living soul who knows the truth and that's Norm himself." He smiled. "So there you are. I've got a fake Aboriginal brother and it comes in handy when he goes north on business. Every man and his dog believes he's dinky-di."

"Dinky-di?"

"The real thing. A genuine blackfella."

"But how did you find him?" Polly asked.

"When I got my arts degree, I decided to try and find Norm over here. It was a tough job as there were no official papers. The only record of him was on a list of Aboriginal people who were eligible to vote. He'd managed to make a living doing this and that. He spent a fair bit of time up in the Territory on cattle stations and he's pretty good on a horse. I've seen him ride." He paused and gave Polly a hug. "But if he ever wanted to get a passport, I don't know what he'd have to do. He still doesn't exist."

"What about money? Didn't he have to pay income tax and other stuff?"

"Lucky bastard's never had to pay a skerrick of tax in his life. He's the invisible man. Oh, I should point out that most Aussies call people *bastard* almost as a term of endearment," Bill explained.

"And at the end of the day, he really is one," Polly added with little laugh. "Jeez, that's quite a story."

"And it's definitely one you, Miss Journalist, must never write."

Polly snuggled under the covers again and wriggled her head into the pillows. She tucked the bedsheet up under her chin and shut her eyes. "I wasn't sure about Norm at first, I have to confess, but his story has painted a totally different picture of him."

# *Twenty*

For the next few weeks, Polly enjoyed her new lifestyle in Melbourne. While Bill was busy at the gallery, she took herself off to explore the city and came to enjoy riding on its trams. On a few occasions she helped Bill in the gallery, dusting and tidying up and on one particularly busy Saturday morning, she sold a large Aboriginal dot-painting for eight-hundred-and-fifty pounds—cash. Bill was so appreciative he took her to Steak Diana that night for a slap-up dinner with French champagne.

As Polly slowly stirred her second cup of coffee, she locked eyes with Bill dreamily. "I know what you're thinking," Bill smirked. "You've got *that* look."

She tapped her spoon twice on the rim of her cup and replaced it gingerly on the saucer. "You know what..." Polly said thoughtfully, "this time I don't think you do know what I'm thinking."

"Tell me then."

She put her elbows on the table rested her chin on her hands. "I'm ready to do more."

"More what?"

"I'm toying with the idea of going back to journalism."

"What!" Bill gasped. "Why? I thought all that was behind you, all the strife and upset. Are you serious or just winding me up?"

"Sort of semi-serious."

"I don't get it. I thought you were happy with our lifestyle, with...well...us?"

"I am, I am, Bill, but I'm a teeny-weeny bit bored. Don't get me wrong, I'm very grateful for everything I've got and everything you've done for me, but I need to find something to occupy my time, especially when you're out doing business deals and finding clients. What am I supposed to do next time you are away on a sped? Unless, of course, I tag along."

Bill looked at her, but said nothing.

"Melbourne's a great place. I love the shops, the people, the atmosphere, but if I have to go much longer without some sort of distraction, I feel like I'll end up like a pickle in a jar. I don't want to end up like some of the city's trophy wives, whose lives revolve around charity events, theatre opening nights, spending huge amounts of money in Bourke Street or wherever..."

"God, Polly, you've bushwhacked me. I didn't realise you were unhappy."

"I'm not unhappy, Bill, far from it. But I have a need..."

Bill looked crestfallen as he fiddled about rearranging his cutlery then moving it around again. "I'm a bit lost for words."

"Try, Bill, try to talk to me. Tell me I'm a spoilt brat or something. Reassure me. Tell me I'm stupid and things will change."

"I'm just digesting your comment about trophy wives. I have to tell you this, Polly, and hope it doesn't hurt you, that at this stage in my life, I'm not ready to marry and certainly not in the right frame of mind for children. I don't really know whether I could ever be a father. It's all hit me like train...like a bomb's just gone off."

"I need another drink," Polly grumbled. "Waiter! Can I have a large gin and tonic, please? What about you, Bill?"

"Same."

They sipped their gins in sombre silence. It was as if a dark cloud was hanging over their table. After about five minutes, Bill broke the silence. "Polly, I'm so sorry. I haven't brought you all this way to be unhappy. What can we do, do together, to make things right, take you back to being the wonderful, beautiful Polly?"

"First of all, you didn't bring me here. I'm a big girl and I chose to come. Remember? I gave up Cardwell to be with you. My choice. If it's a mistake, it's mine. I own it."

"Are you saying it's a mistake, my angel?"

"Stop that! None of the smoothy angel stuff. You should know by now I'm no angel." She looked him directly in the eye. "No, I'm not saying it's a mistake. Everything is fine, *very* fine, but, and it's a big *but,* I need something to do. I'm not looking to retire." She shrugged and breathed in deeply. "I've got to say I'm a bit shocked by your thoughts on marriage and fatherhood, but right now that's on the back burner for me. I would definitely like children one day, but not now. Maybe that's something we can talk about down the track, as most Aussies seem to say. Just help me, Bill. See my point of view and, if nothing else, humour me," Polly pleaded.

Bill reached across the table and took Polly's hands. This brought an immediate smile to her face.

"Let's forget tonight, Polly, write it off. Give me a little time and I'll come up with something. I don't want to lose what we've got. I certainly don't want to lose you. All this has come like a hand grenade and knocked me for six. I haven't handled it well, I know. I'm sorry. Tonight is not me. Please let me make amends."

"Okay, but *you* haven't done anything wrong. It's my fault. I thought I was on a solid foundation, but now I don't know. I think I've just had an earthquake of my own making."

"There are obviously things we should have talked about and haven't."

"You're right. Let's rewind and delete tonight. Just take me home, Bill, please."

Polly woke the next morning a little muzzy in the head. The smell of frying bacon wafting from the kitchen perked up her senses.

"Good morning," Bill said cheerfully when Polly peered round the kitchen door. "Want breakfast? I'm doing bacon, eggs, fried tomatoes, mushrooms...the lot."

"Sounds good to me," Polly replied as she stifled a yawn. "What time is it?'

"Nine-thirty."

"Shouldn't you be at work at the gallery?"

"Not today. I've put Norm in charge. Today we have a few things to sort out after last night's...what shall I call it?"

"A bloody disaster is what I'd call it. I'm sorry. I acted like a nincompoop and ruined the mood."

"It's all right. Let's forget last night and start all over again, as if you'd just arrived."

"Can't do that. It's impossible to take back what I said, but I've had an idea."

Bill put down the kitchen tongs and spatula he was using. He undid the cook's apron and tossed it onto the kitchen worktop. "Wait till I serve up the brekkie, then tell me your plan."

As they tucked in to the food, Bill waited patiently for her to start the conversation.

"Are you making a bacon sandwich?" Bill asked with childish delight as Polly wrapped a slice of buttered bread around two rashers of bacon.

"You betcha," Polly grinned and methodically dipped the sandwich into the soft, runny yolk of one of her two fried eggs. "Don't you know they are bacon butties where I come from?"

"I haven't made a bacon sanger for ages," Bill lamented.

"Well, don't get green over bacon—get to it and make your own. God, this tastes so good. Just what I needed," she mumbled as she chomped into the sandwich. "Okay, Bill, listen up. I've come up with two things, no three things, I'd like to do. None of them involves going back to reporting, although there's one paper called *The Age*, which I suppose is Melbourne's answer to *The Times* of London. It looks pretty good. Staid, but good writing, good reporting, full of detail and devoid of sensationalism."

"So...?" Bill said hesitantly.

"So..." she echoed, "... first I'd like to work in the gallery and get to know the business. Second, go to the Top End and see what it's like. Third, I definitely want to see the Aboriginal artists at work doing their dot-paintings and other stuff. Fourth...well, there isn't a fourth, just yet, but I'll keeping adding to the list as my curiosity grows."

Bill stroked his chin and thought for a moment. Then he gestured with a forefinger to indicate Polly had runny egg yolk trickling from her lips and down her chin.

"The gallery work I can arrange without a problem. Going north I'm not sure. It's wild, rough, hot, sticky, full of flies and dozens of other creatures that want to eat you or kill you."

"Sounds just like journalism," Polly joked as she took another bite of her sandwich.

"Let me think about that one," Bill said in a tone Polly assessed to be placatory.

"Are you trying to dissuade me from seeing the Top End? What have you got up there that you're trying to hide?'

Bill's face froze momentarily. Then he burst out laughing. "You caught me! Guilty! I have a harem of gorgeous, naked, dusky women just pining for me to go back."

Polly picked up a piece of bread crust she had left on her plate and threw it at Bill, hitting him on the nose. "Yeah right. Now I definitely want to go to the Top End. There's gotta be gorgeous naked men as well. Let's pack our rucksacks right now!"

They both laughed heartily and Bill's face lit up with an expression of relief. "God, I'm glad we can have fun again," he said.

"I'd say the fun is just starting," Polly added gleefully.

~ * ~

Three weeks passed and Polly was making inroads into the business. She could readily distinguish the different forms of indigenous works of art, was clear on prices and how much she could discount if clients wanted to barter, and was becoming quite an accomplished salesperson. As with journalism, her beauty and killer figure were appreciated by the majority of men who, when not in the presence of their spouses, seemed to spend readily, without too much sales pitch. Bill knew this and was happy to keep the status quo as long as the cash register was ringing.

Then the day arrived when Bill announced he needed to go north to collect more stock. At first he was reluctant to take Polly along, but his hand was forced and he eventually capitulated. Polly played her trump card when she strongly suggested she might apply for a job at *The Age* newspaper and reminded Bill, in no uncertain terms, that they had agreed on a new start.

For the next two days, they made preparations for the long, arduous trip. They crammed six large containers of drinking water, as much clothing and food as would fit into Bill's Land Rover. On a sturdy trailer hitched behind the ex-Army four-wheel drive vehicle, they loaded six spare wheels and tyres for the Land Rover and four for the trailer, more containers of water, both for drinking and washing, three tents and three sleeping bags, two car jacks, various spanner sets and extra equipment such as shovels, ropes, tarpaulins, three camp stoves, and boxes of things that might come in handy such as candles, matches and an old suitcase containing medical supplies. On a sturdy metal roof-rack were four more tyres and six jerry cans of fuel. All were strapped down with metal cables, secured by strong brass locks.

"I see what Norm meant when he said you were off on a sped. I'll bet the expedition that conquered Everest didn't have this much equipment," Polly marvelled as she climbed in and out of the Land Rover's passenger door. She was abuzz with questions. Bill spent ten minutes explaining that the enormous metal *contraption,* as Polly had called it, welded on the front of the Land Rover was a bull-bar.

"It's vital for fending off wildlife at speed. On a long journey in the Outback there's a fifty-fifty chance we'll hit a kangaroo wandering across our path at some time, or an emu. Farther north it could be a water buffalo. There's a menagerie of animals out there that can cause a deadly accident.

"By the way, I'll warn you now, Polly that by the time we hit Humpty Doo, your pretty little backside will feel like it's been..."

"Spanked?" Polly interjected in a flash.

Bill groaned in mock exasperation. Gently he took the wide-eyed Polly by her shoulders and slowly shook her in fun. "Oh, Polly, I truly worry about you. Where is that crazy mind of yours taking you?" He ran his fingers through her hair and took a deep breath. "I was about to say it will feel like it's been through a meat grinder. A huge chunk of the roads we're going on are just gravel and are rutted."

"And you think my mind's weird," Polly scoffed. "Who do you know who's had their bum in a meat grinder?"

"Fair enough," he conceded. "Just an expression. I freely admit, I'm not as good with words as you, Miss Jordan."

Polly tilted her head, looked him in full the face and fluttered her eyelids.

Bill couldn't stop himself from smiling. "You...Polly Jordan...are just too damn cute for your own good. One thing you will need to take is a head scarf or two if you have them."

Polly's puzzled look told him he needed to elaborate.

"Out in the sticks, there's red dust everywhere and if the wind gets under it, the conditions will seem like a sandstorm. It'll get everywhere, in every part of your body."

"*Everywhere?*" Polly said with startled incredulity.

Bill ignored her remark. "You'll need it to keep your eyes, nose and mouth clear, or you'll be eating dust for days and if it gets into your lungs, it's a serious problem and one we definitely do not want on this trip."

Polly sensed this was a serious warning from Bill and complied by saying, "I'll see what I've got. I'll find something even if I have to tear up one or two of my blouses."

"You'll also need strong but light and loose clothing and be prepared to rough it when nature calls. Towns along the Stuart Highway are few and far between and in some places there are hundreds of miles between toilets and running water."

"Yikes," Polly exclaimed. "That's *not* so convenient."

~ * ~

Norm had already set off early that morning in the huge zebra-striped truck, also with a collection of spare wheels, tool kits, spare parts for both vehicles, and plenty of oil and drinking water. He had arranged to meet Bill and Polly at a truck stop on the other side of Adelaide which they had often used as a rendezvous. After a relatively uneventful nine-hour drive west, they crossed the Victoria-South Australia state border. Late afternoon traffic was light and they quickly weaved their way through Adelaide and met with Norm about twenty miles farther north at the designated highway truck stop. This served as a last chance to take stock of what they had and what they might need for the next gruelling leg of the expedition, which Polly was already referring to, in just about every other sentence, as her first *sped*.

Bill let it go, assuming that by the time they reached their destination, the word would be long forgotten, crowded out of Polly's mind by a myriad of greater distractions.

The two men talked for a few minutes at the rear of the big zebra-striped truck while Polly remained in the Land Rover quenching her thirst. Hours on the road in late temperatures had warmed the water, but Polly drank it gratefully.

Bill returned and took a metal grid from the trailer. He carefully fitted it across the windscreen then climbed back into the driver's seat.

Polly worked out its purpose. "Is that to stop stones smashing the windscreen?"

"Exactly," Bill confirmed. "It's not so much stones from vehicles ahead. We steer well clear of them, but anything going in the other direction can flick up a stone and ruin your day. It happened to me once when I didn't have a stone-guard and I can tell you, driving in this heat without a windscreen is like sitting in front of a blast furnace. Okay, here we go...this is where the real driving starts," he said as he clunked the Land Rover into first gear. "Norm's going to drive on for a mile or two, then we'll set off."

"Why don't we drive in convoy?"

"I like to leave a fair gap between us and the truck, and when we set off, you'll see why. When we leave the bitumen, any vehicle ahead will kick up that much red choking dust, it'll be like red fog. We'd practically be driving blind. You'll see why most people give the Stuart Highway its nickname, The Track. I know it's hot in the Rover behind glass, but we might have to close the windows to keep out the dust and flies, so it will get hotter. Great vehicles these, and tough, but not built for comfort."

"You're telling me. You were right about one thing…my bum is already numb and we've not hit the main highway yet," Polly moaned.

"Any time now," Bill advised "the sun will start to go down on your side, the west, so you might want to put something across your window to block it or you'll be *really* hot."

"Hah, right. I didn't think of that. Typical town girl."

"You can't think of everything on your first *sped*," he joked.

"Drive on, Flint. I think you're taking the piss."

"Sorry Polly, but you have been a bit *sped* happy."

"Yeah, I think you're right. Banned word of the day is…*sped*. Don't worry, I've got a new catchphrase…*The Track*!"

"Lord help us," Bill protested with a grin.

For the next hundred miles or so, Polly spoke little as her mind wandered back to England, to all the events that had collided and orchestrated her decision to be in Australia with Bill, especially Doc's death. The silence didn't bother Bill as he concentrated on the road, which comprised stretches of poorly maintained bitumen or loose gravel surface. Harsh on vehicles as this was, there was worse to come as it eventually gave way to red earth, stones and the occasional bone-jarring rut.

Polly was starting to get sleepy despite the uncomfortable journey. Her head had started to nod when the Land Rover hit a pothole with its passenger side front wheel and the vehicle lurched dangerously to the left. "Bloody hell!" she screeched "What was that? I thought we'd had a crash."

"It's all right, just a pothole," Bill said calmly. "I'll pull over and check the wheel and suspension just in case, but I'd say it would take more than that to bugger up this old jalopy." He pulled over to a long patch of gravel to the side of the road and checked for damage. "Nah, she's fine."

As he climbed back in, Polly suddenly squealed as she looked out at the vast expanse of flat red land strewn with small rocks and stones. "Look! Look, Bill. Look at that heat haze. It's like a silvery shimmering mist, all blurry. Everything is distorted."

"There you go again, Polly. You really *are* amazing with words."

"Wait, wait!" she cried. "There's someone out there. I can see people. Right out there about as far as the eye can see...people. She looked at Bill. "Won't they die in this heat, Bill? Should we check out that they're all right. Isn't that what you're supposed to do in the Outback?"

"Nah, leave them alone. It's their problem," Bill said with an air of indifference as he fired up the Land Rover again.

"What the hell, Bill! I can't believe you'd leave those people out there to die in this heat. What sort of man are you?"

"Relax, Polly," he laughed. "Do you know who those people are?"

"What, Aborigines?"

"No, silly. They're emus."

"Oh wow, emus. Can we stop and look at them?"

"No way, Polly. That would be madness. Apart from them being at least a mile away, maybe more, they'd take off when we got anywhere near them. Added to that, we'd risk heatstroke and tripping, and maybe breaking an ankle. Even more to the point, we'd take up precious time and our journey has a long way to go."

"Oh, right," Polly said sheepishly. "Sorry. Is that me being scolded?"

Bill turned to her and smiled. "No, not at all. You're new to the bush and it is, after all, your first...

"Expedition," Polly yelled, then stuck out her tongue and playfully punched Bill's left shoulder.

"Aaaagh!" Bill shouted and yanked on the steering wheel, causing the Land Rover to veer violently.

"Stop it, Bill! There's enough rough stuff on this road without you adding to it."

"Sorry," he said, "Let's both concentrate on the road."

"Gotcha! Wilco, Captain," Polly replied with a cheeky salute.

As the day wore on, they were forced to stop twice to refill the petrol tank from jerry cans, once to change a punctured trailer wheel and several times to clear dust from the windscreen and side windows.

"It won't be long before the sun sets," Bill said. "Judging by the sky, it will be okay, but not spectacular. When you get clouds, the sunsets out here can be nothing short of sensational."

"Oh, heavens, I've been so taken up watching the countryside, not that there's been much change for the last five million miles, I've not looked up once," Polly said.

"Norm knows when to stop just as the sun disappears, so we should catch up with him in the next ten miles or so...about twenty minutes."

"Thank goodness we'll be stopping. My back is killing me and my bottom is..."

"Feeling like it's been through a meat grinder, perhaps?" Bill joked.

"For once I agree," Polly grumbled as she wriggled to ease the discomfort.

Bill's estimate was almost perfect to the minute. Polly had already spotted the zebra-striped truck parked about thirty yards off the road. It was on a patch of flat ground that was reasonably clear of rocks and stones.

"This looks like it's a popular lay-by," Bill said as they slowly drove towards where Norm had already lit a fire from dried out twigs and tree branches he had gathered.

"Why the fire in this heat?" Polly said.

"Once the sun goes down and there's no cloud cover, it will get bloody cold. We'll throw some sausages, a bit of steak and some onions in a pan and have a bit of dinner, then set up for the night."

Polly was surprised. "What, we're staying here for the night?"

"Yes, that's why we brought all that equipment...tents and stuff."

"Aren't there any towns or motels?"

"There are, but miles away."

"I need to pee," Polly admitted. "I've drunk a lot of water."

"That's good," said Bill.

"What, that I need to pee?"

"No, that you've drunk a lot of water," Bill said with a laugh.

"So...where do I go?" Polly said hesitantly.

"Anywhere you like. You're in the world's biggest loo."

"But there's no cover."

"Polly, just go behind the Land Rover's trailer. Nobody's watching, unless there are emus around. Just watch out for snakes."

Polly stuck up two fingers and blew a raspberry. "Bastard!" she said, with a passable attempt at an Aussie accent.

As night closed in and the temperature started to drop rapidly, Norm wandered off to look for more firewood.

"We'll keep the fire going through the night if we can," he shouted as he disappeared into the gloom.

"How come there's firewood here when for the past few hundred miles there hasn't been a tree in sight?" Polly asked.

"There are times even out here when the land gets a deluge of rain, when some of your famous clouds do their job. Dry creeks flow again, little billabongs fill again and water seeps into the earth and forms basins. Nature takes over and stuff grows...acacias and eucalypts. All manner of things, even desert flowers. Then after a few years, it dries up and everything dies off. It's a never-ending cycle."

"Mr Flint, I'm impressed by your knowledge. You're not just a pretty face," she teased. "So where are we going to sleep? Do we put the tents up?"

"Norm and I will sleep under the stars tonight," Bill said casually. "There's a really comfy mattress in the truck, so you sleep in there. We'll bunk down in sleeping bags and keep the fire going."

"Sounds romantic," Polly replied.

There was no response from Bill. He just looked at the dancing flames and threw on more branches. "You were right, Bill, I can feel the chill," she said as she crossed her arms across her chest to hug her shoulders. She drew nearer the fire and warmed her hands, rubbing them together before holding her palms closer to the flames. Slowly her eyes followed little trails of sparks propelled by crackling wood into the inky sky.

"Oh, how wonderful!" she exclaimed in awe. "Just look at the stars. Millions of them. Everywhere. That must be the Milky Way. Jeez, look...a shooting star. Did you see it? And another. I've never seen anything so magnificent in my life. Every single one looks like a diamond. And they seem so close you feel you could reach out and touch them. I'm absolutely flabbergasted. It's truly miraculous. God, I wish Doc were here to see this. He'd want to photograph it," Polly said excitedly, then she clammed up. *I hope I haven't offended Bill by mentioning Doc's name.* Silently she decided to let her wish drift into the night, just like the campfire sparks.

"I'm going to turn in, Bill. I'll see you in the morning. I hope you manage to sleep well on the ground. Tell Norm I said good night."

"Will do," Bill answered. "Oh, by the way, you'll find a flashlight next to the handbrake."

Polly clambered into the truck through the driver's door and climbed over the seat. She made a space to lay the mattress which she found secured upright with ropes. After a few minutes of rearranging some of the expedition equipment, she flopped onto the mattress, happy to be under cover and, more importantly, off the ground.

As Polly settled, she could hear the men chatting quietly around the campfire. She tried to make out what they were saying, but nothing was clear and within the space of ten minutes, she drifted off to sleep.

Just after midnight Polly woke. She was cold and began to shiver. The bulk of her clothes were in the Land Rover, which she assumed would be locked. The only way to get warm, she reasoned, was to get to the campfire then gently wake Bill and ask him for the Rover's keys. In the confined space, she had difficulty putting on her clothes, a flimsy cotton blouse, underwear and khaki shorts. She found a large towel and draped it around her shoulders while she slipped her feet into thick woollen socks and sturdy boots. She climbed out of the driver's door as quietly as she could and picked her way carefully through stones and low-growing scrubby weeds to the fire. It was still aglow but the flames had died. She found more branches nearby and placed them on the pile of red-hot embers. In less than thirty seconds welcome tongues of fire were leaping above knee height into the cold night air. She looked around and saw the men's sleeping bags. They were empty. Bill and Norm were gone.

Polly waited for a few minutes, hoping they would return. By the time thirty minutes had elapsed, she was racked with worry. She could hear nothing but the sounds of the desert night, faint rustling on the ground, a few fluttering moths drawn by the firelight and a strange bird as it called mournfully in the dark distance.

"Bill, where are you?" she called. There was no answer. She called again, this time louder. Nothing was returned from the blackness.

Now Polly really was scared. What could have happened to them, out in the middle of nowhere? In the endless black Outback, the stars provided scant relief and the moon, two nights after its new phase, was little more than a sliver. She looked round for a light, perhaps a lonely little township or a car on the highway. Gripped by fear, she screamed at the top of her voice. "Bill! Bill! For Pete's sake, where are you? If this is some sort of weird game, please stop. I'm really scared."

About five minutes elapsed before, through the eerie curtain of night, two figures slowly emerged. They were whispering as they approached the fire. Polly thought she saw Norm's arm round Bill's shoulders.

"Polly, what are you doing up? I thought you'd be sound asleep," Bill said. Both he and Norm had towels around their waists and their shirts were unbuttoned.

"We thought we heard something out there," Norm said hastily. "Could have been dingoes. The little beggars sneak around in the night and they can be dangerous."

"Did you find any?" Polly said, with some relief in her voice.

"Nah," Bill said. "Nothing, but we did find a little billabong about half a mile away so we thought we'd wander back for towels and have a dip. We couldn't sleep, so why not?"

"What, in this cold weather?" Polly said incredulously. "I was cold so I was going to the Land Rover to get more clothes. Mind you, I thought the Land Rover would be locked."

"Yeah, you're right about the cold. It was bloody freezing when we put our toes in, so we quickly ditched that idea. Then we heard you calling so we hurried back as best we could without tripping."

Still tired and a little shaken but mightily relieved, Polly readily accepted their explanation and thought no more about it. "Okay, as long as everything's safe and you lads are all right, just let me have the keys and then I'll head back to the truck. Good night, or should I say good morning?"

"See you in the morning," Bill said sheepishly then adding, "The Land Rover isn't locked."

"Okay, I'll be off then," Polly said and scooted off to find some warm clothes.

"Yeah, see you, Polly," Norm added. His face was lit by flickering firelight. His usual nonchalant expression seemed to have given way to tension.

Polly was up early next morning after a disturbed night in the truck. Her mind was trying to see reason in what the men had told her about a billabong. Carefully and quietly, she dropped her clothes out of the driver's window then deftly opened the door. The air was cool, but not freezing like the night just passed. Her naked skin had goosebumps, but after a moment her nakedness felt soothing...cleansing. She dressed and looked round for a way to head off in search of the billabong, avoiding the two green sleeping bags, still occupied a couple of paces from the remains of the campfire. Trying to avoid crunching stones or dead twigs that might snap, Polly wandered off towards the west. The terrain was flat, studded with low shrubs and boulders. There were also a lot of strange looking plants with black trunks and heads of bushy vegetation that looked like long grass. Some had tall brown spikes growing vertically from their grassy clumps.

She walked for about twenty minutes but could see no signs of a billabong, in fact no signs of anything other than plant life until she suddenly took fright when she disturbed a gigantic lizard feeding on some sort of carrion. The lizard ran straight across her path and disappeared between two boulders. Polly guessed it must have been four feet long.

"Phew!" she exclaimed, her heart thudding in her chest. "What a horrible thing. Looked like a dragon."

The search seemed hopeless and the terrain seemed to look the same no matter where she turned. Already, Polly had lost sight of the zebra-striped truck, so she decided to return to the camp before she became disoriented. As she got within thirty yards of the now dead fire, she noticed the sleeping bags were gone and the men were up, dressed and talking. With no mention of last night's events, Bill and Norm greeted her with a cheery good morning.

"Where have you been?" Bill enquired.

"Trying to find your billabong."

"Oh, dear, you must have gone in the wrong direction. It's easily done out here. There are no landmarks to guide you," Bill said as he started to kick and scatter the campfire remains. "Gotta make sure you always put the fire out. Heaps of wildlife perish when there's a bushfire."

"Hang on!" Norm told him. "What about breakfast? Don't kick the bloody thing out yet."

With that, conversation stalled and thoughts turned to having something to eat and hitting the highway before sunrise.

Polly cooked scrambled eggs while the men checked the vehicles and, just as the sun came up, they hit the road once again.

"All being well, we'll be in Alice Springs by about lunchtime, so we'll find a pub and have a counter lunch."

"Brilliant. I'm looking forward to seeing Alice," Polly said.

"Aussies always say *the* Alice, not just Alice," Bill corrected her gently.

"I loved Nevil Shute's novel. I'd love to write like that one day, when I get journalism out of my blood."

"Well, you've got the words, Polly. You're a born wordsmith."

"It was great literature, but a story of terrible cruelty to prisoners of war. Did you know Shute's full name was Nevil Shute Norway?"

"You're a mine of information, Polly. I don't tend to read stories about the war. They bring back too many bad memories."

"Oh, sorry, Bill. That was thoughtless of me. I'll be careful what I say in future."

In the Alice, Bill, Polly and Norm enjoyed a steak lunch at the Todd Tavern, with just one cold beer apiece. After a good wash and brush-up and allowing Polly to tend to her untidy hair, they headed north once again. The track followed arrow-straight lengths of rugged, red road that sliced through endless flat and featureless scrubland. From her window, Polly spotted kangaroos by the hundreds as they bounded away, unnerved by the sound of the Land Rover's engine.

"Have you noticed how the kangaroos hop away to a safe distance, then they stop and turn around? They sort of rest back on their big tails and just stand and stare at us. It's like they've been hypnotised," Polly remarked gleefully.

Twenty or thirty miles up the road, three mature camels and a juvenile munched without a care at the side of the road. Polly even persuaded Bill to stop for a few minutes while she tried to stroke them.

"Be careful," Bill advised. "They're wild animals and can bite really hard."

"They look docile enough," Polly countered, although she stopped in her tracks as she weighed up the warning.

"I heard that one cameleer got his ear bitten clean off by his own camel. It was a male and coming into rut. I've heard the cameleers call it *musth,* although I think that's related to elephants, not camels."

"Bloody hell! See you later, camel," Polly gasped and hastily retreated back to the Rover. "Just like a bloke to get macho before sex."

"Okay let's go," Bill said and tooted the horn. "Daylight's burning and we need to try and get to the other side of Tennant Creek before nightfall. If we can reach Three Ways, I've heard there's an old pub there that does great bed and breakfast. So we'll stay there for the night. A bit of civilisation."

"That's the best idea I've heard since we left Melbourne. Put your foot down, mate, and drive like the wind."

It was close to six o'clock when Bill pulled on the Land Rover's handbrake outside an old, tired looking pub. "Wait here, Polly and I'll see if they have rooms."

The town was equally old and tired looking. On the opposite side of the road was a service station with petrol bowsers Polly thought would look perfectly at home on the set of a nineteen-forties movie. *Blimey, I hope the beds in the pub are not as worn out as those petrol pumps*, she mused.

About ten minutes later Bill came back out, smiling. "Good news and bad news," he reported unfazed. "They can accommodate us all, but they only have single rooms left."

"That's no problem," Polly replied. "I'd sleep in the back yard as long as I have a decent bed, a hot shower and a real lavatory. Sorry, Bill, you're on your own again tonight, so behave yourself."

Bill cast an inquisitive glance at Polly. She returned his glance with a searching gaze. For a split-second it took him aback. Then he winked and with a jolly laugh went back inside. That night the mood was light and relaxed as they tucked into meat pie, chips and seasonal salad. This time, they downed two beers each and rounded them off with a whisky for the men and a gin and tonic for Polly.

"Let's get an early night and get on the road really early in the morning before the sun's up," Bill suggested.

"You won't have to twist my arm for that," Polly chipped in. "I'm feeling sleepy already and it's only nine-thirty." She took her leave and climbed a creaky staircase up to the first floor. Her room, number six, was pleasantly furnished and next door to a communal bathroom. She flopped onto her bed. *Oh lovely! A soft bed and super soft pillows. They must be duck down.* By ten o'clock, she was sound asleep and did not stir when Bill tapped gently on her door and peeped in around midnight.

~ * ~

Over a hearty bacon and eggs breakfast with all the trimmings, followed by toast and jam and several cups of coffee, they discussed the final leg of the journey and their destination, Humpty Doo. Polly recalled the frivolous, cannabis-fuelled mood she and Bill were in when she had first heard the name.

"It still makes me laugh," she told Bill, "although the rest of that night wasn't my finest hour. I know that."

As they were about leave, Norm announced he would be making a detour at Katherine.

"Oh, yes," Bill said knowingly. "Is that the favour you're doing picking something up for a mate in Jabiru?"

Norm nodded in an exaggerated fashion. "Yeah. It'll take me off the Track, but I'll catch you up if you pull in and wait for me in Adelaide River township. There's a truck stop on the right, going south. Cross over and wait round the back and I'll find you."

"No worries," said Bill, "good as gold."

Two or three times back on the Stuart Highway, Bill had to pull over and let huge trucks and trailers thunder past him going both north and south. The rigs were enormous and carried mainly live cattle or sheep, or industrial machinery for the mining industry.

"You wouldn't want to get in the way of those gigantic things," Polly said as they obligingly pulled the Land Rover over for about the tenth time.

Fifty miles further on, Polly notice a shadow on her left that seemed to be keeping pace with the Land Rover. She wound down the window and stuck her head out into the hot afternoon air. Her hair flew back as if it had been caught in a bomb blast. "Bill, I think there's a plane up here following us. The wind and the Land Rover rattling along are noisy, but I'm sure I heard the drone of an engine."

"You sure? Can you see what it is?"

"Not really, but it's definitely a plane and looks sort of blue colour. What do you think's happening?"

Bill went quiet for a moment or two. "Ha, I'll bet it's a crop spraying plane."

"Don't think so," Polly replied. "I can't see any spray tubes and all the paraphernalia they usually have fitted on them. In any case, what the hell is there to spray out here? Only endless scrub, weeds and stones?"

"If it's not that, it's a pilot trying to land on the highway. If a plane gets into trouble out here or has to land for any other reason, they land on the road. It doubles as a runway. He'll just be looking for a safe gap in the trucks and other traffic, then he can touch down. Nothing to worry about."

Polly was content with the logic she saw in Bill's reasoning and closed her window. Within minutes the shadow had gone.

"It's over on my side now," Bill said. "I'll give him a wave to let him know we've seen him."

Bill stuck his arm out and signalled. "There he goes, he's banked off to the east. He must have changed his mind."

Within thirty minutes, Bill had to stop the Land Rover to refuel. As he was just emptying another jerry can into the tank, the plane returned. It flew towards them from the north at a height of a few hundred feet. Once past the Rover, it circled twice and left the scene for the last time.

"That's got me stumped," Bill admitted. "I don't know what the pilot's playing at unless he's mistaken us for somebody else."

At the end of their third gruelling day on The Track, Bill and Polly finally reached Adelaide River. The truck stop was easy to find, but where was Norm?

They called into the office and asked if anyone fitting the description they provided had called in. "Has anyone seen a large truck painted in black and white stripes like a zebra?" Bill asked everyone who called in at the truck stop for the next hour or more. "I'm getting concerned," Bill said, wringing his hands. "It's not like Norm to go missing."

The truck stop had a small café attached, so they went in and ordered two coffees. Just as a young Aboriginal girl brought them to their table, Norm walked in, dishevelled and dirty. "I'm bogged down about three miles from here along the road to Jabiru."

"What happened?" Bill asked. "Did you get the stuff all right?

"Yes, it's all loaded on, but you know what the weather's like up here this time of year. Monsoon rain half the time. The Adelaide has burst its banks in some places and I just happened to pull in for a...you know...a pee, and got the truck stuck. I stopped for a while watching a plane doing circuits in the sky for about ten minutes, and by the time I was ready to leave, the wheels were just spinning and tore up the ground. I'll need a pull with the Land Rover to get her free."

Bill had a frown on his face. "What did the plane look like?"

"Hard to say. Single-engine, small plane, nothing striking. Could have been blue."

With his elbow on the table, Bill ran his left hand across his forehead and, deep in thought, pushed back his hair.

"Is everything all right?" Norm asked.

"Yeah, course it is. I'll bet it was some trainee pilot having a lesson or flying solo for the first time. Planes are everywhere up here. The Northern Territory is huge. There's probably more planes than cars. Don't worry about it." After contemplating their situation for a few moments, Bill continued, "Well, we'd better all pile in the Land Rover and find the truck. It'll be dusk soon, so we'll set up camp for the night and sort out the rescue job in the morning. Hey, Norm, I forgot to ask. How did you get to the truck stop?"

"I had to bloody walk. Three or four miles is a flamin' long way in this heat."

"A long way?" Bill said in jest. "I thought you Abo boys covered endless miles on your walkabouts."

"Watch it, Billy boy, we Indigenous brothers are not averse to belting you white blokes' heads with a boomerang or two."

As Bill started the vehicle, they all broke out into peals of laughter, and talk of planes and bogged trucks was forgotten for a short while.

~ * ~

Once they reached the stranded truck, Bill and Norm jumped out quickly, leaving Polly wondering what, if any, part she would be asked to play. The men were talking in low voices. "How are we going to play this?" Bill said, casting a glance in Polly's direction.

"We'll have to play it cool. If she gets a look inside the truck, who knows what we can do?" Norm said, irritated. "I can't believe I got the bloody thing stuck. I'm sorry, Bill."

"No use being sorry, mate, we have to get the bloody wheels turning and get to Humpty Doo before two o'clock."

"Tyrus and Noah will be waiting with a few of the usual tribal contacts. I managed to ring Tyrus from the hotel in Three Ways. We've got a two-hour window to do the business and get back on the road south with the art works. Tyrus reckons this batch is fantastic, some of the best he's ever seen and will make us absolutely heaps of moola."

"We've gotta keep our lads up here happy, or that new mob from Sydney, the Russians, might get a foothold. That's something we don't need. We can't let it happen."

Norm took a length of thick rope from the cab of the truck. "If you get the trailer off the Land Rover, we could hook it up to the truck and between us pull it clear of the mud."

Once the rope was secure, Bill and Norm fired up their engines and Bill inched the Land Rover forward to put tension on the rope. "Okay, Norm, let's go."

As both vehicles were revved, the truck lurched forward then sideways.

"Try again," Bill shouted with his head out of the driver's window.

Despite repeated efforts, the truck's double back wheels spun without gaining traction in the soft and slowly deepening muddy ground.

"Jeez, what are we gonna do?" Norm said, panic-stricken. "We can't blow this deal."

"The first thing, mate, is don't panic. Let's use brain power if engine power fails. I've got a plan, but it's a last resort and we risk it all with Polly."

"I know what you're going to say," Norm said as he wiped sweat from his brow. "Have you any idea what this load weighs?"

"We have to do it, you idiot," Bill snapped. "We can't wait here for some big rig to come along and yank us free. It could be days before anyone drives down this bloody goat-track of a road. The clock is ticking, mate, and there's no way we can unload the truck to lighten it." Bill paced back and forth as he gathered his thoughts. "Sorry, Norm. That was uncalled for. I'm just worried we won't get there on time and everything is lost. This is the big coup we've worked hard for all these years."

Norm gritted his teeth and said, "No use talking about it, let's just do it. If Polly works it out, we'll have to come up with a plan B." He went to the rear of the truck and was about to lower the tailgate when someone yelled out, "How ya doin', fellas?"

"G'day," Bill replied.

"In a bit of strife?"

"Nah, we're right, thanks, mate," Bill replied dismissively.

"Don't look you're right, to me. Stuck in the muck, looks like."

The huge bearded man, wearing faded denim overalls and a big floppy brown hat, drew closer.

"Mate, I said we're right, thanks...really!" Bill insisted.

The stranger's ginger whiskers parted to reveal a toothy smile that lit up his weatherworn, tanned face. "I know stuck when I see it. Hold it there and I'll get some help. If you'll drive me about a mile over in that direction, I'll have you clear in no time." He pointed in a roughly westerly direction to an expanse of scrub land.

"I could walk, but I figure you boys might be wanting to get somewhere in a hurry. Right?"

Bill looked at Norm and the two pondered the proposal. They were unsure of the stranger and how he seemed to come from nowhere.

"We can't do it ourselves," Norm sighed. "I suppose we could drive you..."

"Done deal! I'm Brad, by the way. I have a cattle station over there," and once again he pointed to the west.

"I can't see any station," Bill remarked with suspicion.

"Ah, no mate, the homestead's about twenty miles away. It's over the horizon. Me and the boys are doing some fence repairs. Kenny, one of my boys, picked you up with the binoculars while he was checking for strays that might have wandered off."

Within thirty minutes, Brad and son Kenny had driven back with an enormous tractor and had the truck hauled clear and onto the road with ease.

"Can't thank you enough," Bill said, shaking Brad's podgy callused hand. "How can I repay you?"

"Just put it down to Northern Territory friendship and hospitality," he said, beaming from ear to ear. "It's what we folks do up here."

"Well, thanks again," Bill said as he stuffed twenty pounds into the man's overall pocket.

"Whoa, you don't have to do that, sir," Brad protested.

"No, I insist, Brad, buy yourselves a drink or two at the pub. You don't know how big a help you've been. You saved our bacon."

"No worries, and thanks for the cash," Brad said as he and Kenny bumped their way across the road on the tractor. Within minutes they were lost from sight and Bill and Norm were ready to get back behind the wheel.

Bill went over to Norm. "Well, we're out, but don't you find it odd that Brad, if that's his name, just popped up from out of the blue."

"You don't trust anybody, do you?" Norm said as he patted Bill's hand resting on the open window.

"Only you," Bill said. "Only you, Norm."

The journey to Humpty Doo was uneventful except having to crawl past a herd of big white cattle grazing on the sparse grass and other vegetation along the side of the road.

Polly was fascinated. "What kind of cows are those? I've never seen anything like them."

"Brahmans," Bill replied cheerily. "And they're bulls, beef cattle."

"They're huge," Polly marvelled. "But why are they eating at the roadside?"

"When the weather doesn't provide enough grass, the drovers graze them along the roads where there's sometimes enough to tide them over. They call it grazing the long paddock, for obvious reasons. They could wander a hundred miles sometimes. Sometimes they're just changing grazing areas or they might be rounding up for sale and slaughter. It's just one of the many things that make Australian Outback farmers and ranchers different," Bill commented with a measure of admiration in his voice. "It's a tough life out here on the land."

"Weird looking things, but I like their floppy ears. They look like they've just been told off," Polly said with a giggle. "There must be a hundred of them...all sulking."

Bill glanced at his watch and it was almost five o'clock when they turned off towards Humpty Doo. "Ten more minutes and we'll be there, thank the Lord," Bill announced, his voice a little dry and croaky from thirst and the heat. It told a story of both relief and fatigue.

The Land Rover was jolting and jumping along a rutted dirt track that snaked through skinny shoulder-high bushes and finally came to rest in a fenced compound surrounded by big trees that provided shade.

Polly jumped out and stretched. "Oh, that feels so good. I don't think my body will ever be straight again. This shade is worth bottling. I might just wander for a minute and get the circulation going again in my legs."

Bill was quick to respond. "Whatever you do, don't go near the big metal shed over there," he said, as he gesticulated to an area about two hundred yards away where there was obvious activity.

What Polly could see of the shed, she assumed was an old aircraft hangar covered, camouflage-style, in random patches of brown, green, black and grey paint. "Why, what's happening in there?"

"They're busy and they don't like people getting in the way."

"What is this place anyway?' she said. "Why all the secrecy?"

"Polly, we're all tired, so just for now, let your curiosity have a welcome night off."

"Oh, well if that's your attitude, Bill Flint, I'll sit in the Land Rover until you've finished."

"You know I didn't mean it like that. There's no secrecy, truly. Give me five minutes and I'll check progress, then you can take a look." He calculated that Norm had arrived up to thirty minutes before Polly and him, and hoped this had been enough time to complete their work on the truck.

Polly sat back in the passenger seat and tried to straighten her windblown hair. Satisfied it was relatively tidy, she casually dangled her arm out of the window. She was startled by a deep voice. In fading light, she was confronted by a black face. "Hello, missus, ya waiting for Mister Billiam? He not be long away."

The owner of the voice was an old Aboriginal man. It was the first time Polly had seen any Indigenous person close up. His face, looking like it was carved from leather, sported a large, flat nose with flared nostrils and was framed with long silver hair. His appearance scared Polly and she closed the window as fast as she could. Quivering fingers fumbled for a lever that might lock the door.

"It's okay, missus. I friend of Mister Billiam. We work mates. Don't be terror." The leathery face slowly produced a grin that contained one silver denture on a top row that had more gaps than teeth. The grin transformed his leather face to a mask of creases, dotted with several scars. "Sorry, missus. I scare you, sorry. Come on, Mister Billiam says come now. All is all right."

Polly plucked up courage, slowly opened the door and slipped out from her seat.

"I name am Noah. Follow behind me."

Polly's tension eased as Noah guided her to the shed, although she wondered why she needed someone to take her to a place she could see from the Land Rover.

"Mister Billiam busy man, but his loading work is done finished by now."

She was amused by Noah's quaint spoken English, but managed to keep a straight face.

"Ah, Polly," Bill said as she entered the shed. "Thanks Noah," he said, shaking the old man's hand and then to Polly, "Noah is one of the elders here in Humpty Doo and he helps me negotiate with tribal artists. He's part of our business, but part of his role is also to ensure the artists get a fair price for their work. As you can see, we've got a huge load to take back," Bill said proudly and pointed to the truck. Its lowered tailgate allowed Polly to see scores of wooden crates. Many were tall and quite thin, and had been stood on their ends, secured to the truck's inner rails with strong rope.

"Look at all that wonderful native art. Overseas buyers clamour for it and it brings high prices. There've been times when the demand has been so great, I've had to auction stuff off to the highest bidder and some of them are very rich," he said, rubbing together his first two fingers and thumb.

"Moola! Money, Polly, that's a truck full of money."

"Is money your only goal?" she asked coolly.

"Right, yes, that probably sounded mercenary, but for a lot of these people it's a way of getting a better lifestyle and—"

"Giving Bill Flint a better lifestyle too?" she interrupted.

"It's been a long day and we're all buggered so let's not get into an argument right now about the noble art of supply and demand."

"I'll drink to that," Polly said light-heartedly. "In fact, I'll drink to anything. I could kill for a scotch or a gin and tonic."

"That's good, because I've ordered us a dinner at a little pub in Humpty Doo. There's very little accommodation so I've managed to get you a single room for the night. You deserve a good night's sleep after putting up with the journey and me for four days."

"What about you and Norm? Where will you stay?"

"Good question, but we'll be sleeping here as best we can. The stuff in that shed is like gold to some people and security is almost non-existent up here. So Norm and I will be on guard duty."

"Let's not waste any more time. I can almost taste that whisky."

As they left the shed through a sturdy metal door, Polly noticed a large green tarpaulin acting as a cover for something large. Some of the hidden items displayed angular outlines in the tarpaulin. Polly guessed it was concealing crates. "Is that the next load, Bill?"

Her keen eyes and powers of deduction had Bill flummoxed for a moment. "Er...not exactly..." He fumbled for an answer that might satisfy her. "It's all part of the deal, sort of a package deal...hard to explain really."

"Oh, boy! Don't bother. If it's that hard to put into words, I'll forget I asked. There's more important stuff to quench my curiosity, such as how good will that first drink taste. And will the second be better? By the way, how long have you been Mister Billiam?"

Bill's laugh seemed to be amplified in the still evening air. "Old Noah's always worth the price of admission. I was first introduced to him as William, but I told him he could call me Bill, so I suppose the confusion was born there and then; I just let him call me that. It's sort of cute."

"Mister Billiam? I like it."

"Don't you dare start calling me that, Polly Jordan...or..."

"Or what? There you go again, all threats and no action. I'm starting to think you're a wimp." She saw his face twitch and he looked hurt. "Sorry, Bill. That was a hit below the belt. You're not a wimp. You're just a sensitive guy I'm still trying to fathom after all this time."

"What do you mean?" The look on Bill's face roused up Polly's inquisitiveness.

"You're a bit of an enigma."

"Whoa, Miss Jordan! I might know art, but my English language skills are no match for yours. Spell it out."

"I sense there's more to you than meets the eye. You have a deep well of mystery inside that lovely head."

"Blimey, I don't know whether that's a compliment or an insult. If we're being honest, Polly, I could say the same about you."

"Hold it!" Polly said with her hands in the air. "Truce. Let's not get into a deep and meaningful conversation tonight. There's food and drink to be had." She kissed him lightly on the cheek and they climbed into the Land Rover. Norm was already seated in the rear.

The saloon of the old pub was practically deserted except for two elderly Aboriginal men and two younger women whose looks were Asian. A tall, bespectacled man who had been standing at the bar slowly walked over to greet Bill and Norm. He had grey hair and a long ponytail, and he whispered something to Bill.

"Oh, this is Polly. She a very good friend of mine. She's new and not long in Australia. She's getting to know the lie of the land," he said pointedly.

The bespectacled man nodded, then held out his hand to Polly. "Welcome to the Territory and a special welcome to Humpty Doo. It should be renamed Dumpy Doo, but I suppose some people call it home. It's a goldmine to us, mind you. I'm Tytus Kowalski. It's Polish. Most people call me Titan."

"Pleased to meet you, Titan," Polly responded. As she looked down to their clasped hands, she noticed a blue cross that seemed to be etched into his right thumb nail.

"You have a strong grip, Mister Kowalski," Polly said as she reclaimed her hand.

"I'm so sorry. Forgive me, Polly. May I call you Polly?'

"Absolutely. My real name is Mary, but I've been Polly for as long as I can remember."

"Ha, ha! Then neither of us is who we say we are," Titan said and roared with laughter.

"Hey, Titan," Bill called, "let's go into the dining room and get started."

"Just be a minute. I'll get my drink from the bar and make a quick call to the little boys' room." Again he let out a loud laugh.

The dining room was little more than an empty room with a wooden floor and a round uncovered table. It was set out for six people. The room could best be described as seedy. A single light globe dangled above the table. Its light was weak and barely lit the area. Polly looked up at the ceiling and noticed damp patches and places where ages-old wallpaper was peeling away. Little patches of white plaster were dotted across the table top. As the three travellers took their seats, Polly asked, "Who's Titan and where does he fit in?"

"I've known him for years. He's the main cog in our wheel up here in the Far North. He has hundreds of contacts to Aboriginal artists. He's a great bloke. Without him we'd be struggling to keep the business afloat," Bill said reassuringly.

"This place isn't exactly The Ritz," Polly lamented.

"You can say that again, but it's close to the shed, close to Noah's people and well isolated from prying eyes."

"Whose eyes would be prying?"

Bill tapped his fingers nervously on the table and stared across the table at Norm. "I might have been a bit melodramatic. However, we have competition now. There's a Russian mob trying to undercut us. We have to keep our deals strictly hush-hush. Even so, word gets around like wildfire. It's impossible to keep anything totally confidential up here."

Titan entered the room followed by Noah. A third man appeared at the doorway. He was about six feet tall, barrel-chested and wide across the shoulders. His thick neck, craggy face and a severely broken and bent nose completed a picture, Polly quickly conjured up, of a wrestler or boxer. She was surprised when Titan introduced the stranger to Bill and Norm.

"This is Emir, everybody. He's my...shall we say, security man. It's just a precaution in case the Russians decide to make a move."

Bill put his right hand to his mouth and whispered to Polly. "Don't know who this bloke is. Looks like a thug to me."

"Shush, don't let him hear you. He looks like he could tear your head off," Polly whispered back from the corner of her mouth.

As luck would have it, Emir had turned away to close the dining room door.

"How are you, Emir?" Bill said in a friendly fashion.

Emir's answer was as brief as it was brusque. "Good."

"Not much English, I'm afraid. He's Turkish," Titan interjected helpfully.

Bill had a perplexed look on his face. "Is it going to be a problem, you know, with language?"

Any answer from Titan was cut short. "No," Emir grunted. "No problem. Okay understand, not talk it good."

"No worries," Bill said as he tried to ease the sudden air of tension. "We'll be right. The old saying still applies...no problems, only solutions. Yes? Am I right?"

All around the table muttered *right*. All except Polly, who felt alarmed by Emir's size. His gruff demeanour did not help endear the big man to her. Alarm bells were ringing. Her senses seemed to be reading him as hostile.

Titan also tried to thaw the icy atmosphere. "Okay, the formalities are over. We're all friends, hungry friends, let's order and get the party started. We're all here to celebrate the biggest and best shipment ever. So let's celebrate." As he spoke, he made an exaggerated gesture with his right hand as if he were casting a spell over the gathering.

A sharp-eyed Polly noticed that the cross she had noticed earlier on Titan's thumb was gone. *Maybe it's on his other thumb. I know I saw it; it wasn't my imagination.*

When everyone was seated, Bill stood and said, "It's been another successful coup. I think we should all slap each other on the back, eat well and drink even better, and look forward to the next expedition. *Sped* to you, Polly," Bill joked as he turned to her and gave her a double thumbs-up.

Just then a middle-aged woman with long jet-black hair entered the room and produced a notebook and stubby pencil from the front pocket of her faded floral apron.

"Ready to order, lads?" she chirped. "Tonight's special is roast beef, sausages, boiled or mashed potatoes, gravy and vegetables."

Bill told Polly in a whisper, "It's been the special every time we've been here."

"What's the alternative, Sophia?" Norm asked. "Any lamb shanks?"

"Not tonight, darl," she replied, stroking her hair. "We've got burger and chips or pie and chips. I could fry you some barramundi. Oh, no, wait, the barramundi supply didn't come today. Mustn't be biting."

Polly, wide-eyed, leaned towards Bill. "What's barramundi?" she asked quietly.

"Barramundi," Titan responded in a flash, "is the most beautiful, tasty fish you will ever eat. Except not tonight, by the sound of things. But next time you come to the Top End, you must try it."

"I've eaten flake in Melbourne," Polly offered with enthusiasm.

"Flake? That's crap compared to barramundi. Sorry about the language. Better still, when you come back, try a mud crab. There is nothing better in the whole world than chilli mud crab."

"Mud crab? That sounds revolting," Polly replied scrunching up her nose. "What, you eat something that's crawling through mud and eating heaven knows what?"

"My dear, they are like manna from heaven. Am I not right, Bill?"

Bill ran his finger under his nose and smiled. "They're pretty damn good, yes. The only problem is, they're not on the menu tonight and Sophia wants to know what we all want to eat that's actually available, so it looks to me like it's a simple choice.

Noah was alone in not ordering roast beef. He asked Sophia for a bowl of gravy and some bread.

"Don't you like roast beef?" Polly asked Noah.

"Not for Noah, missus. I know where it comes from. I like better to eat a goanna or a nice big fat snake."

Polly was stunned and, for once, lost for words.

"Oh, Sophia," Bill called as she was about to leave the room, "Keep the drinks coming...beers, whisky, anything this bunch of bad boys wants."

Polly dug Bill sharply in the ribs with her elbow. "What about me, am I a bad boy or just a bad girl?"

"You know what you are, Polly Jordan," he replied with a wink.

As the night wore on, the conversation got louder and the drinking got harder. Despite the hub-bub, Bill noticed that Emir had been drinking only water from a large jug Sophia brought in before serving their meals.

"Not a drinker, Emir?" Bill asked, his voice raised to be heard.

"No. Religion," was the curt reply.

*I suppose if he's Turkish he's probably a Muslim*, Bill silently reasoned.

It was about eleven o'clock when the party finally broke up and the six walked in into the still night air. A half-moon dodged in and out of the clouds. There was an eerie silence apart from the chirping of insects, but the quiet was shattered by a sound that startled Polly. "Oh! What was that? It sounded awful...like someone vomiting through a megaphone. What the hell was it? Don't tell me Humpty Doo has a werewolf, apart from all the other killer animals."

Noah moved to Polly's side and nudged her arm with his elbow. "Pretty bad, eh, missus! It's father koala want to make love to mother koala."

"God, they have some revolting love talk. If that's foreplay, then I don't know how any gal can be seduced by a sound like her lover's throwing up."

Polly's amusing observation had everyone laughing heartily. In the night air, their burst of laughter seemed to have the decibel rating of a small explosion.

"Sssssh!" someone said. "It's late."

Obligingly Bill lowered his voice. "Polly, listen, Norm and I have drunk a bit more than you. Do you feel up to driving us to the shed, then you can drive back and kip at the pub?"

"Why can't you just drive yourselves? It's such a quiet night and not that far to the shed. I'm not certain I can handle the Land Rover, especially in the dark."

"That's a fair point," Bill replied with a loud burp.

Polly was quick to chide him. "Excuse you! Manners, please!"

"As I was saying," Bill continued undaunted, "the only fly in the ointment is you. You won't be able to get back to the shed and get ready to head south if you're on foot."

"Oops!" Polly said with a giggle. "I must be a bit tiddly. I didn't think that one through, did I? What about the others?"

"They'll be all right. Noah will just melt into the undergrowth, as his mob are inclined to do, and I assume Titan and the big grumpy bast…"

"Emir," Polly prompted sternly. "His name's Emir, and he's right behind us."

"Yeah, Emir…he and Titan must have driven here so they'll be right, too. Simple. Easy as ABC."

Polly said goodnight to everyone and added, "You two boys behave yourselves."

"What do you mean?" Bill asked.

His speech was a little slurred so she simply stuck her hand out of driver's window and waved vigorously to Noah and the other two. "See you blokes bright and early in the morning."

Despite her misgivings, Polly's drive to and from the shed was relatively plain sailing. She quickly mastered the Land Rover controls and surprised herself at how skilfully she tackled the rutted dirt path. The Rover's modest headlights, with helpful moments of moonlight, were just enough for her to pick her way through the densest clumps of trees and bushes.

She parked and locked the Land Rover at the rear of the pub, then collected her room key at the bar. In keeping with the rest of the pub, her bedroom was bordering on shabby, but all she cared about was getting a good night's sleep before the long punishing journey back to Melbourne.

There was an old freestanding double wardrobe and a chest of drawers with a frameless mirror on top, propped up against the wall. An armchair completed the furniture, which was in reasonable condition, but clearly nothing matched. After a quick wash in a small adjoining bathroom, Polly stood in front of the bedroom mirror and treated her hair to a long, slow brushing. Finally, she rolled blissfully onto the single bed. This had been placed next to a small window which was framed with navy blue velvety curtains.

She did several little body bounces to test its springiness and comfort, and happily gave it a mental tick. *Not too bad after all.*

Quickly she sat upright and reached down to the rucksack in which she had brought a few belongings from the Land Rover. She pulled out a large bottle of water and took several long drinks before wiping her mouth with the back of her hand. *Never go to sleep with booze and no water*, she told herself.

The light switch was next to the door. Before she put the room in darkness, Polly tried to secure the door by means of a small hook and eye device. She could see it would be useless in keeping anybody out. One kick and the door would fly open, but she engaged it nevertheless. She closed the curtains. With the light out, they let in a meagre strand of moonlight which lit the edge of her pillows. She was too tired to undress. Within minutes she was sound asleep.

# *Twenty-one*

"**B**loody hell! Look at the time!" Polly cursed. She had planned to be up at seven o'clock and it was almost nine-thirty. She rushed into the bathroom, squeezed some toothpaste onto a finger and rubbed in on her teeth as she clomped down the stairs. "I've come to settle up," she mumbled to the girl behind the bar, toothpaste dribbling from her lips.

"Are you Polly?"

"Yes, that's me. Room three."

"Nothing to pay. Mr Flint has paid in advance."

"Thanks, thanks a lot. Nice stay, thanks. See you," and with that, Polly ran out of the pub to the Land Rover parked out at the back. *No breakfast for you today, Polly Jordan.*

She put the key in the ignition. Drrrrrr...drrrrrr...drrrrrr. "Bloody heap!" she yelled. "Come on, start, you worthless hunk of metal."

At the fourth attempt, the engine spluttered into life. Polly hastily crunched the Land Rover into gear and swung it out onto the road. She banged her foot down hard on the accelerator. Round the first bend, she scattered a flock of cockatoos feeding on grass seeds at the edge of what bitumen there was on the road surface. "Get out of the way, bloody birds. Sorry if I've hit any of you. Truly sorry."

She glanced at her watch as she pulled off the road and drove onto the track leading into woodland and the big shed. Little more than one hundred yards along the track, she was forced to brake. A large dark green car was parked across the track, blocking it.

"What the hell is this guy doing?' she grumbled angrily.

She opened the driver's window and yelled, "Oi! Whoever is in that car, get out of the bloody way. I need to come through."

As there was no response, she searched for the horn and blasted it several times. Suddenly there was a face at the window.

"Good morning, miss."

"Jesus Christ, you scared the crap out of me," Polly said with a gasp. "What the hell's going on? Oh, no, it's you Emir from last night, with Tytus, I mean Titan."

"Yes," he replied. "Can I ask you to turn off the engine, hand me the keys and step out of the vehicle, please?"

"Shit! You speak English. I thought you were Turkish and…"

"I am Turkish, but I was born in Canberra. Can you please do as I ask, Miss Jordan?" he urged politely.

Polly was still wary of the big powerful-looking man and slowly obliged. "What's this about? Why are you suddenly sounding like a traffic cop?"

"My name is Emir Gultekin. I'm an officer in COMPOL, the Australian Commonwealth Police, and I have need to question you."

"Me? What about? What have I done, or supposed to have done?"

"I'll tell you more once we sort the vehicles out. I will reverse off the track, give you back your keys and you will proceed to the shed. I will follow in my car. Thank you."

Shock had turned Polly's mouth so dry she could only mumble "Okay," and meekly did exactly as she had been instructed. Her mind raced in panic and her stomach churned, gripped by jangling nerves.

As the Land Rover rounded the last stand of trees before the shed came into view, Polly saw up to a dozen people going in and out of the old hangar. It wasn't an enormous leap to realise that these people, most in unform, the rest in civilian clothes, were police officers.

Officer Gultekin tooted his car horn and with his arm out of the window, he signalled to Polly to pull over and stop the Land Rover. He walked round to hold the passenger door open and beckoned her to get in. "It's going to be a hot day, so you can leave the passenger door open," he told her. "As long as you don't run away," he added with a faint smile.

"Is it because I'm driving on an English driving licence?" Polly asked.

"No, it's not that. Driving offences are not my concern."

"Then what's happening. Who are those people? Police? What have I got into that warrants all these officers? Is it serious trouble?"

"Now I must tell you at this stage you are not charged with anything, you are not under suspicion and you do not have to comply, but in all honesty, it will benefit you to be frank and cooperative."

"I'll do my best," Polly said with a quivering voice. She took a deep breath. With her bottom lip curled over the top one, she blew out air, launching stray whisps of hair from her forehead.

"Are you Mary Frances Jordan?" he began.

"Yes, I am."

"And are you a British citizen, in possession of a bona fide British passport and currently in Australia under the provisions of a migrant visa?"

"That's right. In fact, I have my passport with me. I seldom go anywhere without it, as a journalist. At least I was."

"That's very good news and will save a lot of time and make life easier for both of us. However, for the time being, I must ask you to surrender the passport to me."

"Okay, but first of all, can I ask you to show me some identity, as you are asking me for mine?"

"Most certainly," he said, and took out a small leather wallet from an inside pocket. He flipped it open and let Polly examine his badge, personal identity number and name.

"It's not that I don't trust you," Polly explained, "but last night at dinner, you deceived everybody."

"Not quite everybody, but that's a story for later."

"I shouldn't really tell you this, but Bill thought you looked like a thug."

"And what do you think, Miss Jordan? May I call you Polly?"

"Hold it there, cowboy, is this part of your chat-up routine? Get a girl in your car and get into her mind?"

He laughed and as he did so, Polly concluded he didn't seem half as brutish as he had the night before.

"No, it's not a line I would use. Beautiful as you are, if I may be so bold as to say, I am a married man with four little children and, I'm sorry to say, I am here to do a very serious job."

"To be honest, Officer Gultekin, I was terrified of you."

"And now?"

"*You're* fishing and *I'm* not biting."

"Right, back to business. For what purpose have you come to the Northern Territory and Humpty Doo in particular?"

"That's easy," Polly replied, "I'm here with my friend, Mr Bill Flint, who has driven up from Melbourne to collect some Aboriginal art works for his gallery."

"Is that the sole purpose of your visit? Are you here to assist him with any other business?"

"Well, first of all, I am not assisting him. I know nothing about the art trade, let alone Aboriginal stuff. I like to look at it. I think it's so brilliant and speaks to you. And yet it's mysterious and primitive, in the nicest possible way. But I don't know the first thing about it. In fact, I was rather hoping Bill would take me to see some of the artists and watch them do that famous dot painting."

"What do you know about Mr Flint? Are married to him, engaged? Or are you his common law wife...de facto?"

"Jeez, you're thorough, Officer Glupekin," Polly told him.

"Almost correct. It's Gultekin," he emphasised.

"I haven't known Bill *that* long, but we've struck up a close friendship. I had some major personal issues back in Cardwell. That's where I've come from, it's not my home town. I was born on the Isle of Man, so when Bill asked me to come to Australia, I decided on a lifestyle change."

"Castletown, Isle of Man, March eighth, nineteen-forty-one."

"If you know all this about me, why the heck are you asking me all these questions? Have you contacted Interpol?"

"No, Interpol only deals in major serious crime. It's not a police force, just a way of exchanging critical information between countries. You'd have to be in rare air to be known at that level. I don't think you qualify. Or do you?" he said jokingly.

Polly sensed the officer was trying to make her feel at ease with a few lighthearted exchanges, but she knew she had to think carefully about every word she said, even though she still had no idea why she was being questioned.

"I admit I do have a little information on you, Polly, but I'm just trying hard to get your measure. I'm sorry if I've deceived you again."

"Some men are born deceivers," she snapped and turned her head away from him.

Officer Gultekin was about to respond, but relaxed his shoulders instead and composed his next question. "What do you know about the man they call Norm?"

"What do you mean the man they *call*...? Norm's not Norm?" Polly suddenly recalled the story Bill had told her about Norm's private, unofficial adoption and knew she needed to take extra care with her answer. "He's Bill's brother. At least half-brother. I've only known him a few months and know little about him."

"What do you know about the big zebra-striped truck?"

"Stuff-all really, apart from its camouflage or whatever the paintwork's supposed to represent. As far as I know, there are no zebras in Australia."

"Only camels," he smiled. "And water buffalos and crocodiles. All sorts of creatures that can kill you. What's in the back of the truck?"

"I don't know. I slept in there the first night of the journey and I haven't seen inside it or been inside it since."

"So when exactly did you last see inside the truck and what precisely did you see?"

"God, all these truck questions? What's the big deal with the truck? I slept overnight at a campsite. I'm not sure now whether it was in South Australia or the Territory. I'm new here, so I don't know where I am half the time, unless I'm in Melbourne. I know Malvern and Prahran. The only things I saw were camping stuff and spare wheels and other equipment we brought with us. That's it."

"So would you swear on oath, if you were called to, that you saw nothing other than that? You didn't perhaps see a number of wooden crates?"

"Nope, not one. I'd put that in writing."

"Okay, Miss Jordan, thank you for your cooperation. We can go to the shed now, but I must ask you not, I repeat not, to talk to anyone but me. Do you understand? Nobody. That must be your absolute guarantee."

"Yeah, if that's what it takes to get whatever is happening over and done with," Polly confirmed as she swung her legs out of Officer Gultekin's car. "Oh, by the way, Officer, I don't think you're that much of a thug after all."

"So I've made a reasonable impression? In an official capacity?"

"I'll see. The jury's out. Maybe if you can reassure me I won't end up in jail for whatever you think is going on here, I might relent and bring in a verdict of not guilty."

Polly was feeling rather uplifted after her interview until she reached the large metal double-doors of the shed. They had been left wide open. "Oh, no! Oh, no, Bill. What the hell...?" The site of Bill Flint and Norm sitting on the concrete floor staggered Polly. They were both handcuffed and clasps around their ankles were shackled to each other with a sturdy chain. "Christ, Bill, what's happening here? What are...?"

Officer Gultekin grabbed Polly by the shoulder. "I'm sorry, Miss Jordan, you cannot ask any questions at this time. I did ask you for your assurance and you gave it."

"I'm sorry. I'm in a state of absolute disbelief. Can you please explain what has happened and why they are in chains? Have they been arrested for something? Please...I need to know."

"I can't say much here but I must ask you one final time, and you must answer me honestly—have you seen those before or anything like them?" He pointed to a pile of wooden crates and at the side a large green tarpaulin that had been used to cover them.

"Honestly, you said? I might have seen the tarpaulin thing before but I can't be certain. That's all. I've never seen the crates and I certainly don't know what they contain. I presume there's something in them."

Bill attempted to get up from the floor but failed.

"I told them you didn't know anything, Polly. I've told them you're innocent," he whimpered with tears welling in his eyes.

"Sorry, Mr Flint, you cannot speak to anybody right now," Gultekin said.

"All I want to know is why," Polly insisted. "He's a good friend. Surely I have the right to know why he's under arrest, which I assume is the case."

"At this very moment I am unable to answer your question. I must wait for word from my superiors before we can take this any further."

"Why is Tytus not under arrest, or Noah?"

"Mr Kowalski is elsewhere and is assisting us with our enquiries."

"Into what? You said I could talk only to you, but you won't bloody tell me anything. I feel like I'm talking to a stuffed parrot. If I put two and two together and recall how you didn't drink alcohol last night, obviously because of today's raid, and if I also recall that Bill said he didn't know, then am I getting the answer four? And does this mean that you and Kowalski were working in collusion?"

"You have a sharp mind, Miss Jordan, but you must know I can't comment on that."

"And where's the old bloke, Noah?" Polly persisted. "Is he helping too?"

"I'd hazard a guess that Noah is somewhere in the Outback by now and that's the last we'll see of him. The blackfellas can live for months off the land. They've done it for thousands of years. Nah, we won't be seeing Noah again. If *they* hide, you don't find 'em."

"So what happens now? What do I do?"

"The uniformed officers are from the Northern Territory police and they'll take charge of the truck and its contents. My

COMPOL crew and I will go separately to Darwin with Mr Flint and Norm. I can give you a lift to Darwin, if you wish."

"No, I'll take the Land Rover," Polly announced with an air of independence.

"Sorry, but that vehicle has been impounded and may be part of the brief of evidence in the event of a prosecution."

"Do you coppers *always* talk in jargon?" Polly asked sarcastically.

"Only on days ending with y."

"Ha bloody ha! Oops! I'd better be good or I'll be walking to Darwin."

"I wouldn't advise that, it's about twenty-three miles."

"I don't know why I'm making a joke of all this. I'm still reeling and my gut tells me there's worse to come." Polly looked at Officer Gultekin's face. It wore a stony expression and showed no hint of being ready to reveal information.

# Twenty-two

A van with smoked glass side windows took Bill Flint and Norm in handcuffs to Darwin. Officer Gultekin, with Polly as a passenger, left the shed and also headed for the Territory's capital city. Three armed uniformed officers had been posted to guard the shed and its contents.

When they were about halfway there, dark clouds filled the sky and within minutes a torrential downpour forced most of the traffic heading into Darwin to stop at the side of the highway and wait until it was safe to proceed. Most vehicles' windscreen wipers just could not cope with the deluge.

"That's one thing you can bet on up here," Gultekin said turning to Polly. "The monsoon season is nearly over, but you never really know when it's over until it's over."

As the rain began to clear and the car picked its way through massive puddles skirting the highway, Officer Gultekin looked away from the road and turned to Polly. "Tell me, Miss Jordan, you saw crates in the shed. Do you still say you did not know what was in them?"

Through gritted teeth she yelled, "No!" She pushed her hair back from her face and said in a more subdued voice, "I'm saying, for the umpteenth and absolutely final time, I have no idea what they contained or where they came from. I can't be any clearer than that. I'm happy to take a lie detector test, but I don't know why you are obsessed with them."

"You've seen too many American movies, I think. We don't have lie detectors in Australia."

"Well, I'll swear on a crateful of Bibles," she responded.

As the car entered Darwin, Office Gultekin said, "I'll have to take you in for more questioning, but if things go as I think they should, you'll be free to leave later. Is there anywhere you want to stay or anyone you'd like to stay with?"

"How am I supposed to know? I've never been to Darwin and I don't know anyone in the whole of Australia except the people you have put behind bars." Polly was a little annoyed with his seeming lack of perception, but her mood soon changed to one of optimism. "I've just had an epiphany."

"A what?" Officer Gultekin was puzzled.

"Epiphany...oh never mind, it's not important. I've remembered, I do know someone here. There's a doctor I met in England who's working right here in Darwin. At least he was a few weeks ago."

"Can you contact him?"

"I assume you'll be interviewing me in an office. Will I be able to use a phone?"

"I think the Commonwealth Police can afford to shout you a free phone call."

"Isn't that my legal right?"

"There's that American movie influence again. To be honest, I don't really know if it's in legislation."

"Well, I'm relying on your honesty, because if I can't make a call, I'll be sleeping in a cell."

"That won't happen," he said.

The officer and Polly went up two flights of stairs in central police station headquarters and stopped at a door with a handwritten sign that read *COMPOL*. He knocked lightly and a voice replied, "Enter."

An untidy arrangement of desks greeted Polly. There were two or three phones on each, wire filing trays that seemed to be overflowing and several people who had stopped what they were doing to monitor the intrusion. Early afternoon sun was partially blocked by large windows of smoked glass and an air-conditioner hummed gently on a wall. Officer Gultekin escorted Polly through the maze and knocked lightly on a second door. Again there was a handwritten sign. This one read *Inspector N. Hastings, Operation H. Doo.*

"Come on in," a woman's voice instructed.

The officer stood back while Polly entered first.

"Miss Jordan?"

"That's me."

The woman standing next to a large wooden desk was middle-aged, wore a pale pink blouse and a pencil skirt. "I'm Inspector Nancy Hastings, please sit down, Miss Jordan. May I call you Polly?"

"Yes," said Polly as she quickly let her eyes scan the office. This, unlike the office she had come through was the essence of order. Papers were neatly arranged on her desk and there was even a small bowl of what looked like wild flowers between two green telephones.

"I know today has probably been something of an ordeal for you, Polly. Perhaps even a trauma. You'll notice from my accent that I am from England...Kent, actually. I'm not here to trap you in any way or to scare you. I just need your cooperation and understanding while we have what I will try to ensure remains an informal exchange."

Inspector Hastings took her seat and invited Polly to sit in a leather chair facing her. Polly was surprised and impressed by this officer's English language skills, and having a woman on the other side of the desk helped her to feel more at ease.

The inspector looked up to Officer Gultekin and said gently, "Emir, I think we'll be better off alone, so if you'll stay outside for a while."

He nodded and went towards the door.

"Oh, before you go, Emir, can you get someone to organise some tea and maybe some biscuits for us? Is tea all right for you, Polly, or do you prefer coffee?"

"Tea's fine, thanks," Polly affirmed.

"Before we start, do you need the loo? Or do you want to freshen up?"

Polly politely declined. "I'd just like to get the bottom of whatever is going on," she said wearily.

Just as Inspector Hastings was about to speak, they were interrupted by a sharp knock on the door and a young Aboriginal girl wearing a blue waitress-type uniform wheeled in a trolley. The girl took a tray bearing typical afternoon tea fare and walked over to the officer's desk. As she approached, Polly noticed the girl was unsteady and had a pronounced left limp. Polly jumped up from her chair and went to help the girl by taking the tray from her.

"It's all right, miss, I can manage," the girl said politely but firmly and then with a flashing smile she said, "Your tea, ma'am."

"Thank you, Yindi. That's all for the moment."

Yindi hobbled back to the door and closed it with a gentle click.

"Poor girl," Inspector Hastings said. "She was hoping to become part of the Darwin police force. It had been a dream of hers since she was thirteen. She was attacked by a saltwater crocodile and lost her left foot. She was devastated. The force was keen to have Indigenous officers as law enforcers but, of greater importance, someone able to liaise with people of the Aboriginal and Chinese communities. We have many nationalities in the Territory, especially in Darwin."

"That's so sad," Polly said. "She seems such a lovely attractive girl. And that smile is dazzling."

Inspector Hastings continued, "We wanted to employ her and make a tiny part of her dream happen. It's not just charity. She works hard and helps both COMPOL and the Territory force with paperwork. She's happy and she often acts as a conduit between the police and the people, so she's doubly useful." She poured the tea before she continued.

"Polly, I am at a crossroads. First let me say that Officer Gultekin contacted me this morning after his interview with you and has stated that he sees you as being an unwilling and unwitting pawn in the commission of several serious federal offences. It sounds as if a number of Territory laws may have been breached and perhaps laws involving three other states, New South Wales, South Australia and Victoria. Working on the premise that you know nothing of what is alleged to have happened, I will explain."

Polly visibly relaxed. "At last! Thank you."

"Operation Flint was established three years ago. Federal officers have been investigating Bill Flint and his so-called half-brother, Norm, on and off since then."

"Sorry, but can I just interrupt?" Polly asked anxiously. She received a nod of approval. "Why do people keep referring to Norm as though he and Bill are not related?"

"It's a good question and, if I may, I'll leave the explanation until later. All will be revealed, I promise, Polly. As you're new, or relatively new to Australia, you may not be aware that for many years, there has been a huge and socially destructive problem with alcohol in the Indigenous communities. It has led to widespread family and domestic crises, sickness, violence, an increased crime rate, marital breakdowns, in fact a host of issues.

Alcohol has indirectly been involved with deaths in custody, killings and dreadful accidents." She took a sip of her tea. "Over the past three years, we have compiled evidence and we have absolute proof that Mr Flint has been using illicit, illegally-produced alcohol as currency to buy Aboriginal artworks which he then sold for outrageous profits in his gallery."

"Are you sure it's Bill? I can't believe it. He's not like that. There *has* to be an explanation. It can't be true." She leaned forward and held her head in her hands, her elbows resting on her knees. *What the hell have I got myself into?*

Inspector Hastings stood and went to put her arm around Polly's shoulders. "I know that's a shock, but I'm afraid there is not a shadow of a doubt. We asked you many times if you knew what was in the crates in the shed. We believe your story. Those crates contain absolute proof and they are covered with Mr Flint's fingerprints and Norm's. Two days ago, officers working out of Katherine arrested five men who were operating an illegal still on a remote farm that turned out pure spirit from potatoes.

"The consignment of alcohol Mr Flint is accused of supplying is enormous. There are approximately six hundred gallons and it is believed it has been blended with ethanol which we suspect was manufactured in either Queensland or New South Wales. We have forensic chemists conducting tests.

"Ethanol is difficult to manufacture, so there must be other illegal sources that still have to be tracked down. We are dealing with a very large criminal organisation."

Polly remained completely still.

Inspector Hastings continued. "We have testimony from dozens of indigenous witnesses who have done business with Mr Flint's company, and hundreds of artists have signed statements that they received alcohol distributed by Mr Flint and his employees in exchange for their work. Small amounts of cash were included in the payments, but the bulk of the remuneration was alcohol. In crude terms, it was home-distilled vodka, which has a massive alcohol proof and can be destructive to health if consumed over a long period. If you want to call it our trump card, Tytus Kowalski has made a full confession and has provided detailed evidence of his and everybody else's involvement."

"So he knew last night when he came into the pub with Officer Gulp...Emir...that this raid was to take place?" Polly asked.

"Yes, that's right. He has been cooperating with us for some months. Officer Gultekin has been working closely with him."

"Why would Titan...Tytus...do that? What has he got to gain? If Bill crashes and burns, so does he."

"He had little choice. We have information on Mister Kowalski that could land him behind bars for life."

"What information?" Polly said, growing angry.

"Let me hold fire on that, just for a short while."

Polly looked up and sat up straight in the chair. "This is an absolute nightmare. We're talking about the man who asked me to join him in Australia being a crook. I'm shattered. After all we did and talked about, I'm here. I've given up my career and my life for him. I am such a fool. I've been played for a sucker. Oh, hell, what am I going to do? I've got nothing here without Bill," Polly wailed, beating her knees with her fists. She tried to gather her thoughts and took deep gulps of air. "He was so nice, so perfect. He made me laugh. We enjoyed each other's company in and out of bed. I've never been so shocked and I'm feeling so hollow and useless since..."

She wanted to evoke memories of the Doc trauma, but felt reluctant to sully his memory. "I'm just going over what you said, Inspector," Polly said, trying to compose herself, with the impact still making her head spin.

"Would you like a drink?" Inspector Hastings offered. "And I don't mean tea this time."

"You must be joking. You're offering me alcohol when that's the very thing that has just brought my entire world crashing down?"

"I suppose it could have seemed insensitive, but sometimes a small amount of brandy can help to counter shock. I always keep a bottle handy for times such as this."

"Thanks, but no thanks, as they say. What happens now? What happens to Bill?"

"He and Norm are in custody. They have been charged with contravening federal excise laws as holding charges—"

Polly jumped in, "What, booze tax evasion? They couldn't even convict Al Capone on that one."

"I don't know if your history is accurate, Polly, but as I said, they are holding charges. There will be more serious charges to come."

Polly looked wide-eyed at the inspector. "What could happen to Bill, worst case scenario?"

"I'm afraid he faces quite a long time in prison if convicted."

"Oh, Jesus, I feel sick," Polly said. "I honestly think I'm going to throw up."

"Shall I send for a doctor?" Inspector Hastings offered sympathetically.

The mention of a doctor reminded Polly that she had been promised a phone call to Conor Docherty. "I have a friend who's a doctor and I think he's working right here in Darwin. Officer Gulp..." Polly stalled.

Inspector Hastings came to her rescue. "Gultekin."

"Yes, him. He said I could ring my friend from here."

"You certainly can, but I have more information I think you should know. It's not exactly pertinent to our enquiries involving Bill, yet it does involve him and you."

"Oh, no," Polly wailed. "I couldn't bear any more shocks today. My life is already a bloody fantasy. Please don't make it a laughing stock."

"Do you recall I said we had fingerprints of Mister Flint and Norm from the crates? Those fingerprints match some which were taken, I think, towards the end of November." 1941. Polly looked totally nonplussed and held out her hands as if waiting for the next body blow.

"Polly...how well do you know Mister Flint...Bill?" Hastings' voice was soft and calm. She spoke to Polly like a caring mother. "What I am going to tell you may affect you emotionally. I am concerned, but I think it is something you should know and I know it will hurt you, really hurt, if my reading of your character is correct."

"Is it time I had that brandy?"

"It might be useful. You will suffer, I'm sure."

Polly finally relented. "Pour me one and don't make me drink alone."

With the glasses of brandy in place, Inspector Hastings took a sip of hers and cleared her throat several times. "You might be aware that Bill Flint took part in the military evacuation of Allied troops at Dunkirk in 1941."

Polly sat up straight and put her shoulders back. Proudly she said, "Yes, Bill was a hero."

Inspector Hastings continued. "I might have to refer to my notes at times, so please excuse me. Our investigations into Mister Flint are a little unclear about those particular events, and War Office records help little. We do know that Bill and his father managed to re-patriate three men in uniform and they certainly risked their lives doing so, given that the Luftwaffe mounted machine-gun and rocket attacks on shipping and small boats alike. One man they took into their craft was shot and killed and fell overboard. He was a French soldier from Lyon, records tell us. They were unable to recover the body as the tide was nearing full, and the current was too fast.

"One of the others was James Gledhill, a teenager from Manchester and about the same age as young Mister Flint. The third was a Scottish man, age about twenty. He was Bruce Cameron from Paisley. There was a fourth evacuee...Tytus Kowalski."

Polly gasped.

"The return journey to the English coast was rough, but uneventful, that is until the small boat was within two hundred yards of land when Mr Kowalski shouted *'See ya, boys.'* He jumped over the side and started to swim south, parallel to shore. No one saw him again, at that juncture.

Polly was aghast. "This is turning out to be some story."

"Over the coming months, Mr Flint and James Gledhill struck up a friendship. This in turn became more than a friendship. The outcome, to cut the story short, was that both were convicted of engaging in homosexual acts with two other men. All four were imprisoned for five years."

"I can't stand this. Please tell me this is a lie," Polly said, not trying to hide her distress. "He told his mother he was recuperating in the Isle of Man after suffering severe trauma from being strafed by the German fighter aircraft. None of this makes sense. It seems everything he told me was lies," she said. She glugged down the brandy and coughed as it burned her throat.

"Polly, I'm really sorry to be telling you all this. I can see you are completely disillusioned."

Polly could hardly speak, but managed to croak, "Bill, a homosexual? I must be utterly gullible. I thought he...desired me for me. Was it some other weird fantasy?"

"I know it won't help really, but there is a transitional stage of bisexuality," Inspector Hastings counselled. "Perhaps..."

Polly held up her hand. "Stop! Stop what you're saying. I have to have time to think this through. I feel like Alice Through the Looking Glass, but the glass has shattered into a million pieces and I've been cut and left bleeding by every single shard. Is there anything else I should know about the man who isn't?"

"I'm loathe to go on, but I feel it is my duty, although none of this is pertinent to the alcohol case. Mr Flint was sent to Strangeways Prison, Manchester and shared a cell with Wilfred Normansel, a convicted confidence trickster and pickpocket. They each spent time in solitary confinement for committing lewd acts and received extensions to their sentences, but, incongruously, remained cell mates. They were released separately in 1949."

Polly shook her head over and over. Dejectedly she announced, "My head is bursting with all this. I need a break."

"Yes, goodness gracious! I have put through you the mill, Polly. Frankly, I don't know how you are coping so well. There is just one more piece to a huge puzzle that I must put in place before we take time out. After Tytus Kowalski jumped overboard, Mr Flint senior reported it to the police in Ramsgate. Because of the unpredictable tides, Kowalski was soon found and placed under arrest. He had been in Paris at the outbreak of war and roamed round France even as the Germans were advancing. We're not sure where he was heading, but evidence points to this: either he murdered a British soldier, or he found him dead. He allegedly stole his uniform and identification tags, which enabled him to escape to England by way of the Dunkirk evacuation. He left his own identification papers on the dead body. One week after being arrested, he escaped and had been evading capture ever since, until we tracked him down and found him in Melbourne."

"You couldn't make this up," Polly said reflectively.

"With that last bit of knowledge, we were able to, let's say, persuade Mr Kowalski to help in Operation Flint. He will be a prosecution witness in any case against Mister Flint and Mister Normantel. After that he will be deported to face trial on the outstanding charge or charges involving the British soldier whose name was Frederick Carmichael.

"You can imagine how tricky this investigation has been, apart from mounting a case against Mr Flint. We've had many, many international challenges to overcome."

Polly leaned back in her chair. "My mind is having a hard time holding all this, let alone being able to process it. This is the sort of story I would have loved as a journalist, but it's now my life story, one big fucking mess. Sorry for the bad language, Inspector."

"No problems! In our line of work we hear much worse," she said. Her voice carried a soothing blend, in equal measures of kindness and understanding.

There was a knock on the door. Yindi entered to tell her boss she was finished for the day.

"Oh, Yindi, I've a massive favour to ask before you go," Inspector Hastings said.

"Another round of tea and biscuits, ma'am?"

"Yes, please. You read my mind. That would be greatly appreciated. It's been a long day," she said, looking at Polly. "I've been here since five o'clock this morning." And then to the girl, "Yindi, thank you, I'll make sure you're paid overtime."

"That's not necessary, ma'am. I'm happy to help."

Once Yindi had left, Inspector Hastings said, "She's such a darling. There's a story behind Yindi's tragic accident, Polly, and one that I hope will make you realise why some of us are determined to stop illegal alcohol reaching the Indigenous community. As I said earlier, Yindi was thirteen when her accident happened. She and two male cousins, a bit older, went out in a small boat on a tributary of the Adelaide River, not far from their homes. The boys had gained access to some illegal alcohol. We think it was supplied by Mr Flint's enterprise. Maybe they couldn't be classed as drunk, but their senses were impaired. On the water, they capsized the boat and were attacked by a saltwater crocodile estimated to be sixteen-foot-long."

"Oh, jeez!" Polly responded.

"Yindi was bitten on her left foot so severely that amputation was the only way to save her. She wears a prosthesis, but she will never be able to achieve her ambition of becoming a police officer. One cousin lost a leg in the same way. The second boy, Yarran, was never seen again. An inquest ruled that he had been taken. Unfortunately, there was not enough evidence to prove conclusively Mr Flint was culpable, but unofficially, we all know the alcohol was supplied by him."

Polly was ashen faced. "I feel sick. I'm so sorry. I'd love to apologise for Bill and his dreadful crime, because what you've told me *is* a crime, but I knew nothing about his so-called business. That man has so much to answer for. In a single day, he has turned my world upside down and now I am being told he is nothing short of a murderer, at least an accessory to the gruesome, brutal death of a child. Please, God, make this day end. I can't take anymore."

~ * ~

After their refreshments, Inspector Hastings told Polly of her immediate future. "My recommendation is that you will not face prosecution," Inspector Hastings advised Polly to her immense and visible relief. "What I expect, therefore, is that in the event of any prosecution against Mr Flint and Mr Normantel, which is virtually guaranteed, you will appear as a witness for the prosecution."

Polly pondered this proposition for a moment. "I don't see I have much choice. I assume the usual restrictions apply...you keep my passport, I have to stay in the immediate area, and I do not consort with anyone who is likely to be a witness or a defendant?"

"I see you know the drill," Inspector Hastings said with admiration.

"I've spent years as a reporter and some of those have involved covering court cases and legal affairs," Polly said.

"Okay. That's it for now and you are free to go, but you must inform us of your contact details as soon as you arrange accommodation."

"I understand," Polly replied. She picked up her rucksack and was about to leave the room. "Before I go, what about my phone call to my friend?"

The inspector pressed an intercom button. "Is that Constable Sharp? Oh, good, will you come to my office and escort Miss Jordan out of the building? But before she leaves take her to the phone room and find her a booth where she can make an outside call." Then to Polly, "Just wait for an operator to answer and give them your number. They'll connect you."

When the young constable arrived, Polly left Inspector Hastings with a curt, "Goodbye! Thanks!" She waited for several minutes for a connection then waited again for a reply. The minutes ticked by and Polly was on the verge of hanging up and trying to call again when someone picked up.

"Hello, Royal Darwin Hospital, can I help you?"

"Oh, hello, yes," Polly said hurriedly, "My name is Polly Jordan and I'd like to speak to Doctor Conor Docherty, please. It's rather urgent."

"Hold the line, please. I'll see if he's available. What name was it again?"

"Polly, Polly Jordan, I'm a personal friend."

The line fell silent, then Polly heard a faint noise as the receiver was picked up.

"Hello, Polly, how good to hear from you. I'm sorry, I'm a bit busy right now so I don't have much time to chat, I'm afraid."

"Oh, Conor, it's so good to hear your voice."

"Where are you, in Melbourne?"

"I'm here in Darwin."

"Oh, my goodness, that's brilliant. We must meet up."

"Conor?"

"Yes, Polly?"

"Conor?" Polly repeated as she tried to control her emotions, "Conor, I need a friend." With that she burst into tears.

"Polly! Polly. What's wrong? Why are you crying? Has somebody done something to you? Are you safe?"

"I need you, Conor. I'm in trouble. I'm at Darwin police headquarters. I'm not under arrest, but Bill is. He's in terrible trouble. I saw him in handcuffs this morning."

"Holy shit!" Conor blurted. "Stay right where you are. I'm coming to collect you. Don't wander away, stay right there. I'll be with you in less than ten minutes."

## *Twenty-three*

Conor led Polly into the two-storey apartment he was renting in Tiwi. She sat on the leather settee close to a picture window that overlooked a garden lush with tropical fruit trees.

"Are those actual bananas on that tree? And I can see mangoes. Wow!"

He poured Polly a gin and tonic. "How can I help?" he said calmly. "Have a good drink, slow down your breathing and try to relax. Do you do yoga?"

"No," Polly sniffled. "I thought yoga was a cartoon bear."

They both laughed briefly then Polly began to tell Conor of her dreadful day.

"Wait for a second. I'll just call work and tell them I have a family emergency and won't be back today."

"Family?" Polly questioned hesitantly.

"Well, sort of. I feel we know each other..." Conor stopped and caught Polly's gaze. "You were one of Dad's closest friends so...the phone's one of those wall things and it's in the hall. I won't be long."

Polly took another sip of the gin and tonic he had made for her.

When he came back, he sat opposite her in an armchair that was part of the loungeroom suite. "All fixed, and tomorrow's my day off...so far. You can never really be sure you're not going to be called in for an emergency. I'm in general admission at the moment so anything can happen."

"I see you've remembered I sometimes like a gin and tonic," she remarked and held up the glass as if to make a toast.

"How can I forget? I often recall that night in the hotel."

"Oi, that sounds like a lot more happened than just talk, Doctor Docherty."

"Oh, yes, sorry. Don't forget, I don't have your word skills."

After another drink and more brief, subdued laughter, Polly told Conor everything she could remember about her day from hell and the journey leading up to it.

Conor shook his head slowly. "I'm totally shocked that anyone could be so callous as to ply those poor people with homemade and probably dangerous booze. And worse still, it was for profit—to get rich on their wonderful artistic talent while they or members of their community drink themselves into oblivion. I've seen first-hand what alcohol can do to them. They've come in with knife wounds, injuries from beatings and some are just about comatose with drink. It's a curse for those lovely people. Even if they *were* being paid some part of their fee with cash, it's the liquor that was doing the damage and lining Mr Flint's pockets even further."

Polly put her hands behind her head and looked up to the high ceiling. She watched a large ceiling fan designed to keep cool air circulating. As her eyes tried to follow each revolution of the blades, she seemed transfixed. She felt the tension, the fear that had gripped her since mid-morning, slowly ebbing. "I feel rotten having learned what Bill Flint has been doing. I feel a crushing guilt even though I had nothing to do with it. The thought of just knowing him makes me feel sick."

"Don't blame yourself, Polly. He was obviously brilliant at deception. Didn't you tell me his cell-mate was a confidence trickster? He could have influenced him, unless Mr Flint himself was an accomplished born liar." Conor suddenly put his hand up to his forehead. "Oh, hell, I forgot to ask. Where are you staying, Polly? Have you got clothes and stuff?"

"I've got more or less what you see me in, and I don't have anywhere..."

She hadn't finished the sentence before Conor jumped in and insisted, "You're staying here with me."

"Thanks, Conor. But it could be a long stay. I have to wait around in Darwin for the court case."

"No worries. The longer you stay, the better I get to know you. There's just one problem though, not that it's a *real* problem..."

Polly looked crestfallen. "You've got a girlfriend? Fiancée? You're married?"

"No, none of the above. There is a girl staying with me sharing the rent. Diana is the fiancée of a fellow doctor. He's in England studying for his master's degree in paediatrics. They had a lovely apartment, but too big for one person, so I suggested Diana move in on a share basis. Half the rent, half the bills. It works well, except we rarely see each other because our shifts just about never coincide. We mostly communicate via scribbled notes or phone calls."

"Well, where would you fit me in? It sounds too complicated, too hectic."

"There are only two bedrooms, but there's a great sort of box room that has a single bed and a smallish set of drawers. I'm not being rude, or personal, but you're not exactly a giant, or I could go in there and you could use my room."

"No way! I wouldn't come under those circumstances. If you're working, you need proper sleep. I know I'm pint-sized, so the teeny room will do for me."

Conor rubbed his hands together and smiled. His eyes seemed to sparkle in the evening sunlight that streamed in almost horizontally as the sun began to set. "That's settled then," he said happily. "We can call the police headquarters or call in and see if they will release any of your personal belongings from the Land Rover. If you're not implicated, I can't see any reason to refuse. Surely nothing you have can constitute evidence."

For the remainder of the evening until late, they chatted over a few glasses of Australian chardonnay. Polly took a shower while Conor cooked a light fish supper.

"I tend to eat at all hours of the day, depending on work," he told Polly from the small, kitchen.

"I know the feeling. Journalists sometimes never know what time they'll get to eat when they're out on a job."

"That's another thing we have in common," Conor said as he opened another bottle of wine.

"I don't suppose you have any plans for tomorrow, but I was thinking we could go for a drive around the area. I can show you a few landmarks and stuff and I reckon a change of scenery might take your mind off...well, you know what I'm referring to."

"Thanks, that's a cracking idea," Polly agreed as she pushed off each shoe with her heels. "Is Ayers Rock anywhere close? I'd love to climb it."

Conor was taken by surprise. "Polly, have you any idea how far..."

"Gotcha," she said with a girlish giggle. "I know it's a zillion miles away!"

"You little teaser, Polly Jordan. Dad, er Doc, often said you were a handful. Who taught you to say zillion anyway?"

"Oh, just some bloke I met. I wanna sound like an Aussie. By the way, what do you mean I'm a handful? What sort of handful was Doc alluding to?"

"Nothing in particular, I think he just meant you were a playful little minx."

*Minx? Okay. As long as he had not told Conor about the darkroom debacle. I'm sure Doc would never tell tales.*

~ * ~

Polly had not slept well in her little room. Not that there was anything wrong with it or her bed. She just could not get the Bill Flint bombshell out of her mind. She was up at six and went into the kitchen to make a cup of tea. No sooner had she put the kettle on than a girl in short-legged pyjamas breezed in. "Oh, hello. You must be Polly, right? I'm Diana. Pleased to meet you," she said as she held out her hand.

"Hope I didn't wake you," Polly said.

"Nope, not at all. When I'm asleep it takes an earthquake to wake me. No, I'm off to work. Did Conor explain our relationship? Perhaps relationship isn't...well, I think you know what I mean. I'm sorry, but if you were about to make toast, can I jump in ahead of you? I'm a bit pushed for time."

"I'll make toast if you want to get ready," Polly said.

"Oh, that would be so good of you. I'll owe you one." She ran back upstairs shouting, "Conor, I'm up and getting ready to leave. See you tomorrow if you're not at work."

There was a muffled "Right-o!"

Five minutes later, Conor appeared wearing just a pair of beach shorts. Polly was surprised, but took him in with some pleasure. His broad shoulders and muscular frame were an impressive sight first thing in the morning.

Polly buttered Diana's toast and put it on a plate and set about making more toast for Conor and herself. *Not a bad way to start the day,* she mused.

"Good morning, girls," Conor said with a yawn and a stretch. "You on until ten tonight?" he asked Diana.

"'Fraid so. We're absolutely flat out in medical at the moment."

"I'll get a coffee at work." She grabbed the toast, thanked Polly and disappeared through the front door.

"There's goes Diana Dynamite! She's in a perpetual rush, but she's a great flat-mate and she and Karl are a lovely couple."

"She's gorgeous. Her looks are so exotic and she's so tall and slim. I often wish I were six inches taller."

"You're the perfect size," Conor said in a fatherly tone. "What's the old saying? Diamonds are never the size of house bricks. Something like that." He winked at Polly. "Diana is a looker, that's for sure. I'm sure she told me one of her ancestors came to Australia from Japan to make his fortune in the pearl-diving industry in Western Australia many moons ago."

"She's stunning." Polly sighed.

"And so are you," Conor replied, "Petite, yes, but perfect."

"You've definitely got the Irish gift of the gab, Doctor Docherty. The blarney. I can just imagine all the nurses fawning over you in your white coat, with your stethoscope hanging round your neck."

Conor chose to ignore Polly's dig. "I thought today we'd just pile in the car and head north-east. One of the Aboriginal nurses told me there's a beautiful remote gorge with fantastic scenery that way. She reckons it's really remote so there's not going to be many people around, maybe nobody."

"Do we need a picnic blanket or anything? I'd say loads of water, right?"

"Yes, you're learning fast. Maybe we should buy some fruit on the way. I don't think there'll be any shops once we leave the city."

They got into Conor's car and drove towards police headquarters. "I'll come in with you," he told Polly.

"No, it's all right. You stay with the car in case parking's a problem You don't want to get a ticket in front of the cop shop."

"You're not just a pretty face," Conor said with a smile. "And what a pretty face it is."

"Are you flirting, Doctor?" Polly said as she walked towards the main doors.

Conor put his hand up behind his ear as if he couldn't catch what she was saying. Then he shrugged and grinned.

About ten minutes later, Polly returned empty handed. "They agreed to return my stuff, but the Land Rover is being forensically examined. I can collect the rest of my belongings the day after tomorrow. I've had a bit of a shock. Inspector Hastings told me Bill Flint wants to see me. He's in custody."

"What will you do? Would it upset you?"

"It might upset *him*. If I go, he'll get both barrels and I mean buckshot. That man has ruined my life."

"Well, there's one bonus, for me, I mean. I've been reunited with you."

Polly looked him in the eyes as if she were reading his innermost thoughts. He returned her gaze.

"We should get going, I think. Killara, the nurse, said it was about thirty miles."

Polly opened the passenger door and let out a little squeal. "I didn't take much notice of this before, but how cute is this front seat. It goes all the way across to your side like a park bench."

"Yes, they call them bench seats. Holden, that's the make of this car, are famous for them."

Polly sounded perplexed. "So where is the gear stick?"

"It's here. This is it," Conor said, and he wiggled a lever to the left of the steering wheel. "It's automatic transmission."

"Slow down and don't baffle me with technical terms. You mean to say the car picks the gears to drive in?"

"In a nutshell, yes."

"Aussies are years ahead of the Brits then. I don't know of any cars over there that have auto, except maybe Rolls-Royces and Bentleys."

"I think it's because distances are so great in Australia. The fewer gear changes on a drive, the less tiring it is."

Conor set off, and the city limits quickly gave way to interesting countryside. Polly marvelled at palm trees and paddocks where hundreds of bananas trees were fruiting.

"Just about every garden in Darwin seems to have bananas growing," she remarked.

Before long, the palms and bananas were replaced by more rugged terrain. Scattered about were the weird tall bushes that seemed to Polly as if they had grass growing out of them. "What are those things?" she asked. "Those things with grass on top."

"The locals call them blackboys, but I haven't a clue what the real botanic name is."

Suddenly, as Conor's Holden turned a bend, a small range of hills came into view.

"Look at the shape of those," Polly remarked with amazement. "If hills were designed by people, I'd say the creator of those was aged four. I've never seen hills that shape. They're like triangles cut off at the top."

"I think that's where we're heading," Conor replied, slowing almost to a stop.

"Right. This is where you say we've run out of petrol and we'll have to spend the night," Polly said and she laughed.

"Nope, just letting that goanna get across to the other side."

"What's a goanna?" She peered over the dashboard. "Oh, one of those ugly dragon things. I saw one of those, even bigger, on the journey up here. They look fierce."

"They can be. They have a wicked bite and can crush your fingers."

"Is there anything in Australia that doesn't bite or sting?"

"Me."

"Me what?"

"I don't bite or sting or take advantage of young ladies."

"Holy moly, Conor, you certainly are your father's son. The more I learn about you, the more I see Doc, bless him."

Polly turned away to look through the passenger window.

Conor sensed she might be upset by the mention of Doc, and tried to reach her. He touched her shoulder and without looking his way, she slid along the bench seat. He slid his arm around her and cuddled her for a moment. She laid her head on his shoulder.

"Don't cry. Isn't being Doc's boy a good thing?"

Polly deftly brushed away a tear and slid back to her side. "It's the best, Conor. The absolute best. Okay," she sniffled. "Let's drive."

Conor parked the Holden next to a huge boulder under some trees. "This will give us a little shade for now, until the sun moves west." He locked all the doors and he and Polly walked down a stony path towards a cliff face. As they approached, Polly seemed amazed by its size and composition. "I can't believe how high it is. The rock looks like crimson flintstone, and look how steep it is. I bet that's not far off dead vertical."

"It's pretty special, isn't it?" Conor said as his eyes slowly focused on the top where small trees were growing from crevices. "I have a feeling it might be sandstone, but geology isn't my forte."

"Imagine trying to climb it. I reckon the men on John Hunt's Everest expedition wouldn't have been able to scale that face." She started to say *sped*, but refrained. She made a silent pledge...*I'll never say that word again as long as I live.*

"Let's follow this path around these big rocks," she continued excitedly. "I want to explore. It's so quiet, it's a bit eerie, but I want to know where this path takes us."

Around the rocky fortress, they picked their way carefully. They came to an area with trees with huge roots shooting out from halfway up the trunk and forming a strange looking buttress before they buried themselves in the ground. The leaves looked similar to those of the palm trees Polly had seen on her journey north, but the weird roots were baffling. "What are *those* crazy trees?"

"I think they're called pandanus. There are some growing around the beaches where we live. A few of the doctors and nurses had a barbecue near Casuarina Beach one weekend and Killara called them pandanus. Many Indigenous people eat the fruit they produce and make all sorts of stuff from the leaves: hats, baskets, rope...I can't remember the whole list of things she said they use them for."

Polly was quick to appreciate the way Conor said *where we live* and smiled to herself. "Some of those roots are thicker than my legs," she said in awe.

"Yes, that's right...pandanus, but I hear some folk call them screw palms," Conor continued.

"I'm not going to comment; I'm not going to say a word."

They both laughed heartily and their eyes met in a lingering gaze before Conor conjured a little cough and said, "Let's walk on, there might be water nearby. I was told pandanus flourish where there's good ground water."

"What time is it?" Polly asked. "My watch is in my rucksack and I can't be bothered fishing it out."

"It's ten minutes past noon."

"Gosh, I thought it was getting hot. I could do with a drink."

"Oh, bugger, we've left the water in the boot of the car," Conor said. "We'll give it another five minutes and if we don't find water, we'll turn round and go back."

Polly nodded and wiped her face. Little beads of perspiration had gathered under her eyes and along her nose. "Blimey, it must be hot today. That's the first time in my life I've had sweat on my face."

"The humidity at the Top End is a killer. Sometimes it's only thirty centigrade, but feels like fifty. We're on the tail end of the wet season, but I think the weather people said there was another cyclone building north-west, in the Indian Ocean."

"Phew, I'll have to rest for a minute," Polly said and brushed dead leaves from the top of a knee-high boulder to sit.

"Room for me?" Conor asked.

"No, find your own rock," Polly joked with a giggle.

After a ten-minute sit-down and a chat, mainly about the weather and the plant life, they set off again. The path twisted and turned through the pandanus and palms and gradually got denser.

"I think we're about to get lost," Polly muttered. "And you said we'd turn back if we didn't find water in ten minutes! I'm going to die of thirst!"

No sooner had she said that than the vegetation cleared and they were confronted by a strip of water. It was roughly fifty yards wide and framed by two steep and rugged cliff faces even higher than the first they had encountered.

"This must be the gorge Killara told me about," Connor said as he gazed at the majesty of the flooded canyon. "It's spectacular. That's the only word I can use to describe it. I wonder how far it goes. It seems to go for about two or three hundred yards then bends off to the left."

"Look how fabulous the water is. It looked dark from a distance, but now we're close up, it's pristine," Polly marvelled. "I've never seen water so crystal clear. It must be six or seven feet deep here, yet I can see every little pebble on the bottom and tiny, teeny fish are darting about. I wonder how old this water is? Do you reckon its new or hundreds, maybe thousands of years old? This is paradise."

"Polly, my knowledge of natural history, including geology, is non-existent."

They sat on a small rock ledge overhanging the water. There was a patch of shade to the back of the ledge. Polly inched her way on her bottom towards it to find a cool spot. "Come over here," she suggested. "There's a nice cool place near the base of the cliff."

"I'd rather be in that water," Conor said. "It looks so cool and inviting."

"Pity we didn't bring towels," Polly remarked casually. "Or bathers."

"Mmmm, that would have been perfect," he replied with an air of disappointment. He laughed and said, "I suppose we could skinny dip."

"Swimming in the nude? Out here? No way,"

"There's no one to see you if you did," Conor reasoned.

"Mate, my days as a stripper are over," Polly joked, "and before you ask, I'm not going to explain. There's only one member of the Docherty family ever going to know that story and it ain't you."

"God, now you've got me intrigued. You and...my father? Doc?"

"It was an innocent drunken mistake on my part and it's now ancient history. So forget about it."

"That's me shot down in flames," Conor sighed. "I won't breathe another word, but you can't stop my mind going into overdrive."

"Shall we see how far the gorge goes before we head off home?" Polly asked enthusiastically.

"Are you up to it? Not too tired?"

Polly sprung up with renewed energy "Nah, I've got my second wind. I'll follow you. It looks a bit narrow ahead, so don't wander off too far and leave me behind."

"Wouldn't do that," Conor promised.

The farther they went, the narrower and steeper the ledge became until it was a mere two feet wide and beginning to turn crumbly underfoot.

"We can't go any farther," Conor announced. "It's too dangerous. We'd better turn around and go back to the car. Just be careful, Polly."

Conor had barely said *Polly* when she tripped, lost her balance and plunged backward into the water with a loud scream and a splash. Both sounds bounced off the cliffs and echoed through the still air. As she fell, she dropped her rucksack which Conor managed to save by planting his foot on one of the straps.

"Jesus, are you okay, Polly? Hang on! Try to grab my hand."

"You're right, the water is beautiful, but I didn't plan on testing it like this," she spluttered and squirted a jet of water out of her mouth. "I'm all right. I'm a fair swimmer. I'll just plod on down to the next gap in the ledge where it's low enough to get out safely."

She eventually reached a gap where the sandstone ledge had worn over time and provided a tiny beach, just big enough for her to access. When she reached shallower water, she managed to stand on the lake's bed of fine pebbles, with her head and shoulders out of the water. "Bloody hell, that was not one of my best entries. I think I've just lost my place in the high diving team at this year's Tokyo Olympics."

Conor couldn't stop himself from laughing. The more he laughed, the more Polly laughed until they were almost helpless. To make matters worse, they began punctuating the uncontrollable guffaws with little snorts, which in turn made them laugh more.

When they finally settled down, Polly said, "God, I needed that. Not the plunge but the good laugh." Her hair hung down over her face, ears protruding from the dripping blonde mop and her cotton blouse clung to her provocatively. She pulled it away from her breasts, but the water just drew it back to the skin.

"Well, there you are," she said, taking Conor's outstretched hand and climbing out of the water. "Not quite a skinny dip, but the next best thing."

Conor stood and stared, his mouth slightly agape.

"Now kind sir, would you escort me to some warm little spot where I can get out of some of these wet clothes and dry off?"

Polly's feet made damp footprints as she made her way along the ledge carrying the saturated sandals she had been wearing. Within seconds, heat baked into the sandstone made the footprints vanish.

Once at the car Polly said, "I need to take my underwear and shorts off to dry. If I get behind the car and hang them on this pandanus, will you promise to look the other way until they're ready to put back on? Shouldn't take long in this heat."

"Of course," Conor said.

Polly lay down on a grassy patch on the other side of the Holden while Conor wiled away the fifteen or twenty minutes it took to dry Polly's clothes by throwing small pebbles into the water. Their *plop* as they hit the still surface and sank was amplified many times over by the gorge. Suddenly he was startled by a shriek and Polly raced round to his side. With hands and arms, she tried to hide her nakedness. "Oh, crikey!  I've just seen a snake. It scared the bejaysus out of me. Go and kill it, Conor."

"What happened?"

"I was reaching for my blouse on the pandanus thing and this snake slithered along a leaf and almost touched my hand. It was yellow with big googly eyes."

Conor put his hand to his mouth in an attempt to stop another round of laughter. "Polly, Polly, Polly...you are so funny sometimes."

"Funny! That slimy thing could have killed me. Don't laugh, you horrible doctor."

"It's a tree snake. We have dozens in the garden at home. They don't have fangs and they don't produce venom. It was probably more scared of you than you were of it. Harmless little creatures."

"Harmless, shmarmless. I'm not going back there. And I'm definitely staying out of the garden. You go and get my clothes. Pretty please," she entreated. "I'll be in the car."

In the back seat of the Holden, she managed to wriggle and twist her still damp body into her clothes. Then she clambered over to the front bench seat. "I'm back," she said as Conor put his key into the ignition.

"You were lucky today," he said as the car fired into life.

"Lucky how? How is plunging into water from a height of, er, let's say six feet, lucky?" Polly grumbled. The grin she tried to hide told Conor she had actually enjoyed the misadventure.

"No crocodiles around," he said casually, putting the car into drive.

"Bullshit!" Polly exclaimed. "How could a saltwater crocodile find this place? It's miles from the ocean."

"Don't be fooled. They can travel miles over land to water."

Polly hesitated. "You're teasing."

"No, I'm not. I'm deadly serious this time. What you get mostly are freshwater crocs. I think they're called Johnstone's crocodiles, or freshies. Estuarine crocs, or salties, live mainly in rivers and sea areas, which obviously gives them their name."

"I'm not listening. You're trying to scare me," Polly said and playfully slapped his arm with the back of her hand.

"These are only tiny bits of second-hand knowledge," Conor confided with genuine sincerity. "I haven't been here long enough to have personal experience, but I remember someone telling me there's a river south of here that flows through a popular gorge. Wildlife rangers tie red buoys to trees along the river bank. If the buoys show no crocodile teeth marks for a month, the authorities open the gorge to canoes and kayaks, and let visitors swim."

"My blood's just run cold," Polly admitted and folded herself in her arms. "I'll never swim up here again unless it's in a proper pool...with a handsome lifeguard on hand."

When they reached Conor's apartment, they found an envelope pushed under the front door. It was handwritten and was signed by Officer Gultekin, complete with his rank and badge number. It informed Polly there would be an initial hearing, followed by a probable committal hearing and then a full trial with jury. To Polly, this all made sense. She was used to the way law courts operate from her experience as a reporter.

The officer estimated the time frame could be one to two months. He reminded her that she must not change any contact details or move accommodation without informing COMPOL.

"Bad news?" Conor asked as he threw himself on the settee.

"No, at least not for me. It's from COMPOL telling me about the court schedule for Bill Flint's trial. It also says that a time has been arranged for me to see Bill in custody, if I want to see him. And it's tomorrow at eleven-thirty at Darwin Police headquarters."

"Will you go?" Conor asked matter-of-factly.

With a frown on her face, Polly mulled over Conor's question for a little while. She wrung her hands and turned her head to look out to the garden. "You know what! I think I will. I think I must," she decided. "I know you're working tomorrow, Conor, so I'll get a taxi to town."

~ * ~

The wall clock had a loud tick and it was showing close to eleven-thirty-five. Polly fidgeted. She tried to stay calm, but the knot of nerves in her stomach had her on a knife's edge. *God, I feel like a schoolgirl in trouble waiting to be called in to see the headmistress.* Suddenly, to her left, a door slowly opened and a young woman in police uniform beckoned.

"Miss Jordan? Polly Jordan?"

"That's me," Polly said hoarsely. Her mouth was dry and her hands had started to tremble.

"Sorry for the delay. We can't always get things organised to the second." The officer had a pleasant face and short-cropped hair, and was taller than Polly by at least six inches.

She took Polly down several corridors and stopped at a metal door where a young constable was on guard. The guard unlocked the door and Polly was allowed through with the female officer.

"I'm afraid I can't leave you alone and there is a time limit of ten minutes."

"That's not very long," Polly complained.

"I suppose not, but those are the rules of custody. Sometimes prisoners on remand are not allowed visits."

Polly was taken to a darkened window and told to sit facing it on a metal seat bolted to the concrete floor. The officer picked up a red telephone and said something Polly couldn't quite hear. Suddenly, the darkened window was lit and Bill Flint was seated facing her. A metal grille separated them. It looked impregnable.

"You're not allowed to put your hands anywhere near the grille," the young officer announced sternly. "And your ten minutes start now."

There was an awkward silence for a few moments until Bill started to weep. "I'm so sorry, Polly, to have dragged you into all this mess. I'm guessing you don't want anything to do with me again, and I can't blame you for that. I just had to tell you how much I regret hurting you. I never meant to let myself be attracted to you, but it just happened."

"Oh wow! That certainly makes me feel good," Polly snapped.

"I'm sure you must be devastated. I want you to know I told them you were totally innocent and knew nothing about the business."

"Oh, you mean the business of cheating native artists out of their work and part-paying them with lethal alcohol. You mean the business of—"

Bill burst in. "I wanted you to steer clear. I never wanted you to go up to Humpty Doo."

"You're so full of lies and deceit," Polly said caustically. "I'll bet you never even had a degree in arts, did you?"

"I always wanted to, but I got greedy. The way I worked, it was easy, and nine out of ten people who bought from me were ignorant, rich people who, in my opinion, deserved to be fleeced. When it came to Aboriginal art, they couldn't tell crap from clay. They just bought pretty patterns. They wanted it because it was trendy, and gambled that it could make them money when they got tired of it. They didn't care about the people who created it."

Polly seethed with anger. "And you *did* care?" she said scathingly. "You cared so much you effectively robbed them. To those artists, those so-called pretty patterns were expressions of thousands of years of culture and history. You are a bigger philistine than the customers you despise."

Polly swallowed hard and took several deep breaths to control what her emotions were screaming at her to do. "I just want to know why. Why me? Was I an easy target, too? Can you tell me this? Are your answers going to be the truth? Was everything you ever said to me a lie, or just most of it? The so-called recuperation from trauma in a place that closed in the last century? Your half-brother Norm?" Her tone was caustic.

"You even lied about your own mother. You lied about her having a bastard child. You lied about the so-called Polish-Russian vodka. Lies! You and your evil gang were making it, making poison to exploit innocent Indigenous people, families. Your disgusting potion is responsible for a young boy's death. Another child, a beautiful young girl, lost a foot and her career dream."

"I know nothing about that," Bill wailed. "I swear to God, I know nothing of it."

"Oh, but you will," she spat. "Before very long you will, fella. Justice will catch up with you and it might not be in a court of law. You've played me. The times we made love, or should I say the times we had sex? How could you do it when you were just an empty shell? Who was that man I was ready to commit to? Why did you bring me across the globe?" The questions just kept coming. "Was I some sort of trophy or something to use while you made your mind up about who or what you are and what you wanted to be? Maybe you saw me as some sort of miracle cure. Is that it, Bill?"

She eyed Bill with contempt. "Now I see why Norm's clothes were in your bedroom. Why you disappeared in the Outback that night. And he's not your half-brother, is he? He's your lover and he's not even Norm. His name is Wilfred."

Bill covered his eyes with his hands. His head was bowed. "I can't explain it. The way I felt back then when I..." He took in a long breath. "It was something I couldn't control. I was young, naïve, scared of life. Please try not to punish me for that. I was lost."

"You're not young and naïve now. I doubt whether you've been that for years. How many other women have you defiled, Bill? How many broken clowns have you left in your wake?"

"You're the first, Polly, I swear. May the Lord strike me down if I'm lying. You're the only woman I've ever had, the only one I've ever cared for."

"You call it caring? Now I realise you never once told me you loved me. They don't write songs and poems about people caring for each other. I thought there might be love in there somewhere, sometime. I'm not punishing you, Bill. You can do that for yourself while you rot in jail."

She needed to make sure she had said everything she wanted to say in the short time allotted. "You used me for whatever purpose was in your imagination and enjoyed me. But even by that stage, you had already betrayed me from that very first day you started spinning your web of lies and deceit. I feel dirty. Soiled. I don't condemn you for your life choices, Bill, or your differences. I don't judge you for that. It's something I don't understand and I don't think I ever will. When it comes to matters of the heart and more basic urges, I am in no position to judge. I've been at my crossroads and Lord knows I've made plenty of mistakes. But I do feel debased by all your deceit.

"And going back to what you said a few moments ago—you, naïve, Bill? No, I'm the naïve one. I thought I was *so* worldly-wise, but it turns out I was a child, maybe a brat sometimes, but jeez, I've grown up overnight.

"But you know, Bill, it's not all about me. I want you to think of those wonderful, lovely souls whose lives you have ruined with that poison. The ones you robbed for the good of your own luxurious lifestyle. They're the naïve ones. You preyed on their innocence and vulnerability." For a brief moment, Polly's anger subsided. Her voice slowed, and for a time, resumed its calm. "I remember the time on the moors when we lay back on the grass and you talked about the Aboriginal Dreaming and stories of clouds and corroborees. We had fun. You had me hooked. Was that fantasy too? All bullshit?"

She paused to get her breath and compose her thoughts, then she attacked once more. "Your greed and disregard for other people's wellbeing make me sick in the guts. You're like a filthy, fat pig rolling around in muck, thinking about nothing but your next bucket of swill," she railed once more. "I want to hate you but I can't. Believe me, I've tried. The only thing I see through this grille is a cardboard cut-out of a man I used to know, or thought I knew. I'd like to take you out of my mind, my memory and tip you out with the rubbish, scrub myself clean of you. But I can't. I'm stuck with your dreadful stink for the rest of my life.

"I do pity you, though. I have the feeling that retribution will be harsh. I don't seek revenge, but if your pain is anything like the pain in me, I will take comfort from that. I remember once telling you I thought pain was relevant. Pain was the sure way you knew you were alive. Well, I know real pain now, thanks to you."

"Can you ever forgive me, Polly?" Bill asked as he wrung his hands. His eyes were red and his face wet from tears. "All I ask is that sometime, maybe years from now, you at least try."

"Forgive? I don't know, Bill. For you, finding forgiveness will always be like looking for the proverbial needle in a haystack. As for forgiving myself? That will *never* happen. For a so-called journalist to be so blind, to miss all the signals and not follow up when tiny clues to *your* life and laughable business empire presented themselves is...well...unforgivable. I'm a spectacular failure all round." She paused momentarily. "I'm just thankful that your mother, Lizzie, is at peace and will never learn what her son, her *only* son, has turned into. I'm turning my back on you, Bill Flint, and please don't try to say goodbye."

With that Polly stood quickly. "Let me out of here," she snapped to the officer.

"Your time isn't up yet, miss," came the reply.

"Oh, yes, it is...unlike that animal's," she said. She twice jabbed her thumb over her right shoulder and walked out the door.

# Twenty-four

At the apartment, Polly was still downstairs, dozing on the settee, when Conor returned from work at the hospital.

"You're up late, Polly. How did the visit go? Did you unload on Bill?" he asked as he poured a glass of chardonnay.

"I gave him something to remember me by, but I'm not sure it did either of us any good. It drove home to me, though, what the power of words can do. I said some things that will leave deep wounds. I just hope I never have to talk to anyone like that again. Never." She thought back to the situation with Jocelyn Duckworth. "Not all that long ago, I blasted my news editor in a way I bet she's never been spoken to before. I absolutely tore strips off her and used language I'm not proud of. I felt so good. It actually got me fired, which was the beginning of why I'm here today. So it wasn't all bad." She shrugged. "But my guilt grew and grew, and in the end, I was sorry to have been so belligerent, in fact downright nasty. She deserved my wrath, but she didn't deserve some of the things I said.

"I swore then I would never unleash my anger on anybody again. But today, I did. My tongue lashed that man as sure as any whip."

"How's it left you feeling?' Conor said gently.

"Not good. I feel depressed. I desperately need a friend tonight."

"Well, you have me," Conor said. "Will I do?"

"Absolutely. I think you've been my friend for longer than either of us knows. I'm going to take a shower. Oh, by the way," she shouted from the bedroom landing, "Diana phoned about six o'clock and said she's been roped in for a late shift and won't be home until...whenever...I think that was the word she used."

Conor lifted his glass to his lips. He stopped. He looked around towards Polly then poured the chardonnay into a plant-pot that contained a small rubber plant close to the settee. Then he followed her upstairs.

Once on the landing, Conor walked slowly towards his bedroom, passing the open door of Polly's small room.

Polly was just about to undress. She began to slide her top up over head, but quickly pulled it down as she realised Connor had stopped at the doorway. "Good night, Polly," he said. "Sleep well."

She stared at Conor for a moment. Her eyes searched his. For a fleeting moment there was a strange air of tension before Polly said, "Can we talk?" She swept long strands of hair from her face.

"Yep, sure," he answered with a smile. "Now? Right here? It sounds a bit serious. Is it something I've done?"

"Yes, yes, and no...in that order," Polly said hesitantly. She slowly lowered herself onto her bed. "You haven't done anything, Doctor. Nothing at all. After today's massive outburst, I suddenly feel free and the tension has gone. Is that normal?"

Conor drew a little closer. "Maybe you just need to be cared for."

"Maybe," Polly said quietly.

"Sorry!" he apologised, "I...er...I thought..."

"Are you offering to take care of me, Doc? I think I would like that."

Conor looked questioningly at her. "I thought you reserved that name for my dad. I thought..."

"Please don't think, Conor, just come in and close the door," Polly said hoarsely. "I desperately need a hug."

~ * ~

Three weeks sailed by and Polly was still awaiting news about a court appearance. She tried to busy herself to avoid becoming bored. She read paperbacks and books she found in a cupboard below the stairs. Stories about the Aboriginal Dreaming were of great interest. She enjoyed the mystique and history of Australia's ancient people and tried to understand how important art was in the telling of Aboriginal visions of creation and lore.

When she was not engrossed in reading, Polly took up writing short stories for pleasure and occasionally taking a taxi trip into town for a coffee and cake. To her surprise, she found herself developing a taste for lamingtons, a favourite Australian jam sponge cake. The *lammo* is dipped in chocolate sauce and always sprinkled with a coating of desiccated coconut. Until then, the very smell of coconut had made her wretch.

During the following weeks, she prepared an application letter for a job at *The Northern Territory News* in answer to an advertisement for a senior reporter. When she first saw the advertisement, she ignored it, but started the think that the way back to anything like a *normal* life would be to return to the career she had put on the back burner.

On the same day, Conor received news from lawyers in England that Doc's estate had been finalised and that Conor was the major beneficiary. The lawyers' letter advised, however, that the settlement and disbursal should be delayed until an outcome was reached in joint civil proceedings between *The Cardwell*

*Express* and the journalists' union against the owners of the circus where Doc met his end.

"I've decided to take the legal advice," Conor told Polly over dinner. "But there's a little surprise for you." He produced the lawyers' letter and read out a relevant part. "It's written in legal jargon, but it means Doc added a codicil to his will. Reading between the lines, and that's not meant to be a pun, Doc knew he was on borrowed time." He paused.

"Okay, well, I'm the main beneficiary, but Doc wanted you to have his Mini Cooper, his cameras and a little over ten thousand pounds was left in trust for you."

"You have to be kidding! That's so much money. And the car? He loved that Mini Cooper. But I can't accept any of it," she said her eyes filling with unshed tears. "I think I've done enough blubbering for one lifetime, so these are happy tears. Thank you, Doc, wherever you are."

"Dad..er...Doc would have wanted you to be happy and accept it with fond memories. He wrote a little note, too, which the lawyers have included in their letter. It's in Doc's handwriting. I have it here."

*Be happy, Polly. Sorry to leave you. Take the money, invest it well and make enough to buy the bloody Cardwell Express and close it down. Just a joke, babe. Love always, Doc.*

Polly smiled. "He always knew what to say, bless him, even though sometimes he tried to wind me up. We were a team, Conor. Such a great team. If you have no objection, I'd just like to keep the note."

"No objection at all. It was meant for you."

"I'll treasure it for the rest of my life. Thank you, Conor," Polly said and put it gently to her lips for the lightest of kisses.

~ * ~

Some days later, Polly and Diana were eating breakfast. Conor brushed past them saying he had been called in to assist with an emergency. A car had struck a kangaroo thirty miles south of Darwin and three people were seriously injured in the ensuing crash.

As he picked up his medical bag and looked for car keys, Connor said, "I was supposed to attend a meeting to finalise details for the group of doctors involved in the Aboriginal health project, but that will have to wait for today. See you ladies later, but I don't know when."

"Busy life, this doctoring business," Polly said, turning to Diana.

"You're not wrong. I'm thinking of becoming a general practitioner. At least I'll have steady hours, five days a week and hopefully a slower pace of life."

"Can I be your first patient then?" Polly asked with a hint of trepidation.

"Well, I suppose so...but that's a fair way down the track yet."

"No, I mean right now. Today."

"Heavens, what's the problem?"

"I don't know whether I'm asking you this as a woman, a friend or a doctor. I'll let you decide."

"I'm intrigued," Diana responded. "Please feel to ask me whatever you want."

"Will you check my breasts for me? They don't feel right." She unbuttoned her blouse and presented them to Diana.

"They look fine to me," she said. "But please go on. Tell me your concern."

"I hate bras, if you are wondering," Polly told her. "Anyway, I know my boobs. I look after them, I feel them, all the usual things a woman does, but they seem strange—tingly and a bit sore."

"Mind if I examine them?" Diana said.

"No, go for it."

She felt them and squeezed them a little and checked for suspicious lumps. She asked Polly a few general questions about her medical history then gave her medical opinion.

"I can't find anything wrong."

"Oh, great. I was worried. I wondered if it was because I had come off the pill. Not through choice, I just ran out and I don't think I qualify for them here in Australia. Not yet, anyway."

"No, you're supposed to be married and most doctors follow the rules scrupulously. Some turn a blind eye to protocol. I'm not a GP yet so I couldn't prescribe them. It's a bit of a grey area, but I could probably refer you to somebody who specialises in women's health."

"Oh, I wasn't hinting," Polly said earnestly.

"Good," said Diana, "they wouldn't do you any good right now anyway. Oh, listen, I'm bobbing into town in a few minutes, would you like me to drop you off anywhere?"

"Oh, thanks, Diana, I'm fine. I'm feeling a bit bilious, to be honest. I think my breakfast boiled eggs might be making a reappearance." She turned to leave the kitchen, but stopped in her tracks. "I'm pregnant!" Not waiting for an answer, she ran to the bathroom.

"Well, I'm definitely out of here. I see and hear enough vomiting in the wards without you joining in."

"It'll pass soon. It always does. What an idiot I am not to have worked it out for myself."

After lunch Polly went to bed feeling tired and listless. She was just about to doze off when the phone in the hall rang. She eased herself down the stairs, feeling a little lightheaded from getting upright too quickly. She took the receiver from the phone on the wall.

"Hello, Miss Jordan?"

"Yes, speaking."

"It's Inspector Hastings at COMPOL. I have some news for you."

"Okay, fire away," Polly replied, grabbing a notebook and pencil from a shelf below the phone.

"I'm afraid the Flint case has run into a wall of red tape. I'll try to explain as best I can, but the circumstances are so complicated and involve so many different levels of legislation that I am having a hard time understanding it myself.

"You're probably aware, as a journalist, that over the past few years there has been a groundswell of public opinion following huge political upheavals in the United States and South Africa regarding the poor treatment of Black people. Now fingers overseas are being pointed at Australia and its perceived lack of understanding of the needs of its indigenous population. An official body, the Parliament of the Commonwealth of Australia and Indigenous Peoples, was established about five years ago and has a lot of political clout. They, and other Aboriginal lobby groups, want self-determination, racial equality which they claim is not enshrined in the Constitution. They want native title land rights, equal pay prospects and many other social reforms. It's a political hot potato, and is likely to blow up very soon and shake the country to its foundations. These are the words from somebody right at the top.

"At the same time, the Northern Territory admini-stration and the federal government itself are anxious that no hint of exploitation is brought to light. Therefore, the Flint case, for want of a better phrase, is to be whitewashed."

Polly sighed. "I'm not sure I understand totally, but please go on."

"People way above my pay-scale have made it clear that COMPOL is to back off. The fact that the man they call Noah has disappeared without a trace means the Flint case has stalled. Apparently, he was the linchpin and chief negotiator and persuader. Most of the other evidence is now being classed as circumstantial."

Polly listened intently.

"The powers that be say a good defence team would bulldoze any prosecution, therefore the only charges we can lay are like slaps on the wrist, such as excise evasion and handling and possessing illegal alcohol. I know it must be disappointing, but can you imagine my team being told that three years of hard work has brought virtually no reward in court?

"However, COMPOL played *some* hardball and a trump card is now ready to be played. Mr Flint faces breaches of federal excise and duty laws and this could result in a bill of staggering size. The federal government has convened top lawyers and it has been decided they are legally able to seize all his assets and liquidate them to compensate for lost excise, and to pay some of the costs of the COMPOL investigations. Similar penalties apply to the people working the distillery and those who transported component parts across state and territory boundaries. It's all a legal minefield, but at the end of the day, politics is always found in the fine print."

Polly heard the inspector take a sharp intake of breath.

"But, and this is a big *but*, the federal government has exercised its discretionary powers and the minute Mr Flint is clear of any monetary or custodial penalty, his visa will be cancelled and he will be deported...and permanently barred from returning to Australia. The same will apply to all the others. So the outcome will be satisfactory and stop this awful business for the foreseeable future, at least.

"Oh, one last thing, and perhaps I shouldn't tell you this, but I will anyway...we have alerted Scotland Yard and Interpol about Mr Kowalski's imminent deportation. He will be escorted to England and once there, he will no longer be our concern."

Polly weighed up the inspector's information. "They're not the punishments I'd imagined, but it protects the Indigenous communities and gets rid of a crooked, amoral alien, so you've all done a good job. Well done, COMPOL."

"Thank you, Miss Jordan, for your cooperation. I wish you well and good luck for your future."

~ * ~

The minute Conor returned home, he dropped his briefcase to the floor and poured two glasses of white wine.

"Hello, you!" Polly's voice chirped from the kitchen.

"I've had a day from hell at the hospital. I need a drink," Conor announced grumpily, and slowly lowered his large frame onto the settee. He carefully put the wine glasses on the small coffee table close by, then kicked off his shoes.

"I had a phone call from COMPOL," Polly shouted as she fought to be heard above the sound of water boiling in the whistling kettle.

"Hi, good to see you," Conor said as she padded barefooted into the loungeroom. His voice sounded weary from the pressures of the day and he ran his hands through his hair. "What did COMPOL have to say?"

"It was long and complicated and you're tired. So I'll tell you everything tomorrow. The outcome was good."

"Fair enough," Conor said, yawning. "Hey you, you're wearing one of my shirts."

"Just thought I'd put it on. It smells of you. I've missed you today."

"You look funny. It's miles too big for you. Is this what you do while I'm at work? Sneak around in my things?"

"Only on special days," Polly replied in a whisper. She sat next to Conor. Their bodies met.

"How was *your* day?" he asked.

She told him that apart from receiving the message from COMPOL, she had decided to tear up her job application letter to the *Northern Territory News*.

"Why? I thought you wanted to go back to journalism? What do you think you'll do now, Polly? Now that all that awful chapter is behind you?"

"All these questions," Polly teased. "I thought I was the reporter."

"Will you go back to England? You have a car waiting there for you," he said with a sudden broad smile. "Or will you stay?" he probed. Now there was worry etched all over his face.

For the first time, Polly noticed Conor had little crow's feet at the corner of each dancing green eye, just the way Doc had. She reached up and touched them. Her delicate fingers, tenderly traced them. "You look worn out, Doctor," she whispered in his ear. She sighed deeply, pulled herself away from him and lay back on the settee. She let her hands wander over her belly. Looking directly at Conor, she cocked her head to one side. Her elfin face wore the beginnings of a cheeky grin. "Will I stay? Mmmm...let me think about it. Well..." she purred slowly and seductively, "that depends on whether the father of my child asks me to marry him."

For an instant, Conor looked as if he'd turned to stone. Suddenly, with a yell, he leapt from his seat. He pulled Polly to her feet. He reached down and with one arm under her bottom and the other round the small of her back, he swept her up to his chest and pulled her so close their noses touched. He spun them both round and round crazily like kids on a playground roundabout. When he stopped and let Polly slowly slide from his arms and onto her feet, they were both so dizzy they tumbled onto the settee. He smothered her in kisses, her face, lips, neck, ears, her nose.

"Shall we ask that man right this second?" Conor said eagerly.

"I think you better had, Doctor. The child's father is lost for words."

"I've dreamed of this since the day I met you. Oh, my lord. This is the happiest day of my life. Let's drink a toast."

"Let's not," Polly replied, as she carefully drizzled her wine into the rubber tree plant-pot. "No more alcohol. I've drunk enough for at least one lifetime. And it's my bet that any doctor worth his salt would advise against mixing booze and babies." She smiled. "Oh, by the way—do I have to say it? I think I'll stay. And though you haven't asked me, Doctor—you know, with actual grown-up words—my answer is yes, please," Polly chuckled.

~ * ~

After what seemed like an interminable pregnancy, baby Liam Gerrard Docherty was born in Darwin, Northern Territory, Australia. Polly gently rocked him to sleep as she sat in the shade of the scaly ash tree in the back yard. Protecting her eyes from the glare of the afternoon sun, she picked out a wispy white cloud, a fluffy ball of what she knew was simply water vapour that would dissipate and re-form, dissipate and grow many times. She smiled to herself. *All the clouds have gone from my life now. No more talk or stories about favourites.* Her thoughts turned to her beloved Doc. *Just pie in the sky, Polly.*

# *Meet Gordon Campbell*

Gordon Campbell is a former journalist who grew up in a cotton town in Lancashire, England. In 1979 he migrated to Australia with his young family and worked for several Australian newspapers as a writer and senior sub-editor. Since his retirement, he has found an interest in writing fiction as opposed to reporting factual information. *My Favourite Cloud* is his first novel.

## *Dear reader,*

I hope you've enjoyed reading this tale of intrigue spanning
continents.

Your opinion is valuable to other
readers like you,
who may be looking for books like mine.

Please consider taking a few minutes to post a review, however
brief,
on the site where you purchased this book
or on the Wings ePress web page.

You may also want to visit my author page
at the Wings' website, where you can find
all the other books in my series.

Thank you!

Gordon Campbell

# Visit Our Website

*For The Full Inventory*
*Of Quality Books:*

**<u>Wings ePress, Inc</u>**

*Quality trade paperbacks and downloads*
*in multiple formats,*
*in genres ranging from light romantic comedy to general fiction*
*and horror.*
*Wings has something for every reader's taste.*
*Visit the website, then bookmark it.*
**We add new titles each month!**

*Wings ePress, Inc.*
*3000 N. Rock Road*
*Newton, KS 67114*